Time to Heal

A Novel

Linda Pynaker

Copyright © 2003 by Linda Pynaker

ISBN 0-7414-1408-2

Published by:

PUBLISHING.COM

519 West Lancaster Avenue
Haverford, PA 19041-1413
Info@buybooksontheweb.com
www.buybooksontheweb.com
Toll-free (877) BUY BOOK
Local Phone (610) 520-2500
Fax (610) 519-0261

Printed in the United States of America

Printed on Recycled Paper

Published February 2003

Acknowledgements

To my husband, Rob, for his never-ending love and support and his fun-loving nature which brings joy into my life.

To my twin sister, Karen, for loving me since we first met as souls, always believing in me, and introducing me to Healing Touch energy work. She also had the patience to help me edit this book from start to finish. May we soon share another box of Smarties.

CHAPTER ONE

Ted had gone off to work as usual that day. Debra, on the other hand, was numb and could hardly function. The thought of eating breakfast made her sick to her stomach.

She was dragging herself through her morning routine. She had been so preoccupied she hadn't slept well for days. When would be the best time to ask? What would she say? How would he answer? That one scared her the most. Or worse—would he even answer? Lately, he'd become almost impossible to talk to.

She'd finally done it and now she felt even worse.

"Do you feel like you have to work really hard to keep this marriage going?" Debra had asked Ted that morning as he was pulling on his socks.

Without hesitation, he had said, "No."

"Then why do I?"

He had barely glanced at her as he walked into the bathroom. Stunned, she had walked away. She felt as if they were barely surviving. How was she going to make their relationship work without his help?

How could he NOT realize there was a problem? No…he knew it was bad. He certainly didn't look happy to her. Ted had always been easygoing and quick to smooth ruffled feathers rather than get involved in conflict. Lately, he didn't seem to care about anything but work. His sandy brown hair was now marked with salt and pepper gray and his face was often lined with tension. If and when he mentioned work, he spoke through clenched teeth.

She wasn't sure exactly when they started the downward slide—sometime after Ted's promotion and transfer to San Diego just over one year ago. Debra couldn't remember the last time she and Ted had enjoyed each other's company. She couldn't even remember the last time she had had kind thoughts about him!

Almost every morning, Debra told herself, "I'm going to be less demanding. I'll be more cheerful. Today's going to be a better day for us." But, somewhere before the end of the day, usually earlier than later, she'd get frustrated and lose her resolve. Things couldn't continue this way!

Debra showered, applied mousse to her medium length sandy colored hair, and lightly tossed her natural curls before getting dressed in her office clothes. As her blue eyes looked back into the mirror, she hardly noticed her appearance. She had always been a low maintenance woman. Her frame was average, with pleasant curves where they counted most. She could possibly lose five pounds or so, but Ted had always said he didn't like women built like boys, and she had never worried about losing the extra inches.

She hurried downstairs where she joined their two children, Jonathan and Leanne, in the kitchen. Jonathan, a tall gangly redhead, with blue eyes and a freckled nose, was cramming his mouth full of toasted frozen waffle as he grabbed his lunch out of the fridge. Leanne looked at him with disgust as she nudged past him and picked up her lunch bag. She was a first year senior and, at times, was appalled by her brother's early adolescent behavior.

Debra ended up dumping most of her breakfast in the garbage disposal before heading out the door. As she drove down the block, she noticed Leanne had met up with a couple of her friends who walked to school together every morning. Despite her lithe figure, long brown hair, and brown eyes, Leanne was modest about her appearance and was well liked.

Jonathan was straggling down the sidewalk all by himself. He was thirteen and was at a difficult age in terms of finding his place among his peers. He was only just starting to make friends since their move.

Debra's desk phone rang steadily from the moment she arrived at work. She meanwhile typed agendas and a multitude of workshop handouts. She delivered the originals to printing for reproduction and then made phone calls to book conference rooms at Marina Village and ordered food and beverages for workshop participants. Fortunately, she didn't have time to think about the mess her marital relationship was in.

When she got home, she threw a load of laundry in the washer, tidied up the family room, and made dinner. She was folding laundry when Ted arrived home shortly after seven o'clock that evening. Jonathan was playing computer games in his bedroom and Leanne was at a friend's home working on a group school project. They had already eaten dinner. Ted took the plate she'd prepared for him and walked over to the couch where he sat down and turned on the television.

Debra had been waiting for a chance to talk to him. She hoped that, if she could get him to talk to her they could do something about their relationship.

"Ted, we have to talk."

"What about?"

"The ways things are going in our relationship." She sat down in a nearby armchair.

He raised his eyebrows.

"We never do things together anymore," she explained.

"We're together now. As far as I can see, you're here and so am I."

"You know what I mean. We don't go places, we never see anybody. We don't talk."

He'd already tuned out and was absorbed in the television.

"Ted! You're hardly ever home and when you are, your nose is buried in the TV. Ted!"

"O.K.!" He grabbed the remote off the end table and muted the volume on the television. "I'm listening. What do you want me to do?!"

"I want…I want you to spend time with me…and with the kids." She sat forward. "Don't you care what happens to this family?"

"I'm working hard to make a good living so you three can have the comforts of life. I can't be here and at work at the same time." He punched the volume button on the remote and the TV blared to life again.

That was always his response when she talked about his absences from home. How could she argue with that? It was hopeless! Debra went back into the kitchen to finish cleaning up.

The rest of the week, Ted did not arrive home from work before nine o'clock in the evening. The most he said to the children was, "Goodnight", when they poked their heads around the entryway of the den each evening before going upstairs to their bedrooms.

He was apparently working on an insurable loss projection system for a new prospective client, Sprint Telecommunications. He had told Debra he wanted the contract assigned to him no matter how much work he had to do to get it.

One evening, Jonathan approached his mother in the kitchen, "Mom, are you and Dad going to get a divorce?"

She stopped loading dishes into the dishwasher. "What makes you say that?"

"Well, you hardly ever talk to each other. You know Denny, the guy I play soccer with? He said that was what it was like just before his parents split up."

"Jonathan, your father is very busy at work. He's under a lot of pressure to produce a huge project right now to win over a new client. It's very important to him." She put her arm around Jonathan's shoulders. "Things will eventually slow down a bit and he'll be around more." She wasn't sure who she was trying to convince more, Jonathan or herself.

"How about you get ready for bed and I'll make you a snack?" she offered.

He looked up, "Popcorn?—The real stuff, the stuff you cook yourself instead of in the microwave?"

Debra agreed as he scooted off to get ready for bed. By the time it was ready, Jonathan was already in his pajamas. The aroma of freshly popped popcorn and butter alerted Leanne and she arrived in the kitchen right behind Jonathan.

Leanne, who was in a particularly cheerful mood because her team had won their after-school volleyball game, fetched sodas for everybody. The three of them moved into the family room where they sat around the coffee table and took turns reaching into the bowl for handfuls of popcorn. As they munched away, they chatted about things they missed in Sacramento and the things they liked most about San Diego.

Saturday morning arrived and Ted was up at the crack of dawn getting ready to go to the golf course for his weekly eight o'clock tee time. He and a few of the guys at work played golf every Saturday morning, weather permitting. The courses are open year round in San Diego and it rarely rains so that meant he played almost every Saturday. Debra didn't resent his golfing Saturday mornings. What she minded was the fact that he often worked late and, on the days he did not work late, he took off to the squash courts. She felt he was avoiding her.

Debra followed Ted into the bathroom where he picked up his shaver. "Ted, maybe we should see a counselor. Maybe an outsider could help us get things back together again."

Ted looked at Debra as if she was insane. "You go to the counselor. You're the only one here who thinks there's a problem. I don't think we have a problem except for you nagging me." He turned on his electric shaver, which buzzed noisily. There was no point in trying to talk to him with that racket.

"Heck," she muttered, "there's no point trying to talk to him period!"

Debra headed down the stairs and walked outside, slamming the door behind her. She started hoofing it down the block at a steady pace. She had barely gone half a block when she almost collided with one of her neighbors who was coming out of the gate of her own yard.

"I'm sorry. That was close, I almost nailed you," Debra apologized.

"That's O.K. Close only counts in horseshoes, darts, and hand grenades."

"I hadn't heard the hand grenades one before." She laughed. "I tell you, in the mood I'm in, I wish I had a hand grenade."

Debra noticed she was attractive, with long chestnut hair swung up in a ponytail and a trim figure dressed in shorts and a T-shirt. She wore tennis shoes and was carrying a water bottle. She was about Debra's age, but she looked like she was seriously into exercise.

"Liz," her neighbor said as she held out her hand. "I'm new in the neighborhood and I'm about to go on my morning walk. It looks like you have energy to burn. Care to join me?"

"Sure—I'm Debra," she lightly clasped Liz's hand. "I noticed you move in a while back. We moved here a few months earlier."

They started to walk side by side down the sidewalk. "So, who's the hand grenade for?" Liz asked.

"My husband."

"I've got one of those too and some days I wouldn't mind blowing him up either."

They both laughed.

They chatted about the weather and scenery. After they had walked a few blocks, Debra said, "I don't usually go for walks. This feels pretty good. Actually I don't usually do much of anything that doesn't involve work or chores."

Liz looked at Debra and raised her eyebrows, "Why ever not?"

"I work full-time and between that, chauffeuring the kids around, and taking care of household chores, I haven't been able to fit much else in."

"Sounds like you're another one of those Super Mom types. Well, if you give me a chance, I'll sure help you fix that!" Liz declared. "I discovered that sacrificing yourself to your husband and children won't get you anywhere. At least not anywhere I want to be. My kids are grown up now and living on their own and I sure don't see them bending over backwards to stay close. I could give that, 'after all I've done for them' speech, but I long since realized that doesn't carry a lot of weight."

"I can't imagine the kids being gone and having time to myself. I don't know what I would do with it."

"My husband, Kurt, and I have since made some kind of life together, but if it weren't for me taking care of myself, there would be nothing left of me. Granted, I'm still working full-time, but I make sure I get out for walks every Saturday morning and the occasional weekday. Right after we moved here, I signed myself up for aerobics classes and I recently joined a Book Discussion group at the local library. Plus I have my hobbies. If I didn't do those kinds of things, I would die of loneliness here. I miss my life back in Denver."

"It's hard. I still don't have roots here," Debra told her between gasps for breath. It was a long time since she'd had any structured exercise and the pace was starting to get to her. Not only that but, despite the fact that it was January, it was a beautiful, sunny morning and she was wearing bib coveralls over a T-shirt. She was extremely warm.

Liz noticed Debra's jagged breathing. "I was planning on taking a little jaunt around the Bay. I discovered a really nice paved path that winds through the beach and it's very scenic. Now that you're not so fired up about whatever it was that was bugging you, we could slow the pace. Are you up for it?"

"I'd like to. Are you sure I won't slow you down too much?"

"Actually, I'm enjoying your company. Once we get around the Bay there'll be a sea breeze that will make you more comfortable."

Liz gave Debra a couple of squirts from her water bottle. They headed off Honeycutt Street and down the paved road to Crown Point Park. They were soon walking on the beach and Debra welcomed the cool breeze.

Both had moved to San Diego due to their husband's transfers, with Liz having come from Denver and Debra's family having moved from the outskirts of Sacramento.

They talked about how tough it was to get established in a new city. Debra mentioned her job as an executive assistant for a team of consultants who do professional development workshops. She then asked Liz about her employment.

"I'm in advertising. As a matter of fact, I requested a transfer and it just so happened our firm had an opening come up in San Diego, so here I am," said Liz. "It was difficult to leave, though."

She explained that her two grown up daughters continued to attend college in Denver and that, although they talked on the phone occasionally, her daughters were busy with their studies and socializing so it wasn't the same as sharing the same household.

Liz suggested they turn around and head back home. "I don't want to be carrying you home. We'll have to break you in slowly, that is assuming you'd like to do this again."

Debra didn't hesitate to agree. "It's a great chance to let off steam and, God knows, I've got a lot of that lately."

They decided to meet at Liz's gate at nine o'clock the following Saturday morning and Debra headed for home. She was energized after her walk and was humming at the thought of having a new friend as she worked her way through her weekend household chores.

Jonathan came around the doorway all sleepy eyed, just having climbed out of bed, and heard his mother still humming after she returned home from getting groceries. "What are you in such a good mood about?"

She told him about meeting Liz and enjoying their walk around the bay.

Jonathan nodded as he went to the refrigerator to get a glass of orange juice. Leanne had already left earlier to go to another school for a volleyball tournament.

Ted was later than usual returning from his golf game. She felt annoyed figuring that he'd probably hung out at the golf house for a while rather than coming home. He went up to the bedroom without saying so much as a "hello" to Debra or their children.

Ted came down in time for dinner, but he had a newspaper beside his plate. He didn't speak throughout the entire meal, except to ask for another helping of meatloaf.

Debra and the children chatted amiably about their day. Debra asked Leanne how her volleyball team did in their tournament.

"We won four games and lost two. Central won the tournament, as usual. But, we were at a disadvantage because one of our center's sprained her wrist when she fell in practice on Friday so she wasn't able to play."

Jonathan piped in, "Like your team would have won anyway. Your team is full of a bunch of losers!"

"It is not." Leanne wrinkled her nose in disdain. "Like you'd know anyway. You couldn't spike a ball if your life depended on it!"

"I could so!"

"That's enough, you two!" Debra realized she'd raised her voice and Ted hadn't so much as looked up.

Jonathan and Leanne exchanged dirty looks, but didn't resume bickering.

Jonathan headed for the family room to use the phone to arrange to visit a new friend, while Leanne started toward the stairs to get ready for her evening out.

"Hey, you two! Don't forget to put your dishes in the dishwasher before you go."

They rinsed their dishes and put them in the dishwasher amid mutters and grumbling before getting on with their plans for the evening. Debra started to clean up the kitchen as Ted wandered off to his den and shut the door. They didn't see each other for the rest of the evening and Debra was sleeping by the time Ted came out of his den.

Debra groaned to herself as she got out of bed Sunday morning. Her legs were stiff from yesterday's walk and it made her aware of how out of shape she was. She limped down to the kitchen and poured herself a cup of coffee from the pot Ted had made before he left that morning for the squash courts.

In an attempt to distract herself from worrying about what was going on between her and Ted, she tackled the yard work. She enjoyed the earthy smell of freshly dug flowerbeds and the bending and stretching helped her to feel more limber. When she was done gardening, she put the garden tools away, and looked around the yard with satisfaction. Then she headed into the house to wash up and make lunch. Jonathan was already in the kitchen putting a sandwich together. They ate their lunches and Jonathan left to shoot hoops in a neighborhood park.

Debra baked a lemon meringue pie. She put a roast into the oven and surrounded it with carrots, potatoes, and onions.

"I'm just a work horse around here," she thought as she finished washing and drying all of the laundry and then put Yorkshire pudding into the oven. She was putting the folded laundry away when she thought she smelled smoke—it smelled more like burned food—burned Yorkshire! The smoke alarm started to bleat.

"Oh, no!" she rushed to the kitchen and opened the oven door. Smoke billowed out. She grabbed oven mitts and snatched the tray of Yorkshire. "Ouch!" The tray clattered to the floor as she burned her hand through a hole in one of the oven mitts. She reached for a towel and retrieved the pan from the floor, tossing it onto the stove.

Debra grabbed a chair so she could pull the alarm open and dismantle the battery. She only felt slight relief when the thing stopped screaming at her. There were crumbs all over the floor and most of the puddings were burned to a crisp. Only the few toward the front of the oven were salvageable. Debra sat down in the chair in the middle of the kitchen, feeling defeated. It was a while before she got up to clean up the mess.

The whole family ate dinner together, but despite their chatter, Ted did not join in. The children were pleased that Debra had made a typical British dinner, like the ones her mother used to prepare for them when they were still living nearby in Sacramento, even if their small portion of Yorkshire was crispy. Debra was fed up that Ted hadn't even seemed to notice what he ate for dinner. She could have fed him dog meat and he'd be none the wiser.

The next morning Debra tried, again, to bring up the topic of their marriage. "Ted, please, we need to talk. We can't keep living like this. We have to do something!"

"Oh, great. Here we go, again. Debra you pick the worst times to want to talk. Look, I'm under a lot of pressure." He pulled on his suit jacket and picked up his briefcase. "I've got a meeting first thing this morning to find out the outcome on the Sprint project. Can't we do this another time?" He hurried down the hallway with Debra close on his heels.

"Ted, you've always got something more important to do. When will we ever talk?!"

"I can't say right now!" He snapped. "Now, please, I've got to get going," he sighed with exasperation as he headed out the door.

Debra had another busy day at work. There was a huge conference scheduled at the Convention Center. Her first task involved drawing layouts for six conference rooms outlining placement of tables, chairs, and video equipment. She consulted with Convention Center staff regarding the requirements for the Continental breakfast and buffet lunch. Then, she met with her clerical support team to delegate responsibilities for the many handouts that would need to be typed and copies made.

Ted had returned home from work even earlier than Debra that evening. She was surprised to see his car in the driveway. The door to the den was closed when she came through the front door.

She tapped lightly on the door, before opening it. "Ted, how was your meeting?"

He waited briefly before he growled, "That son of a bitch, Brody, took most of the credit for the modules I designed. He was assigned as project manager of the Sprint contract."

She walked behind his desk and put her hand on his shoulder, "Oh, Ted, I'm so sorry. Does that mean you're completely off of it?"

"No, but I'm not going to work under that asshole! He's an idiot who couldn't design a decent program if his life depended on it!" He stood up and went up to their bedroom, slamming the door. He didn't even come down for dinner. Debra, once again, felt shut out.

Ted tossed and turned throughout the night. The sheets were mangled by morning and Debra felt like she had wrestled all night to hang on to a corner of the comforter. As a result, neither got a good night's rest.

Ted was particularly distracted the remainder of the week. He even cancelled his weekend golf and squash games and, instead, spent most of the weekend in his den.

Dressed in shorts and a T-shirt, Debra went over to Liz's Saturday morning. She didn't mention her concerns about her relationship with Ted. At this point, it was all too confusing and she didn't feel ready to talk about it anyway. She was glad to have a chance to relax and think about something else.

The scenery really was incredible. Earlier on in the walk they noticed several kayaks and team skulls gliding across the bay. As the breeze picked up and the water became a little choppier, locals and vacationers took their sailboats out and the bay was dotted with a multitude of colorful sails. There were birds everywhere, seagulls padding along the beach, pelicans dive bombing into the water coming up with fish, and ducks floating along the shore. It was a beautiful day and they encountered people rollerblading, cycling, walking, and pushing strollers around the bay.

Debra and Liz chatted about their jobs and their families. Debra found her time with Liz to be pleasant and they agreed to meet again the following week.

Ted called in sick to work on Monday for the first time in the history of their marriage. His mood, however, seemed to have picked up considerably by that evening. He announced, in a tone that implied she had better not ask questions that he would be going to Sacramento for a few days, "on business". He certainly had her curious about what was going on, but she decided she could wait, for now. As long as he was in a better mood, she wasn't going to provoke him.

CHAPTER TWO

She was crying, of course. Debra always cried when dicing onions and today was no exception as she dropped two handfuls of onions into the frying pan for sautéing. The phone rang shrilly and she hurriedly wiped her hands, letting out a sigh of exasperation as she answered the phone.

"Is that you, Debra?"

"Yes, Mom," she sniffled.

"Is something wrong? You sound like you've been crying."

Debra hesitated before answering, "No, I'm slicing onions. I really can't talk right now. I'm in the middle of making dinner."

Her mother was at least a little peeved and insisted that Debra call soon to make arrangements for her father's 75th birthday celebration in Sacramento the following month.

Debra promised to call and hung up the phone.

Onions or no onions, Debra felt like crying anyway. She was tempted to talk to her mother, but it was not as if she could expect her mother to be supportive. She definitely would not approve of what was happening. Besides, Debra needed time to sort things through herself.

It was only this morning, a couple of days after his return from Sacramento, that Ted had dropped his bomb on her. Her hands trembled as she remembered.

She had walked into the bedroom to find Ted packing a travel bag. "Where are you going?"

"I've decided to move out on my own." What?! She was speechless.

"Look Debra, you're right. We can't keep living like this. We're making each other miserable." He placed his electric shaver in its case before placing it into his leather shaving kit. "I've got enough going on in my career. I don't need anymore pressure."

Debra couldn't believe she had just stood there dumbfounded.

"I'm going back to Sacramento at the end of the month." He told her that George Sadler, a software engineer he had worked with when he first started at Paradigm Software Consulting in Sacramento, had moved on to a smaller software consulting firm and had become management there.

He hurried on to say, "He's got an opening for a Project Manager for a new software project and he's offered it to me. It's a smaller firm…more nuts and bolts…less bureaucracy and less cutthroat." He reached inside the cabinet for his toothpaste and deodorant.

"You can't possibly be serious!"

"I've got to get out of this rat race. It's too dog-eat-dog here in San Diego. I'm nobody here, just another cog in the wheel. This city's too big!"

Debra finally regained her senses enough to say, "We're not uprooting the kids again! They've settled into their new schools. They're making friends and starting to fit in here."

"You and the kids aren't going with me. I'm going alone." He jammed his toothbrush into the kit and yanked the zipper shut.

"What?! You're going without us?! When did you plan all this? I can't believe you didn't have the decency to talk to me about it! Why?" She was hardly making any sense, but then none of this was making any sense to her either.

"You wouldn't understand."

"No, I don't, but help me." Debra pleaded.

"Look, I'm not cut out for this. You can have the house and everything in it." He turned to walk away. "I'll take my personal belongings and my things in the den, but I don't care about the rest of it. I need a simpler life."

"What do you mean you need a simpler life? It was your idea to come here in the first place! What about us?"

He spun around to face her. "I don't want a big job! I don't want a house! I don't want a family and I sure as heck don't want you!"

She had been further shocked when his voice dropped in defeat and he went on to say, "I don't love you…I'm not sure I ever did." With that, he was out the door and within seconds was backing out of the driveway in his SAAB.

Debra had sobbed uncontrollably. She was devastated. They had raised two lovely children and shared many joyous vacations. What did he mean he wasn't sure he had ever loved her? Sure things had been difficult for the past while, but she had never dreamed it would culminate in a separation. He hadn't even tried to work things out with her. He had never even hinted that he was unhappy with her.

Her mother would have a fit! And what about the children? How was she going to explain this to them?

Jonathan still needed a father around. Although she had to admit, it had been a long time since Ted had been much of a father to him. Leanne would be horrified. Only just yesterday she had spoken to her mother about her friend, Samantha, whose parents were divorcing.

Debra recalled Leanne expressed concern that Samantha was stressed due to conflict between her parents and the awkwardness of visitation. Samantha was at an age where she wanted to hang out with her friends and, much as she loved her father, taking time away to visit him was a hardship.

"She's so caught in the middle, Mom. Her dad's got a new girlfriend and her Mom is always asking questions about their relationship. I'm sure glad I'm not her."

Jonathan was away at his soccer tournament in San Bernardino and Leanne was sleeping over at Lisa's. They would both be home in time for dinner. Debra wasn't looking forward to explaining the separation to their children. She hardly understood it herself.

* * * * * * * * * * * * * * * * * * *

Right from the beginning they had been voted couple most likely to succeed. She and Ted had met when they were both seniors. Debra had gone to a beach party with her best friend, Terri. Soon after arriving at the beach they found a log to sit on so they could watch a beach volleyball game in progress. Debra immediately noticed Ted.

He spiked the ball over the net and laughed at himself when he fell onto the sand. He quickly jumped to his feet and tipped the ball back over the net when a player from the other side volleyed the ball toward him. Debra couldn't help but notice his thick, sandy colored hair, beautiful blue eyes, trim physique, and broad shoulders.

He eventually noticed her looking at him and she was pleased to note that he blushed. From that point on, he became self-conscious and his game was off. The other team won, but she was glad to see that he shook hands with his opponents when the game was over. He chatted with various people and eventually meandered toward Debra. Conversation was initially awkward and superficial. They, however, discovered they had several common interests and, before the day ended, they agreed to get together the following Friday evening. This led to further dates.

They shared a pleasant courtship marked by outings with friends, visits to the local drive-in for burgers and shakes, cycling in the park, and movies at the town cinema. It became expected that they would stay in Sacramento and marry.

The wedding was a simple affair attended by family and close friends. Debra worked her way up from clerical to administrative positions. Ted meanwhile attended Sacramento State University and completed a Bachelor's Degree in Computer Science.

Debra became pregnant a couple of years after Ted finished his degree and was settled in a good job designing software. Both were excited about the prospect of having children. They attended prenatal classes and doctor's visits and Ted was a supportive coach at her bedside during the delivery.

Ted hadn't been as involved in parenting as Debra, but he changed diapers occasionally and helped with feedings. Both he and Debra were tickled pink as Leanne completed each of the developmental milestones.

When Jonathan came along three years later, they thought the timing was perfect. Ted was well established in his job. Although Leanne went through a brief phase of jealousy, she soon delighted in playing Mommy to Jonathan. She fetched diapers for her mother, made faces at Jonathan to entertain him, and enjoyed wheeling him around the house in his stroller.

Debra returned to the work force once both children were in preschool. Early on, both children discovered they enjoyed team sports and their parents regularly attended their games. They had enjoyed family vacations at Cancun, Disneyland, and the Grand Canyon. And now, he wanted to walk away from it all!

Whatever had gone wrong?

She briefly wondered whether there was another woman involved. He certainly hadn't been home much. But, no he couldn't have fit that in with all of his work demands. Not only that, but relationships seemed to be a low priority in his life ever since the transfer. Even his parents and sister were complaining that they hardly heard from him anymore.

She almost wished there were another woman. She would prefer to think that someone took him away from her rather than he just plain didn't want her.

Ted had returned a couple of hours later, after he'd made his announcement. Debra had tried to plead with him, but his mind was made up. She had followed him around, sick with grief, as he packed some of the clothes from his closet.

He had told her he would stay in a hotel until the end of the month when he would move to Sacramento to start his new job. He would call her to make arrangements to get the rest of his things.

* * * * * * * * * * * * * * * * * * *

Leanne was the first to arrive home, and almost immediately went up to her bedroom to get her homework done. Jonathan returned home soon afterwards. He was excited and buzzed noisily around his mother as she cooked dinner, telling her all about his weekend in San Bernardino. He had scored a total of three goals throughout the games his team had played so he was very pleased with himself. Debra congratulated him and sent him up for a quick shower before dinner.

When she called them both down to eat, they immediately noticed their father's absence at the table. Despite Ted's recent absences, he rarely missed a Sunday evening meal at home.

Jonathan was the first to ask where his father was. Debra thought she was going to cry, but she managed to hold it together as she explained that he had moved out.

Jonathan immediately became tearful. "I told you! I told you you were going to get a divorce!" He bolted from the table and started to head down the hallway. Debra followed and wrapped her arms around him.

"Jonathan, please, honey, I'm sorry. Come back to the table so we can all talk. We need to talk about what we're going to do."

He slowly made his way back to his chair. Leanne said, "This really isn't much of a surprise. Dad was hardly ever home anymore and when he was, he still wasn't, you know?"

Jonathan glared at her.

Debra said, "I know. It's been hard on all of us. I guess your Dad hasn't been happy ever since the move to San Diego. He feels like he has too much responsibility and he needs a rest from it all."

"Does that mean he's coming back after he takes a vacation?" asked Jonathan.

This time Leanne glared at him, "Don't be an imbecile!"

Debra intervened. "I don't think so. I mean, it's possible, but it doesn't seem likely. He got himself a job at a smaller firm in

Sacramento and he's planning on moving back there at the end of the month."

Jonathan started to cry, again.

"It sounds like Dad is having a mid-life crisis."

Jonathan looked over with disgust.

Leanne ignored him. She had other concerns on her mind. "Mom, are we going to have to move?"

"I'm not sure we can afford to keep this house, but, if we can't, we'll get something smaller nearby. I'm not going to move you away from your schools and friends, okay? We'll manage somehow, I know we will."

Debra went up to say goodnight to Jonathan that night. He asked her if he was ever going to see his father, again. Debra felt certain he couldn't just forget his children completely, so she told Jonathan they just needed to give him some time to figure things out. She didn't know how long it would take, but she thought he would eventually want to spend some time with his children. Jonathan let her tuck him in and she knew that was testimony to how vulnerable he was feeling. It broke her heart to see him like that.

She tried to spend some time with Leanne, too, but Leanne told her she wanted to be alone.

Initially Debra just went through the motions of life—numb with shock, a strict routine helped her to carry on and cope. She automatically showered and dressed each morning, and dragged herself off to work. She carried a hectic workload during the day which, on the whole, served as a good distraction. During the evening, she did chores until late at night so that she would fall into bed exhausted. She was afraid to be alone with her thoughts and feelings. They were so overwhelming.

During her out of work hours, she managed herself much the same as she did on the job. She became adept at writing lists of things to do to ensure that she kept moving. Her greatest temptation was to simply sit on the couch staring into space and let life pass by. Debra knew she owed it to her children to try her best to give them as much of a semblance of order as was possible.

She did errands, bought groceries, and prepared meals like a robot with a script. Needless to say, she was distracted and felt she had little to offer her children emotionally. Jonathan was often angry and sullen. His emotional outbursts tried her patience.

Leanne, on the other hand, seemed quiet and withdrawn. Every day was a tolerance test.

"Mom, where's my soccer jersey? I've got a practice right after school! You promised you'd wash it before this morning!" Jonathan yelled. Yanked out of her reverie, Debra told him she'd forgotten it last night in the dryer. It'd been chilly overnight. With the cold air vented into the dryer, that jersey would look worse than slept in.

By the time Debra had cleaned up after dinner the night before, then reviewed Jonathan's spelling list with him, washed and dried a load of laundry, tidied up the family room, and packed the lunches, she'd fallen into bed exhausted. Not that she'd slept much. She felt like she had hundreds of tapes running in her head. She spent the nighttime hours ruminating about the past, wondering what she should have done to prevent the separation and looking for clues that this would have been the end result. When she wasn't reliving the past, she was worrying about the future. How was she going to manage? What effect would this have on their children? Would she be able to afford to keep the house? She was highly reluctant to move and unsettle the children any more than was absolutely necessary.

With everything on her mind, she'd completely forgotten about the laundry left in the dryer. Just one more failure to add to her list. Just yesterday she had forgotten to sign a field trip permission slip for Jonathan to go to the Old Town Museum, but fortunately they had contacted her at work and she had faxed permission so that he didn't have to stay behind at the school. She was exhausted and she couldn't keep up anymore.

Jonathan had finally grown old enough to care about his appearance and he wasn't going to let her off easy for not taking proper care of his soccer uniform. "Mom, how could you do that to me? I can't go to the game looking like a shar-pei dog!"

"Jonathan, I'm sorry. I completely forgot. I'll turn the dryer on for a few minutes and maybe the hot air will take out some of the wrinkles." Debra pulled the rest of the clothes out and threw them in the empty basket on top of the dryer, then turned it on, and hoped it would work.

That day at work, Debra was setting up a schedule of interviews to hire a new clerk typist and was between phone calls when all of a sudden her chest became tight, she felt her heart palpitating and she was breathing rapidly. She clutched her desk as she struggled to grab a breath. "My God," she thought, "I'm having a heart attack." She told herself to calm down and she tried to breathe more slowly. The anxiety eventually receded, but left her trembling.

She started experiencing intermittent panic attacks throughout the day. They would sneak up on her and she felt like she was losing control. She even had a few at night during the many hours she was unable to sleep. It was very overwhelming.

When Saturday morning arrived, Debra hardly had enough motivation to get out of bed, never mind go for a walk. When she didn't show at Liz's gate, Liz walked over and rang the doorbell. Leanne, who was already up watching Much Music on television, answered the door. Once Liz told her who she was, Leanne went to get her mother.

Debra appeared shortly afterward, wearing her robe, with her hair awry. She told Liz she wasn't up to walking. When Liz realized Debra was upset rather than ill, she insisted that a walk would be the best thing for her. She convinced Debra to get dressed and brush her hair, and off they went.

Liz, in next to no time, drew the story out of her. Debra ended up telling her about the separation, the fact that she wasn't sleeping or eating, and she even told Liz about her panic attacks.

Liz was very sympathetic and understanding. She offered to teach Debra a grounding ritual after they finished their walk.

"What is a grounding ritual?"

"It's sort of like meditating."

Liz explained that it's a tool Debra could use to help her to define her own space so she wouldn't be so affected by negative energy. She told her that the reason Debra was so anxious was because she was anywhere but in the present and a grounding ritual would help her feel more centered.

"I'm desperate enough to try almost anything." They stopped in at Liz's home after their walk. Like Debra, Liz's home was one of the few two-stories in the neighborhood. Liz took her into a small room off of the entryway. It was a cozy space and the sunlight softly filtered through the shades. Debra immediately noticed a massage table, which had several fluffy pillows and a soft fleece blanket laid on it.

She asked Liz if she did massage. "Not exactly. I could show you some time, if you'd like."

There was an overstuffed easy chair in the corner, with a small table and lamp beside it. Liz asked Debra to sit in the chair. Liz stepped over to the shelves on the wall and turned on a CD player. Soft instrumental music filtered through the speakers. It was very pleasant. She could also hear the trickle of water coming from a small Japanese fountain.

Liz lit a few of the candles which were placed intermittently throughout the room and asked Debra to close her eyes, relax, and focus on the music. She asked her to make sure her feet were firmly planted on the floor. She then told her to think about her tailbone at the base of her spine and to imagine it being connected with a long tube going down to the core of the planet.

"Some people can see it and some can't, but it doesn't matter either way, imagine that there is a tube connecting your tailbone to the center of the Earth. Breathe slowly and imagine draining any energy that isn't yours away from your body, into the tube, and down to the center of the Earth."

After a few moments, she instructed Debra to imagine that there was a gold ball above the crown of her head and to imagine bringing back all of her own energy that she has let others have. "You might actually be able to see the gold ball and you might not."

She encouraged Debra to keep breathing slowly in and out. "Now, ask that a gold cocoon envelop your body and your space— to keep negative energy out, but to let positive energy in. Imagine that you're surrounded by a warm golden light."

When she suggested that Debra open her eyes, then take some deep breaths in and let them out, Debra was aware of feeling an incredible sense of calm—one she hadn't experienced in what felt like an eternity. She thanked Liz.

"You can do that yourself for a few minutes every morning to get your day off to a good start. You might also want to do it at bedtime, or any time you're feeling anxious or unsettled. If you're having trouble feeling grounded, it helps to wear red."

"I've never really liked red. I'm more into winter shades."

"Make it rosy red, then. Red will help you feel grounded and the pink will help you to feel loved."

Debra looked around the room. Her eyes scanned the circle of angels with wings holding hands on the bookshelves, the delicate pearly shells hung in spirals from a low wall bracket, the lovely Anne Geddes painting of three angels in gathered satiny dresses wearing orange-yellow halos and wings, the many candles, and particularly the massage table. "So, Liz," she opened her arms expansively to encompass the room. "What is all this?"

"I do Healing Touch." Debra looked puzzled. "It involves the transfer of energy and promotes healing...spiritual, physical and emotional, It doesn't actually have to involve a lot of touching. Energy can be transferred by laying hands on a person or from a distance."

"How did you get into this?"

"I broke my knee rollerblading a couple of years ago when I was still in Denver. People in the Boulder area are very open-minded about alternative healing techniques. Actually it's very popular here in San Diego, too." She explained that one of her neighbors recommended she see a Healing Touch practitioner in Boulder to augment her physiotherapy treatment.

"I found it extremely helpful so I enrolled in some courses and learned how to do it to help others." When Debra expressed curiosity to know more about it, Liz offered to do Healing Touch on her.

"You're not going to go all voodoo on me, are you?" Debra giggled with apprehension as she realized she didn't really know that much about Liz. She seemed trustworthy, but who knows?

"I'm not into witchcraft, if that's what you mean. Think of it as a relaxation session. That's probably something you can relate to."

Picking up on Debra's apprehension, she told her, "We don't have to do it right now. Give me a call one evening this week. It's not a big deal. All you have to do is lie nice and cozy under this Arctic fleece and relax. You'll see. It'll be fine."

They exchanged phone numbers. Liz also recommended she consider visiting her physician to see about getting a sedative. "...Just something mild to help you get some sleep so you can function on a day-to-day basis."

Monday morning, Debra called the doctor's office and was able to slip in to see him later that day. Dr. Watson had been their family doctor since their move to San Diego and she had found him to be straightforward, but compassionate about any concerns she or the children had shared with him. He took one look at her and commented, "Debra, you sure don't look well. Whatever is going on?"

"Things aren't good between Ted and I," she answered, holding back the tears. "As a matter of fact, he moved out. That's why I

21

came to see you. I haven't been sleeping or eating. I was hoping you could give me some sleeping pills. I'm sick about it," she said, as she burst into tears.

Dr. Watson stepped toward her and put a hand on her shoulder. Once she had calmed down, he gave her a brief medical check up.

She told him about her panic attacks. He asked questions to determine the level of depression. Debra told him she wasn't suicidal. She admitted she sometimes wished she were dead just to make the emotional pain go away, but said she wouldn't do anything to make it happen.

He asked, "Have you thought about going to talk to a counselor? Sometimes it helps to talk to someone who's not involved in your day to day life."

"I need to do something. I'm an emotional wreck. I don't know what to do."

She told him she had a health plan at work and she would check to see what coverage was available.

Dr. Watson wrote her a prescription for a mild sedative. "I'm not going to give you a lot of these, because they're very habit forming. But, they'll give you a few nights rest." She thanked him and went out into the waiting room.

By the time she had the prescription filled and picked up a few groceries for dinner, she just wanted to get home and go to bed. But that was not an option. She still had to retrieve Jonathan and some of his buddies from their soccer practice. One of the other mothers had dropped them off and it was her turn to pick them up.

Debra managed to get through the evening. She took one of the pills that night and slept like a baby. It was difficult to get up the next day and she was sluggish until at least ten o'clock. But, it was a welcome relief not to feel like a basket case anymore and she didn't have any panic attacks.

The following day, Debra pulled out the file on her employee health care coverage. It provided a web site address with a preferred provider list she could look up on the Internet during one of her breaks at work. Scanning the list of names and reading the brief summaries of their qualifications online, she decided on a female therapist who was listed near her place of employment in Mission Valley. That would make it more convenient to go during office time. She could work through her lunch hour and start a little earlier to make up any time she needed for travel. Thank goodness, the children were at an age where they could take care of themselves for brief periods.

The summary read:

Elizabeth Goldie MFT
Relationships—Depression
Individual—Couple—Family
Reclaim Your Life Through Brief Solution Focused Therapy

Before she could lose her nerve, she placed a call to the counseling office. The receptionist told Debra the counselor had a cancellation the following week, Wednesday evening at seven o'clock. Debra was pleased she wouldn't have to take time off work. She wasn't ready yet to let anyone at work know she was seeing a counselor. With trepidation, she took the appointment and they exchanged the necessary information. "Oh, my God." She couldn't believe she'd actually scheduled an appointment with a counselor.

She called Liz that night and they arranged to get together the following evening so Liz could give her Healing Touch.

Debra ambled down the sidewalk toward Liz's home the next evening. "I must be truly desperate. I can't believe I'm here," she said as Liz greeted her at the door.

Liz smiled, "It's really not a big deal. You'll see," she reassured her.

Liz instructed Debra to lie on her back on the massage table. She placed one of the pillows under her knees and covered her with the fleece blanket. Liz inserted a *Songbirds At Sunrise* disc in the CD player. Soft music filtered into the room with the faint sounds of birds chirping and singing. She, again, lit a few candles. She told Debra to listen to the birds and the pleasant trickle of the Japanese fountain, and focus on breathing slowly.

Liz took a gold chain and dangled it above Debra's feet. Initially, the bottom of the chain bounced back and forth and then started to swing in clockwise circles.

Liz told her, "This is penduluming. It's to check your energy flow." She dangled the chain over Debra's ankles, knees, hips, root, abdomen, above her navel, and over her heart. Each time, the chain eventually swung clockwise, except over her heart it swung counterclockwise.

"What does that mean?" Debra asked.

"You're leaking energy from your heart chakra." If she'd asked, Debra would have said her heart was long since empty. She felt like Ted had ripped it open!

She then dangled the chain over Debra's throat, forehead, and above her head. The chain swung in clockwise circles for each placement. "The energy flow is good everywhere else."

Liz put the chain on the table. She placed a hand on Debra's chest bone and held one of her hands with the other. She asked Debra to take slow breaths in and out.

"Please allow Debra to accept this energy readily and easily. May the energy go wherever she needs it most. Please send any energy she doesn't need back to the earth to be recycled and reused. If there are any guides that would like to assist, their help would be appreciated."

"First of all, I'm going to remove the stale energy. Lie there, close your eyes, and relax."

Debra was aware that Liz initially stood on her right side and, after a few minutes, switched to her left side. She had to peek, just once. Liz was gliding her hands a few inches above Debra's body...down from over Debra's head to past her feet where she would shake her hands off toward the floor and then repeat the process. It almost looked as if she was sifting imaginary spaghetti and then shaking her hands off.

Liz then said, "I'm going to help you create a fantasy place."

Her voice was soft. "Imagine that you are laying on the grass in a meadow." She then related a fantasy setting to Debra. There was a pool nearby and she could hear water from a waterfall thundering into the pool. It was a beautiful sunny day. She could hear the leaves gently rustling in the breeze and feel the warmth of the sun on her skin. The leaves were various colors, light green, dark green, and some yellow, with even an occasional orange leaf. Debra felt warm and drowsy.

After a while, Liz had her walk over to the pond and dive in. The water was cool and refreshing. When she swam deeper, she saw an underwater tunnel. Liz instructed her to swim through it and come up in a pool inside a cave. The cave had sunlight streaming in through a rock opening above. It was beautiful and serene. A ledge surrounded the pool. Debra looked over and saw a treasure chest on the ledge, as suggested to her by Liz. She climbed up on the ledge and walked over to the chest.

"There is a gift inside. Take the gift," Liz said, softly. When Debra lifted the lid of the chest, her two children rose to greet her. She hugged them one at a time. After a while, Liz told her there was a guest standing behind her. Debra turned and walked over to him.

"He also has a gift for you. Take the gift." The man wrapped his arms around Debra and both of her children.

"Nice, a group hug," Debra thought.

"It is time for you to leave." Liz sent Debra back into the pool, through the tunnel, and up on the other side. She then instructed Debra to go lie on the grass, where she began, again, to feel warm from the sun.

Debra became slowly aware that Liz was massaging her legs separately from the knee down to past her toes. She explained that she was grounding Debra so she wouldn't feel unbalanced.

Liz stepped back and told her, "We're done now. Whenever you're ready, breathe in and out slowly a few times and then open your eyes."

Debra felt like she had woken from a deep sleep. She felt so peaceful and relaxed.

Liz asked her what it had been like and what she had felt. Debra related her experience and Liz told her she was very open to the power of suggestion, which helped her to get more from the fantasy. She asked Debra what her gifts were and told her that whatever a person takes out of the trunk usually symbolizes what is important in that person's life and that the gift received from the visitor usually represents what he or she is looking for in a relationship. Debra found that intriguing.

Liz then used the gold chain to pendulum all of the various points, again. Each time the chain swung in circles, including over her heart, and Liz told her that her energy flow was good everywhere now.

Debra thanked her. She noticed Liz's business cards on the table and asked what she charged for a session. Liz explained that she never charged for initial sessions and that it was more of a hobby to her than anything else. For people who could afford it, she accepted donations, but she said she would rather help Debra as a friend than as a client.

She asked whether Debra would be open to another Healing Touch session. "Who wouldn't? That was incredible! I feel so peaceful and relaxed."

They agreed to meet for their morning walk the following Saturday and would set up another time then, once Liz had a clearer idea of her schedule.

Debra slept peacefully that night. It really meant a lot to her that her children were the gift in the treasure chest. She was so overwhelmed that sometimes she felt she wasn't placing her children as a high enough priority. But, she truly loved them so much that it hurt to have to drag them through this mess. It was no surprise that, if she was going to have a man in her life, she wanted him to embrace her children as well as herself, but she was in no hurry for that at this point in time.

Debra continued to do a grounding ritual every morning and each night before she went to bed. Sometimes she found it difficult to avoid becoming distracted and she would have to consciously re-focus herself, but she always felt more relaxed afterwards.

She found it easier to get up on Saturday mornings because of her walking schedule. It encouraged her to get out of bed in the morning. She knew if she didn't, Liz would come looking for her, but regardless, she looked forward to their jaunts around the bay. She admired Liz's no-nonsense style and found their conversations enjoyable.

Sunday was another story. It certainly was the most difficult day of the week. Most people were with their families and her children were usually off with their friends. Debra found she got more than enough of her own company on Sundays and this one was no exception. Not only that, but she had been procrastinating in calling her mother and she felt unable to put it off any longer. Might as well get it over with now. Her mother would have a lot to say and Debra knew she'd get all the blame.

She dialed her mother's number, part of her hoping she would get an answering machine. "No such luck!" she thought as she heard her mother's voice on the other end.

"It's about time you called. I thought you must have died or something."

Debra told her she'd had a lot on her mind lately, to which her mother responded, "You're always telling me that. If I didn't know any better, I'd say you don't like talking to me."

Debra reassured her that wasn't the case. Who was she kidding? She dreaded talking to her mother!

"Mom, I have some bad news…"

Her mother interrupted her, "One of the kids aren't hurt are they?"

"No. It's Ted, he…"

"Ted's hurt," she interrupted, again.

"No, Mom! He left."

Her mother asked what she was talking about.

"Ted moved out and he's back living in Sacramento."

"I was hoping you'd all come back to Sacramento. It's much nicer than San Diego, you know."

This was even more difficult than she had imagined. "No, Mom, we're not coming back. Ted and I are separating." Next thing she knew her mother lit into her about how she should be willing to move back to Sacramento with him and how it was the wife's job to make the compromises. She wouldn't listen when Debra told her Ted didn't want her and the children to join him in Sacramento.

"Oh, rubbish. I never heard of anything so ridiculous! Of course he wants you and the children with him. Ted's a family man. He's always been a family man."

Debra could argue that, but what would be the point? All of a sudden it occurred to her that she had a history of being unable to get her point across to both Ted and her mother. She'd never noticed the similarity before!

She let her mother rattle on about how Debra would eventually see the light and she and the kids would join Ted in Sacramento. When her mother finally paused for a breath, Debra told her, "I called you so we could make arrangements for Dad's birthday."

That provoked a new tirade. Her mother told her she had rented a hall and hired caterers. "None of you children could see it in your heart to set things up. I decided I'd better take the bull by the horns myself. I'm too old to be cooking and cleaning up for 50 people, so I'll manage to get the money together somehow to pay for someone else to do it!"

More guilt. No wonder she never called. No wonder she had welcomed the move to San Diego.

"Mom, how is Dad doing?"

"Well, his health isn't like it used to be. We're not getting any younger." Her mother went on to tell her about the various people in their neighborhood and church including a litany about which ones were ill and which ones had died. Debra made comments in all the right places and then ended the call by telling her mother that she should phone if there was anything Debra do to help out with her father's birthday celebration. That was one bit of nastiness over with!

CHAPTER THREE

The following week, Debra told the children she had made an appointment with a counselor and she let them know she'd be out on Wednesday evening. She approached the first appointment with great trepidation. What if the counselor thought she was just feeling sorry for herself?

The counselor's name was engraved on a brass doorplate. Debra hesitated, but opened the door and walked into the waiting room. She was about ten minutes ahead of her appointment time. There were several typical waiting room seats, with aluminum frames and cushioned seats and backs. Not real comfortable looking, but the lamps were dim which gave a cozy feel to the room. The end tables were decorated with silk flower arrangements and magazines were carefully spread in the shape of a fan on the tables for easy choosing of titles.

Debra picked up the scent of a mild deodorizer. M-m-m…lilacs. As she had been told, there was no receptionist on duty during the evenings, so she chose a chair and waited.

Debra was more than a little apprehensive. She'd never been to a therapist before. She started to bite her nails and tap her feet. Just when she started to think that she could leave and nobody would ever know she had been there, the door to the inner office opened. A couple stepped into the reception area followed by a tall, attractive woman dressed in professional attire. She said goodbye to them. She then turned and held out her hand to Debra as she introduced herself.

"Hi, I'm Elizabeth Goldie." Her voice was soft, with a gentle lilt.

"Debra Logan," she said as Elizabeth took her hand. Elizabeth's grip was gentle, but firm.

Elizabeth held the door to her office open for Debra to enter. The room was inviting, with a few pastel comfortable armchairs and soft glowing lamps. A glass covered Monet print in an attractive steel blue metal frame hung on the wall and one of the end tables was decorated with a lovely arrangement of silk orchids. A file folder sat on one of the chairs, so Debra chose one of the other two vacant chairs that were adjacent. As Debra had assumed, Elizabeth picked up the folder and sat down in that chair.

Elizabeth recited a brief summary of her therapy background and reassured Debra that everything she shared would be kept confidential.

She asked whether Debra had any questions and when she said she didn't, Elizabeth asked, "So, what brought you here today?"

Debra told her about Ted leaving and her difficulties coping. Elizabeth was attentive. She commented that it was understandable that Debra was feeling overwhelmed and scared.

It felt so good to have a sympathetic ear that she crumbled and next thing she knew she was crying. Elizabeth passed Debra a couple of tissues, but continued to listen while Debra explained about the separation between sobs. "I promised myself I wouldn't do this…I hate crying in front of people. It's just I need somebody to talk to." Elizabeth asked her questions about her current life situation and how it had come about. Debra eventually felt calmer as she talked.

When Elizabeth heard about Ted's lack of emotional availability during the previous year, she asked, "Is there any chance he's involved with another woman?"

Debra laughed, "I wish." When she saw Elizabeth's look of puzzlement, she explained, "It's just, I'd rather he rejected me because of some other woman rather than based solely on my own merits or lack of them."

Elizabeth commented that the past year must have been very painful. "It sounds like he left the relationship emotionally, long before he left physically."

To hear it put into words like that was validating for Debra. That's certainly how it felt to her.

Elizabeth asked whether Debra had ever been to counseling before. Debra told her she hadn't. When she inquired about Debra's support system, Debra told her that her parents live in Sacramento. She, however, explained that her mother wasn't particularly supportive and that, although her father was caring, it was difficult to talk to him. She explained that he was very busy during her childhood and they had never become close. She had three siblings, but they were scattered all over the country and rarely had contact.

"What about friends?" she asked.

"Well, I haven't really made any close friends since my move to San Diego. I'm getting to know one of my neighbors and I think we may become good friends, but we don't know each other really well, yet."

She asked questions similar to Debra's doctor to check for symptoms of depression. Again, Debra was able to answer honestly and told Elizabeth that although she sometimes wished she were dead, she was confident that she wouldn't do anything to harm herself. In response to Elizabeth's questions about drug and alcohol use, Debra replied that she had never really acquired a taste for alcohol so she drank only the occasional glass of wine and she did not use drugs.

Elizabeth then asked, "How are you hoping that I can be helpful?"

"Well, as I said, I need someone to talk to. I need to get my life together. I'm sick of feeling scared. I hardly eat at all and unless I take a sedative, I'm awake almost all night."

Elizabeth explained that she was caught up in "fight or flight syndrome" where the body produces extra adrenaline to help a person cope with a crisis. She asked Debra how she spent her leisure time and what sort of activities she was involved in that provided her with total escape from reality. Debra had to admit that she had pretty much given up all of her leisure activities since the move to San Diego. She said that reading novels used to give her a good escape because she used to become so involved that she almost lived the life of the character while reading, but she hadn't read anything in a long time.

Debra also confided that she had started doing grounding rituals and had been to one Healing Touch session that she found to be relaxing.

"Good," Elizabeth responded. She told Debra that any time she was able to get herself to relax, eat, or sleep, it would fool her body into thinking the crisis was over so it would produce less adrenaline which in turn would help her to relax, sleep, and eat. "What you want to do is get the cycle going in that direction."

Elizabeth then asked, "What would be a first sign to you that things are on the right track?"

"I wouldn't feel so scared and overwhelmed—like I'm almost constantly on the verge of tears. I'd feel more content."

When asked what would have to be happening for her to feel more content and less overwhelmed, Debra didn't hesitate. "I'd have something to look forward to and I'd feel more confident about my future."

"How will you know when our work has been completed? For example, what would have to be happening in your life, for you to know that you no longer need to meet with a counselor?"

"I'd feel good about myself and I'd know I could count on myself. Like I said, I'd have something to look forward to instead of dreading every day."

Elizabeth asked her what was going well and what her strengths were. Debra told her that she enjoyed her job, that it could be stressful, at times, but she liked the people and appreciated the fact that the responsibilities were challenging. She described herself as an independent and determined individual. "Most people see me as cheerful, energetic, and hardworking."

The counselor told her that those would be good characteristics to help her get through the tough times.

When Elizabeth asked whether she had any questions, Debra was quick to respond, "I'm worried sick about my kids. Ted didn't even say 'goodbye' to them. Are they going to be scarred for life by this?"

"Sometimes when people don't know what's wrong, they panic and throw the baby out with the bath water. That is, they don't know what to throw out, so they throw out everything. Ted may become re-involved with the children after he gets more settled in his life and discovers that they aren't part of the problem."

She went on to say that children usually cope well, provided their parents do well. "Let's see how things go and if you want to bring them in later on, we can do that."

She asked Debra what promises she could make to her children to help them to feel more secure. Debra told her she could promise them that both parents love them, she would not interfere with their relationships with their father, and they would not move out of the district. Those were the ones she felt confident she could keep. Elizabeth suggested she reassure the children by sharing those promises with them as soon as possible.

She then said, "Research shows that most people need less than six sessions to get their life on track. How many do you think you will need?" Debra immediately said, "All six."

"O.K., fair enough. Your health care coverage will cover six sessions so you don't need to worry about that. If we decide the children have to come in at some time, we could contract for another set of sessions for them."

She gave Debra some "homework" to do. "Between now and the next time we get together, I want you to experiment with building in things to look forward to and pay close attention to which ones you enjoy the most. Then we'll talk about it when you come back in."

They scheduled another appointment for two weeks later. When Debra expressed disappointment about waiting two weeks, the counselor told Debra she was already doing some things to help get her life on track so she would be fine. She also pointed out that Debra needed time to do her homework. That made sense to Debra and she felt reassured as she headed for home.

Debra decided to stop by the Pacific Beach Library on her way home. It was a new building and it was the most spacious and beautiful library she had ever seen. The shelves were well stocked with the latest books from her favorite authors. She quickly chose two novels and signed up for a library card. Maybe that would encourage her to get back into reading.

Debra was pleased to see that things were harmonious between Jonathan and Leanne when she returned. She was a bit rushed getting things tidied up and lunches made before bedtime, but she felt the time spent with the counselor was beneficial enough that it was worth it.

She noticed she was repeatedly going over the conversation she had shared with Elizabeth, savoring the validation she had received, thinking about the suggestions she had made, and considering things she wanted to talk about next time.

She decided to do her nightly grounding ritual to help settle her thoughts and then treated herself to a half-hour of reading in bed. She was soon wrapped up in a Barbara Delinsky novel and was feeling drowsy by the time she turned the lights off and slipped down deeper under the bed covers.

It was the first night since Ted left that she actually slept for most of it. The next morning, though, was another whole new day. Mornings were always the most difficult part of the day now. She woke up with the frustration of not being able to reach Ted. She needed to talk to him about the house and their bank account.

When Debra returned home from work that evening, she knew instantly that something was wrong. Sure enough, she opened the double glass doors to Ted's den and it was empty. Well, unless you counted a gum wrapper and a couple of paperclips left lying on the floor, it was completely bare. He had removed his computer, desk, and chair. Also missing were the grandfather clock his parents gave them as a wedding gift and all of the contents from the bookshelves. He had even taken the framed hand drawn charcoal drawing of their previous home which used to hang on the wall. Debra slumped onto the carpet. Her immediate feeling was one of defeat. He really wasn't coming back!

All of a sudden she was angry. She jumped up. "That little weasel, he didn't even have the balls to call and tell us he was coming! He snuck into our home, like a thief!" She thought the kids would at least have a chance to talk with him when he returned for his things. He managed to avoid that too! Not only that, but she still didn't have a telephone number. She absolutely had to go over their financial affairs with him.

She stomped out the door and down the sidewalk to Liz's house. Liz was just driving up as she arrived.

Liz looked over at Debra with surprise as she rolled down her car window. "What's happening?"

Debra was so angry the words tumbled out. "You think you know somebody. All those years of marriage! I can't believe it. Everything from the den is gone. He didn't even call first! He walked in and helped himself while we were gone!"

Liz said, "Hang on. Let me put the car away." She parked in the garage and Debra joined her. "Did he take anything else?"

"I don't know. I was so upset, I didn't think to look."

Liz picked out a couple of screwdrivers off the workbench. "Come on, you and I have a little chore to do! Are Leanne and Jonathan home yet?"

Debra said, "Not yet. They both have practices at their schools today. Why?"

"We're going to get your locks re-keyed. He can't come and go as he pleases. You need to have control over your home."

That sounded like a great idea to Debra, but she didn't have a clue how to get a lock re-keyed. Liz put her arm around Debra and said, "Let's go have some fun."

They went over to Debra's home where Liz proceeded to remove the deadbolts on both the front and the back doors. She asked Debra to pay close attention to how the locks were put together so that she could re-install them after they were re-keyed.

She gave Debra instructions to Ace Hardware on Grand Avenue a few blocks away, reminded her to get extra keys made for the children, and told her, "If you have any trouble getting them back together, give me a call." They gave each other a hug and Debra thanked her as she picked up the lock parts to take to her car.

Debra had the locks re-keyed and was surprised it only cost $5.00 for each lock. She returned home and was impressed that she was able to re-install the locks with hardly any difficulty at all. It was simple, all she had to do was put the two halves of the deadbolt in the hole and screw them back together. She was quite proud of herself. "Who needs men?!" she thought.

She checked the bedroom dresser and closet and, sure enough, Ted's belongings were missing. Fine! She pulled out the vacuum cleaner and dragged it into the den. She dusted the built-in shelf unit and vacuumed the carpet with a vengeance, like she was trying to clean Ted out of her life. When she was all done, she brushed her hands off with satisfaction. So there!

She scrambled to get dinner ready before Leanne and Jonathan arrived home from school. Both children were worn out from their practices, but they were ravenous from all the exercise. At least someone felt like eating. Debra was still fuming.

She asked each of them how the day had been. After they shared the details, she announced that their father had been to the house to collect his belongings and she had decided to change the locks on the doors so he would be unable to re-enter without contacting them first.

Debra thought she saw a glimmer of newfound respect in Leanne's eyes. Jonathan, on the other hand, became hysterical. "Why are you trying to drive him away? It's his house, too. Now he'll never come back!"

"Jonathan, your father is confused right now. I don't know what he is going to do. I can't risk coming home to an empty house some day. I'm sorry. Look, I told you I wouldn't do anything to stop you from seeing him or talking to him. I need to know he won't come into the house again, while we're gone."

Leanne spoke up, "Mom, I think you did the right thing." She turned to Jonathan and used his pet name, "J.J., I want to see Dad too, but I don't think it's fair he came into the house when we weren't here. At least this way, he'll have to call if he wants anything."

Debra joined in, "I know he'll miss you once he gets things sorted out. How could he not miss your cute little freckled nose? You're his one and only all star soccer player."

She saw the briefest of smiles from his down-turned head as she walked over to hug him and he protested, "Mom, I'm not a baby anymore!"

"Now go do your homework and we'll play a game together on the Play Station when you're done." She thanked Leanne for her support and asked her how she was doing with all that was going on.

"Okay, I guess. I'm afraid we're going to have to move. I really like my new friends here."

Debra told her, "I promise I'm not going to uproot you. I'd get a second job before I'd do that. But, I don't think that will be necessary. I've been thinking and I think I've got a plan that'll work."

She knew they had put a fairly hefty down payment on their home from the proceeds of the sale of their house in Sacramento. Ted had chosen a short-term mortgage with high payments so they could pay off the house more quickly. If Ted would let her re-mortgage the house, she could reduce the payment to something affordable.

She finished cleaning up the kitchen while Jonathan did his homework, then she joined him for a game of Crash Bandicoot. "Jonathan just give your Dad some time to sort things out, okay? He always used to enjoy spending time with you and Leanne. I'm sure he will, again."

"How can you be sure?"

"Well, okay, I'm not sure, but he probably will. Hang in there, okay?"

"Yeah, okay."

Seeing Jonathan look so crushed gave Debra new resolve. Once he was settled in bed, she called Ted's parents' home in Sacramento. Ted's mother, Louise, answered. They exchanged awkward pleasantries. When Debra asked if she knew Ted's whereabouts, Louise hesitated.

"Louise, I need to talk to him about what to do with the house. I don't know how to contact him. Could you please have him call me? I really need to talk to him."

"Well, I can pass the message along, but I can't guarantee he'll call."

"That's okay. I appreciate you trying."

Then Louise admitted, "I don't have a number for him, so I won't be able to talk to him until he calls...he's not himself lately."

"I know." Debra thanked her and they terminated the call.

When she got off the line, she dialed Liz's home. They chatted briefly before Debra told Liz the purpose of her call.

"Liz, I remember you said you sometimes walk during the week. When I went for my first counseling appointment, she recommended that I spend more time doing things I enjoy. I was wondering whether you'd be open to me joining you on your weekday walks."

"Sure you can, if you want. I go before work, though. You'd have to get up early."

"How early?"

"I walk at six thirty on Wednesdays now. That way I can shower and get ready for work so that I can leave at the usual time."

Debra sighed. "Actually I expected something like that. I think I could manage that. It's not as if the kids need my help getting off to school."

Liz was pleased to have the company. She told her the walkway is usually occupied by lots of people at that time because it is starting to get light by then, but she'd feel more comfortable having someone with her anyway.

Debra was finding her friendship with Liz to be invaluable. The best part was that Liz seemed to enjoy spending time together as much as she did.

Debra was pretty much able to keep pace with Liz during their morning walks although it still took effort on her part. They sometimes chatted and laughed throughout their time together. On other occasions, they walked in companionable silence.

While Debra was walking with Liz the following Saturday morning, Liz asked whether she'd be open to coming over for another Healing Touch session.

"Are you sure you don't mind?"

"Debra, that's the nice thing about Healing Touch, the giver benefits as well as the receiver."

Debra was a little surprised, "What do you get out of it?"

"It helps promote self-healing, too." She stopped to think. "This weekend is jam-packed and I've got a book discussion group meeting on Monday night. Are you by any chance free Tuesday evening?"

Debra, of course, had nothing but chores on her schedule. They agreed to get together at seven o'clock, again.

This time, Debra looked forward to her visit with Liz. Liz had already lit candles and turned on a CD when Debra arrived. After Debra hopped up onto the table, Liz asked if she could remove her socks so she could give her a foot massage. That sounded too inviting for words, so Debra quickly complied.

A pleasant minty scent filled the room as Liz massaged Debra's feet with peppermint lotion. Liz pendulumed the gold chain to check out Debra's energy flow. She explained that each of the points she pendulumed was a different "chakra" which represented particular parts of the body and related emotions.

When she was finished she asked Liz to close her eyes and think about her favorite place on earth. Debra didn't have a favorite place, so she took herself back to the imaginary meadow Liz had described the previous time and Liz proceeded with the session.

After a while Debra began to see a myriad of colors in her mind. There was vivid green, deep red, intense purple and, finally, she looked deep inside an eye of crystalline blue. It was incredible and she gasped.

"Tell me what you see," Liz coaxed.

"I can't even describe it, it's so beautiful. The colors are intense and they keep changing. Wow!"

"Lie back and enjoy them." Debra was only vaguely aware of Liz's hands, she was so enthralled by the kaleidoscope of colors she was seeing.

After a while, Liz reminded her to breathe in and out slowly a few times before opening her eyes.

Debra did so and asked her, "What was that? That was incredible."

"I often see colors, too, while I'm doing the session. Each of the colors represents a different emotion and chakra. What colors did you see?"

Debra told her.

"Green represents the heart chakra and the emotion is love resulting in balance, love, and wisdom. Purple is the crown chakra at the top of the head for higher will or knowing and the emotion is bliss. Blue is communication resulting in creativity, the color of the throat chakra, and is the will to express. The eye you saw is called a "third eye" and is indicative of psychic ability," Liz explained.

As Debra was leaving, Liz suggested she meet her husband, Kurt, who was home this time, watching television in the family room. Debra followed Liz who introduced the two of them. Kurt had a pleasant smile. He didn't look at all as she had imagined when Liz had talked about him. He was strawberry blond instead of dark; thin instead of stocky, and what was most surprising was that his face was like her son's, it was smattered with freckles. She couldn't help but laugh. When he raised his eyebrows, she explained that it's funny how people never look the way you imagine them.

He chuckled and said, "I could say the same about you."

Debra just said, "I don't even want to know how you imagined a crazed neighbor." They all laughed. She excused herself and told Liz she would see her bright and early for their walk the next morning.

Debra's frustration grew each day that she did not hear from Ted. She, however, realized her hands were tied, so she decided to try to make the time as pleasant as possible. She would have to try to focus on other things.

Saturday morning, she went to Jonathan's soccer game immediately after her walk with Liz. She was pleased to find that she was getting to know the players on his team and she cheered them on from the sidelines where she sat in a lawn chair among the other parents. Jonathan scored a goal and he was beaming as he looked over at his mother. She was glad she was there to witness it and briefly wished that Ted had been present also.

Leanne invited some friends over to watch movies that evening. Although Debra was careful to keep a low profile and give them lots of space, she appreciated the fact that there were others in the house. It was pleasant to hear them joking and laughing. She enjoyed a quiet evening reading in bed.

Jonathan checked in with her when he returned home from Tim's house around ten o'clock. "Did you have fun at Tim's house?"

"Yeah, we played computer and video games. His Dad even played a couple with us. I wish my Dad would do that."

Debra nodded. She was glad that somebody's father was spending some time with Jonathan.

The next week started out to be uneventful. But, just when she started to give up hope that Ted would ever call, the phone rang. Debra picked it up on the first ring as she was nearby. It was Ted.

"My mother said you needed to talk to me. What do you want?" She thought he sounded surly.

"Ted, after 22 years of marriage that's not a very nice greeting."

"Fine. What DO you want?"

She decided it was not the time to get into an argument. "I need to talk to you about the house. What are we going to do about it?"

"Why do we need to do anything?"

"You said you don't want the house. I need to give Jonathan and Leanne some sense of security. They're worried sick that we'll have to move. Would you be willing to sign it over to me? I want to re-mortgage it with lower payments so that they're affordable for me.

He hesitated, "Provided it is considered as part of your share in the divorce settlement."

The word "divorce" set her back a moment, but she managed to plod on.

"Do you think I'd have any trouble re-mortgaging the house so I could lower the payments?"

"Probably not. You'd have to talk to the bank."

She needed some time to think things through, find out what the property was worth, and do some calculations. She didn't want to be hasty so she told Ted she needed to think about it.

Ted said, "You want time, take some time. I'm in no hurry. Get some papers drawn up and send them to my parents' home when you decide. I don't want anything to do with it."

She was astounded that she had to get the papers completed. It looked like he wasn't going to take responsibility for taking care of any of this mess! When she asked Ted why she had to get the papers drawn up, his response was, "It's your issue, not mine."

"What about our bank account?"

"What about it?" Gosh, he could be difficult, at times!

"Shouldn't we get separate accounts?"

"I already have."

"I know, Ted, but what do we do about the money already in our joint account and how am I supposed to make the mortgage payments until I decide what to do about the house?"

"I really don't want to deal with this shit right now! Look, there's enough money in the account for the next couple of payments. I always worked hard. You know I always provided well for my family! There's more than enough in there to cover a couple of mortgage payments and still have lots left over," he sighed. "Take enough for your damn mortgage payments, then take half of the remaining balance and write me a check for the other half. Put yours in your own account and we'll close that one. Now, is that all? I have things to do!"

"The kids are really struggling with the separation. They need to see you. When are you going to see them...or at least talk to them?"

"I told you, I need a break from everything! You have to push, don't you?!"

"Ted, please, think about it, okay? We're flying up to Sacramento for the weekend in a couple of weeks for my father's birthday. Maybe you could spend some time with them then. Call me, okay?"

Ted grunted and hung up the phone.

Debra was so upset, she decided to do a grounding ritual to help calm herself. She knew she had a rough night ahead of her. She hoped the latest novel she was reading would provide a good distraction so she could fall asleep. It was with relief that she realized she would have the opportunity to talk this out with her counselor the following day.

CHAPTER FOUR

Debra approached her next counseling appointment with mixed feelings. She was glad to have a chance to talk to Elizabeth, but she was afraid she hadn't devoted herself to her homework as much as she should have. What if Elizabeth was disappointed in her?

She was, once again, feeling overwhelmed. Now she had to find a lawyer she could trust, schedule a visit to the bank about their bank account and mortgage, and get an estimate of the value of their property. All that and still deal with all of her other responsibilities. And there Ted was, merely going about his "simple" life! Her life was anything but simple. It was lucky she didn't have Ted's phone number. She had never wanted to give him a piece of her mind more than she did now.

Debra had gone into work early and eaten lunch at her desk while working so that she could take time off for her one o'clock counseling appointment. She simply told her co-workers she had an appointment, but she didn't clarify what for. Debra was feeling antsy and rushed for time sitting in the counseling waiting room when it occurred to her that she could center herself a bit while she waited. She was feeling more settled when Elizabeth invited her in a few minutes later.

Elizabeth asked how things had been since they last met. Debra gave her a summary of events that, again, raised her feelings of anger toward Ted.

"Unfortunately, he's going to be able to get under your skin for a while. His leaving has provoked a whole chain of events for you and your children."

"No kidding, I feel like I have no control."

"What do you think you have managed well?"

Debra told her about the sense of satisfaction she felt when she had the locks to her home re-keyed. She acknowledged that Liz had been a catalyst, but in the past, she might have refused to go along with Liz's plan and she hadn't this time. She said, "Even if he never tries to enter the house again, it gave me peace of mind and I feel proud that I followed through in changing the locks."

"That was spunky behavior. Anything else you feel you've managed well?"

Debra told her about her phone call to Ted's mother and how she had broached the topic of the house, bank account, and contact with the children when Ted had called her back. She expressed dismay at the extra responsibilities, but she was pleased that she had spoken with Ted.

"Good for you," Elizabeth said. "You're not letting things slide. These are things you need to get settled."

Debra asked if she knew a lawyer she could see about the legal papers.

"I can give you a few names to choose from. They are all experienced in law related to separation and divorce and I've heard positive reports about them from my clients." She wrote the names of three lawyers and their phone numbers on a slip of paper before passing it to Debra.

"So how did the homework go? I believe I asked you to experiment with building in things to look forward to and to notice which ones you enjoyed the most."

"I can see why you wanted me to have two weeks between appointments. You can only accomplish so much in two weeks." Debra said in her own defense before she started.

Elizabeth smiled. "So, what did you experiment with?"

Debra told her about the library card and how she was reading every night at bedtime. She also told Elizabeth she had started reading during her lunch and coffee breaks and this was helping her to relax and forget her problems, if only for a brief time.

She reported that doing a grounding ritual every morning and at bedtime helped to calm her. She then told her about the Healing Touch session with Liz and how much she had marveled at her experience. Finally, she let Elizabeth know that she had upped her weekly morning walks to twice weekly. "I really enjoy chatting with Liz and I find the exercise gets my day off to a good start."

She noticed that Elizabeth jotted notes into her file as she mentioned each activity. It occurred to her that Elizabeth must consider these activities worthwhile. This encouraged her to recall attending Jonathan's soccer game and how pleasant it had been being part of the cheering section with the other parents.

"It sounds like you did a great job of building in positive activities for yourself."

"Thanks. I'm kind of worried. How am I going to take care of all of these financial issues? It's difficult enough keeping on top of family, home, and work responsibilities. The other night, I almost forgot to pack the kids lunches before I went to bed, I was so busy doing other things. Sometimes, it's all I can do to keep pushing forward."

"Have you thought about having Leanne and Jonathan take on more responsibilities? They're old enough to pack their own lunches. They could probably help more with housework, too. Do you give them an allowance?"

Debra replied that she did and told her the amount. She admitted it wasn't generous and both children had been asking for a "raise."

Elizabeth asked whether she could afford to increase their allowance. Debra didn't think it would be a problem provided she could lower her mortgage payment.

"I don't want you to simply give them a raise. What you could do is list some of the chores you would like them to pick up and give them a dollar value. Then negotiate with the children which ones they would like to do in exchange for a higher allowance."

"Isn't that bribery?"

"No, it's reality. Adults often get a raise when they take on more responsibilities at work."

She had a good point.

Elizabeth suggested she give the children a time deadline for getting the chores done. That way she could avoid nagging them. They either completed the chores by the deadline and were paid for it or they didn't.

"I want you to continue to build in things to look forward to and notice which ones you enjoy most. I'd also like you to start rewarding yourself for doing things you don't want to do. For example, if you don't feel like cleaning up after dinner, tell yourself that, if you clean up, you may read a chapter in a book, watch a favorite television program, go for a walk, or do something else you would like to do. Then make sure you reward yourself for getting it done."

Debra wondered how she was going to fit all of that in, but she was willing to try it out. Elizabeth told Debra that she should anticipate a setback and explained that most people take a few steps forward and a couple of steps back before moving forward again.

When it came time to schedule the next appointment, Elizabeth advised her she would be at a workshop on the East Coast during the week they normally would have scheduled. "How do you feel about waiting three weeks for your next appointment, instead of two?"

Debra was quick to respond, "Well, actually, I think I could wait three weeks. I'm going to have an awful lot of appointments during the next couple of weeks and I was wondering how I was going to juggle them all."

They scheduled a time for three weeks later and Debra returned to work.

Once she reviewed her phone messages and checked to see if there were any emergencies to take care of, she called one of the lawyers on the list. She was offered a free consultation during which she could decide whether or not she wanted to proceed. She scheduled an appointment for the following week as that was the earliest available. Unfortunately, it meant having to make up time at work, again.

The next day she took her lunch hour at an earlier time so she could go to the bank and take care of the bank account at a time when it would be less busy. She also made an appointment to see a loan manager about re-mortgaging the house.

As soon as she returned to work she mailed the paperwork to Ted to sign and enclosed a check for the balance of their joint account. He would have to have a Notary Public witness his signature, as he would not be signing in the presence of bank personnel. She hoped Ted was aware he could simply drop in at a Mailboxes Etc. to get it done, but she knew it wouldn't go over well if she attached a note to that effect. Here they were separated and she was still worrying about getting his back up!

Debra made a quick casserole and threw it in the oven when she returned home from work. She left a note on the kitchen counter to let Leanne and Jonathan know her whereabouts, as they would be home soon. She wanted to drive around the neighborhood and check some of the For Sale pamphlets in neighbors' front yards to get an idea of the value of their home.

It took Debra a while to find a couple of homes that had comparable characteristics. Ted had picked out their house while she was still in Sacramento. It was huge, particularly compared to most of the homes in their area. Ted had convinced her they should purchase the property when she had flown down to San Diego to see it. He had thought he needed an impressive home for entertaining colleagues while he moved up the corporate ladder. Ha! They hadn't done any entertaining and he hadn't stuck around long enough to do any ladder climbing! All he'd done was leave her with a monstrosity of a house to clean and care for.

Debra was amazed by their high listing prices. In the process, she noticed a couple of smaller and older ranch style homes with much lower prices. She briefly wondered about the possibility of selling their home and getting a smaller, less expensive home nearby. Their house was modern and spacious as it had only been built a few years ago, but it was too big and cold. The thought of living in a smaller, older home sounded cozy and appealing. But, that was too much to think about right now. If nothing else, she needed to get an estimate on their property before she considered anything. She would call a realtor another day. There was too much going on right now.

Debra decided to bring up the topic of allowances while at the dinner table. Leanne and Jonathan were all ears as she laid out the plan. Both were eager to take on some new chores in exchange for a higher weekly allowance. The chores had to be done by Sunday evening in order to collect their allowance, but they could do them sooner, if they wanted the money earlier in the weekend. They would also be expected to pack their own lunches. They were so excited about the prospect of a higher allowance, they only groaned briefly in response.

That weekend they shared the household chores together. Every once in a while Debra interrupted her work to give them tips on how to do the cleaning. They each had taken on a bathroom for their list of chores and had never cleaned a bathroom before so Debra demonstrated how by cleaning the master bath. When they were finished their individual chores, she did a brief inspection and filled them in on things they had missed. They went back to do the touch ups and she cheerfully gave them their allowance when they were finished.

The opportunity to meet with Barbara Cason, the lawyer with whom she had scheduled the legal consultation appointment, finally came on Thursday of the following week. Barbara was direct and straightforward which was helpful to Debra, particularly considering her own lack of experience with legal matters.

After she filled Barbara in on the details and answered any questions she had with respect to their marriage, separation, and assets, Barbara advised her of her options. She showed Debra a scale for determining the amount of child support based on the non-custodial parent's income. Debra did not know the exact amount of Ted's current income, but she was floored at the possibilities. There was no way she expected Ted to pay that much child support. She balked at claiming alimony, too. The lawyer explained that Ted would be in a position to earn much more money than Debra would and it was costly raising two adolescents and putting them through post-secondary education.

"I only want the house and enough child support to manage. I'm angry with him, but I'm not out for blood. I also don't want to drive him further away from the children."

Barbara indicated she would draw up a Dissolution of Marriage Agreement based upon irreconcilable differences. It was agreed they would negotiate for the assets to be divided down the middle, with the understanding that part of Debra's settlement would include assigning the house over to her through a quitclaim deed. They agreed to request child support in an amount that was higher than the one Debra was willing to settle for, but would give her some room to bargain. Debra's rights for alimony would be waived. They would request full custody of the children for Debra with reasonable access for Ted. Barbara also advised her that the papers would stipulate that they share legal costs for the separation.

If Debra and Ted agreed to an uncontested divorce, they could negotiate the terms in Barbara's office or, if he wanted to dispute the Agreement, he could hire his own lawyer. Barbara said that, either way, they would endeavor to settle out of court. If this was not feasible, it would have to be heard in court in front of a judge. Regardless, Ted would have to provide proof of the amount of his income and information about assets, such as the value of investments, retirement funds, and 401K. She requested that Debra fax a copy of the original mortgage documents, which would include the required legal description of the property for the quitclaim deed.

Debra wrote a check as a deposit for the legal work and returned to work feeling tired and depressed. She was mentally exhausted from trying to estimate values of their assets and debts and emotionally drained due to the finality of consulting a lawyer about divorce papers. If anyone had told her a year ago that she would be involved in this process, she would have called that person crazy!

Debra managed to finish up her workday. She retrieved Jonathan and a few of his neighborhood teammates from soccer practice. She was too bushed to cook supper so she picked up some of her children's favorite cheese buns at a bakery and reheated homemade stew when she got home. Quick and simple. Perfect considering the mood she was in.

She deserved a reward after enduring the meeting with the lawyer. She took the kids to pick out a rental movie at Blockbusters and they all watched it together after Jonathan and Leanne finished their homework. It was with relief that she realized she didn't have to pack their lunches. She dropped into bed and fell asleep as soon as her head hit the pillow.

Tomorrow was another busy day. Debra met with the mortgage loans manager at the bank to find out her options for lowering the mortgage payments. She was shocked when the manager advised her of the high amount of equity in the property. It was very impressive! The manager also reminded her that property values had sky-rocketed in San Diego over the past year, so the value of her property would have gone up considerably, possibly as much as $100,000. She gave Debra a summary of the expenses involved in re-mortgaging which also were considerable. At any rate, Debra told the manager she needed some time to consider how to proceed.

Now she was really overwhelmed! She wondered whether she should re-mortgage the property or, considering the amount of equity, sell it and try to get a smaller home in the neighborhood.

Debra spent a restless night, tossing and turning in bed. There was too much to think about. She was anything but refreshed when she joined Liz for their Saturday morning walk. Liz was quick to notice and ask her what was happening.

Debra filled her in on the details of the previous three days.

"What are you trying to do, do yourself in?" Liz asked. "Rome wasn't built in one day...you don't have to solve this overnight."

"Actually, I would if I could. I can't stand having so much up in the air. It doesn't feel good and it's not fair to the kids."

"I can understand that. I wish I could do something to help."

"I know, it's just I've got so much on my mind. I don't know whether I'm coming or going."

"Maybe, I could do something to help. I could give you a mind clearing—it's another Healing Touch technique. It promotes deep relaxation by altering the energy flow inside the head. It also helps with information retrieval, concentration, and feelings of peacefulness."

They decided they would get together at Liz's house immediately following their walk. They spent the rest of the walk laughing about anecdotes from their childhood. By the time they reached Liz's home, they were both feeling cheerful and relaxed. Debra, who was now very comfortable with the Healing Touch process, laid on the table while Liz put on a CD of soothing ocean sounds accompanied by soft music.

Liz pendulumed her. "Your sacral chakra is blocked. This is the area for decision making and making change, so it's not surprising."

She stood at Debra's side, placed one of her hands on Debra's chestbone and held one of her hands with the other. "Take slow breaths in and out and imagine Mother Earth's Energy which is red, coming up to your ankles...your knees...your hips...and all the way to your heart."

"Circle the red in a clockwise direction in your heart. Now bring God's white light down through your crown to your heart. Mix the white in with the red in a clockwise direction, like a candy cane. Keep mixing it until it's pink unconditional love. It doesn't matter if you can't see it, just pretend."

She told her to allow unconditional love to fill up her heart until she couldn't hold it anymore and then to allow love to seep to her arms and legs...then into her body, mind, and soul.

Liz repeated the phrase for setting a positive intent that Debra had heard previously. She then stood at her head and placed three fingers of each hand lightly on Debra's collarbone. After a while she moved them to various places on Debra's skull, brow, and cheekbones. She gently stroked three times from Debra's hairline of her brow, across the forehead, down both cheeks, and off the chin. She then cupped Debra's face by placing both hands together in a "V" at the base of her chin.

She finished by grounding Debra through putting a hand on each of her shoulders. Debra left for home feeling relaxed and content.

She sat down that evening to write a pros and cons list. Deciding what to do with the house was a major decision for her and she wanted to give it careful consideration before proceeding. It didn't take her long to come up with a list.

Re-mortgage House

Pros	Cons
Don't have to move	Higher payments
Avoid stress of selling	Huge—higher utilities
Showy	More housework
Spacious	Associated with Ted

Buy Smaller House

Pros	Cons
Lower payments	Have to move
Smaller—less utilities	Not as new
Less housework	Less space
Cozy	
New beginning	

It was clear to her. She was going to have to list their house for sale and find a smaller house nearby.

When Sunday morning arrived, Debra's mind was reeling, again. There she was with no plans and no pressing household chores to do. She found herself worrying about Ted. How was he managing? Ted was all alone and he didn't even have the children to keep him company. He must be missing them! What would it be like to get up in the morning to nobody? She shuddered at the thought.

Ted used to be cheerful and there were times when he was so considerate. She recalled one Mother's Day when he had corralled the kids into the kitchen and together they had made her breakfast. They had insisted she stay in bed. Jonathan had ended up spilling the glass of orange juice on the comforter when he had handed it to her, Leanne hadn't buttered the corners of her toast, and Ted had made her tea too strong. But they had been well intentioned and Debra had felt so loved that morning. How could it have gone from that to this? She started to get stuffed up with tears thinking about it.

She felt so depressed and hopeless she started to panic. Oh my God, it was just like the first week after Ted left. "I can't bear to go back to feeling that bad, again," she thought. Then she remembered that Elizabeth had warned her she was due for a setback. "This is only temporary. I can do something." She racked her brain. Sunday mornings were always the toughest. What could she do to get them off to a good start?

The first thing Debra decided to do was to stop moping in bed. She got up, showered, and dressed. She quickly completed a grounding ritual before leaving a note on the kitchen counter in case the kids got up and noticed her gone, then she walked over to Crown Point Park. It was a beautiful morning. The water on the bay was glassy smooth. There was nobody on the water except for the occasional kayaker. It looked so peaceful, she wished she were out there with them.

It struck her. There was no reason she couldn't be. Anybody could paddle a kayak. Pumped with the idea she headed for home. She would eat breakfast, tidy up, and go to Sports Chalet to see about getting a kayak. Jonathan and Leanne were getting up when she left for the store and neither wanted to accompany her.

She wandered around the kayak section, but there were so many choices she felt overwhelmed. She approached one of the sales reps for advice. He was knowledgeable and told her the ins and outs of the various kayaks. He also told her she would need a lifejacket, paddle, and possibly a clip-in padded seat, depending upon the type of kayak she bought. Debra was disappointed. It was much more expensive than she had expected.

When she started to waffle, he suggested she might want to consider an inflatable kayak. "It costs a lot less. It's easy to carry around and if you decide you want to kayak places other than within walking distance, the whole thing packs up into this carry-all bag that you can toss into the trunk of your car. It would also save you the cost of roof racks, if you don't already have them."

That sounded appealing to Debra, but how much work was it to inflate a kayak?

"It only takes a few minutes to pump it up. Granted you have to get a pump, but that would only cost you ten dollars and you wouldn't have the expense of a clip-in seat because the Stearns IK-116 provides lots of cushioning and back support all on its own."

He offered to take it down off the wall so she could sit in it. It was made of sturdy fabric that Debra equated to that of a heavy-duty air mattress. It occurred to her that the orange/black design would stand out on the water so that motorboat and Jet Ski drivers would notice it.

She slipped off her shoes, climbed in, and sat down. "It's really comfortable." Debra was surprised. "How much did you say this one is?"

"Two hundred ninety-nine dollars. Actually it's our demo and it's the last one we have left so I could give you ten per cent off. If you're going to have an inflatable, you might as well have a paddle that is pieced together so you can throw it in the carry bag as well. They're only eighteen dollars and ninety-nine cents."

Wow! That was a lot less expensive than the paddles they had looked at. "What else would I need?"

"Only a life jacket … and you didn't hear it from me, but you could pick one up for twenty to twenty-five dollars at Target or Wal-Mart."

That cinched it. "Okay, I'll take it."

He showed her how to deflate it. The kayak had two compartments so that if one deflated for any reason, it was still floatable. He also showed her how to screw the paddle's five pieces together. Once disassembled, everything fit neatly into the carryall bag.

Debra felt excited as he rung in her purchases. She was really going to do something special for herself.

She drove the couple of blocks to the Target store on Sports Arena Boulevard and purchased a lifejacket. As soon as she got home, she laid out the kayak in the driveway. It took less than ten minutes to pump it up. It was sharp looking! She could hardly wait to get out on the water!

CHAPTER FIVE

Debra returned home from kayaking feeling peaceful and content. She was so pleased with herself. She had ended up deflating the kayak and driving to Crown Point Park to put it in the water. Once she had hefted the kayak up onto her shoulder while inflated, she realized it would be too difficult to carry the kayak and paddle all the way to the bay. It wasn't heavy, but it was awkward to carry for any great distance. Besides, it was so easy to re-inflate. Why not drive to the park?

The water was choppy by the time she got there, so she took the kayak for a short trip to try it out. As she started to paddle, she noticed a gentle pull across her abdomen. "Oh, good," she thought, "exercise where I need it most." That made kayaking even more motivating.

She discovered it didn't take long to get into a rhythm paddling and it was therapeutic. Her worries faded away as she looked around. She could see seaweed swaying deep in the water and huge pinky brown jellyfish floating near the surface. She paddled close to the ducks and they hardly seemed to care. She even saw a fish jump out of the water less than 15 feet away. It was a whole different view on the water. It was wonderful and invigorating.

She decided to make one of her children's favorite meals for dinner—chicken wings and potato skins, with Caesar salad. It was a lot of work, but well worth the hearty responses she received when Jonathan and Leanne joined her at the dinner table.

The evening was quiet, with the children finishing up their chores and homework while Debra busied herself cleaning the kitchen after dinner. She prepared a few things in readiness for returning to work the next day. She spent the rest of the evening reading in the family room and chatting with her children whenever they came into the room.

Monday morning was the start of another hectic week. She finalized the arrangements for several workshops at Point Loma Nazarene University and faxed set-up diagrams for the rooms according to the requests of each of the speakers. There were continental breakfasts and buffet luncheons to arrange for each day the workshops were scheduled. Point Loma provided free parking, so at least she didn't have to worry about sending parking permits to all of the participants. She asked one of her assistants to type the various agendas and make copies. Two of the other clerks were given the responsibility of typing and copying information handouts for each of the workshops.

One of the scheduled companies called to advise that several members of their Human Resources Department would be joining their conference. Debra contacted Point Loma to ask for another table and more chairs. She also informed the catering service of the increase. This, of course, necessitated modification of the bill for services and additions to the number of handouts required. It was a good distraction.

Debra was dreading their visit to Sacramento for her father's 75th birthday. Neither Jonathan nor Leanne wanted to go either. It was a crime that none of them were excited about spending time with her parents.

Sacramento no longer held much interest for her children. They had been back a couple of times in the beginning when they had missed their friends. They had soon discovered the friends they had when they lived in the area had since moved on. None of them sent email anymore and both Leanne and Jonathan now felt like outsiders.

Leanne was upset that her San Diego friends were going to a Brittany Spears concert at Sports Arena without her that weekend. Debra didn't know why Jonathan didn't want to go, but he was being miserable about it.

Every time she asked him what was the matter, he kept insisting there was nothing, but his behavior said otherwise. When the time finally came for him to pack his bag Thursday evening, he was throwing his clothes in, with eyes downcast and bottom lip protruding. Debra, who had come into his bedroom to remind him to bring his loafers so he would look a little more dressed up Saturday night, finally snapped. "What is eating you?!"

"Nothin'."

"Don't give me that. I know there's something. You're like a bear with a sore head."

"I don't want to talk about it," he mumbled.

Debra could see he was on the verge of tears and her voice softened, "I can't help you if I don't know what it is."

He crumbled, "It's gonna' feel awful to be so close and yet Dad still won't want to see me."

"Oh Jonathan, I'm sorry," she said as she hugged him. "We need to give him some time. He'll come around. I know he will."

He had to didn't he? He couldn't turn his back on them forever. She helped Jonathan collect the rest of his belongings for the trip.

They were flying to Sacramento tomorrow right after work. Liz had offered to drop them off at the airport. Other than the Saturday evening birthday celebration there was nothing else planned until they left for home Sunday in the late afternoon. If only Ted had called to arrange to see them. They certainly had enough time for an outing with him.

Ted hadn't called by the time they went to bed that night and she doubted he would try to reach her at her parents' home. She was surprised when she answered the phone at work the next morning and heard Ted's voice.

"It's Ted," he told her. As if she wouldn't recognize his voice after 22 years of marriage. He went on to say. "I thought about it and if it's still okay, I'd like to see Jonathan and Leanne this weekend."

"I'd like to take them for lunch on Sunday. Look Debra, I don't feel up to meeting with your parents. Could you bring them to meet me at a restaurant?"

He was such a candy ass! He just didn't want to face the music. She couldn't believe this was the man she had married and had two children with. It's not as if she would have her own car in Sacramento. But, she knew the children needed to see him.

"I could probably borrow Dad's car. Tell me where and when."

They agreed she would drop the children off at the Cattleman's Restaurant in Folsom, just outside of Sacramento, at eleven-thirty on Sunday and then pick them up at three o'clock.

"Ted, could you please bring the paperwork for closing our joint bank account? Also, I need to talk to you about my meeting with the lawyer. When can we talk?"

"One thing at a time, okay? I'll bring the paperwork for the bank. I only want to see the kids for now," he said as he hung up the phone.

Why does he get to call all the shots? "Because I let him," she muttered to herself. She was sick of being tired. All of this made her so tired.

It occurred to her that the legal documentation might be ready for her to give to Ted. She contacted her lawyer's office. The legal assistant said the quitclaim deed was complete and she was just finishing up the divorce agreement. Debra could pick it up at noon, if she wanted. So much for a lunch break.

Debra was motivated, though. She was in no hurry to finalize the divorce, but she needed to get their financial affairs settled as soon as possible.

Debra scanned the papers when she picked them up, skipping through as much of the legal mumbo jumbo as she could. Everything was as they had agreed. There shouldn't be anything there to upset Ted except the request for child support. She would throw his copy into her travel bag and give it to him after his visit with Jonathan and Leanne.

She hurried back to work. She wondered how the kids would respond when they heard about the visit with their father.

Leanne and Jonathan were waiting for her when she arrived home, their bags packed and waiting at the door as she had requested. She told them both, "Your father called today. He wants to take you for lunch on Sunday." Jonathan's face lit up and he hugged his mother with glee. Leanne didn't say anything so Debra asked, "Are you okay with that, honey?"

"I guess so. Is he sure he could fit us into his busy schedule?"

Unsure how to respond to the sarcasm, Debra told them he would be spending the afternoon with them until it was time to go to the airport.

Leanne just said, "Whatever."

"I know you're hurt and I don't blame you. Give him a chance, okay? You know he loves you and I'm sure he has missed both of you."

Leanne nodded. Debra called Liz to let her know they were ready and Liz arrived within minutes to pick them up.

Her parents greeted them at the airport as they came through the gate that evening. Her mother was dressed in a light tailored suit that fit her petite figure perfectly. Her hair was neatly coifed, as usual, and she was careful not to muss it as she buzzed Debra's cheek. Her father, on the other hand, was dressed more casual in khaki pants and a golf shirt. He crushed her against his robust frame as he pulled her close for a hug. He wasn't a man of many words, but he sure gave warm hugs.

He reached over and mussed Jonathan's hair as he teased him about how tall he was. Then he put his arm around Leanne and asked if any of the local boys had married her yet.

"Grandpa!" she protested as he chuckled and winked at her.

Debra's mother was fussing already. "Come on, let's get out of here. These crowds are driving me crazy."

"Short trip," Debra's father said. Both Jonathan and Leanne giggled and Debra's mother gave them all a disdainful look.

They hadn't checked any luggage and were soon on their way out of the airport parking lot. Debra sighed, she really wasn't much of a traveler and it was a relief to leave the airport with all of its hustle and bustle. "Good Lord," she thought. "I'm getting to be just like my mother!"

Debra's mother disappeared into the kitchen to prepare a late dinner as soon as they were inside the door of her parents' home. She set out a variety of deli meats and cheeses, with pickles, tomatoes, lettuce, and soft dinner rolls. She refused to let Debra help and insisted that she sit down and relax. Once they were all seated around the table, she busied herself fetching beverages until Debra's father finally said, "Sit down, Eileen. You're making us dizzy with all your fluttering around."

"I want to make sure everybody has everything they need."

"That's okay, Mom. If we need anything we can get it ourselves. This looks great." Debra reassured her.

Conversation revolved around Leanne and Jonathan's school and sports. Debra was asked about her job. Eileen filled them in on all the latest changes in the neighborhood and at church. Everyone was careful to avoid discussion about Ted and Debra's separation.

Eileen commented that it was too bad Debra's childhood friend, Terri, had moved to Chicago or they could have got together. Debra agreed and used this as an intro to mention the children's visit with Ted. Her father did not hesitate to agree to lend her his car, but her mother was obviously offended that Ted wouldn't be stopping by to visit.

Debra was glad when bedtime finally arrived. They had long since run out of conversation. What could she talk about that her mother would approve of, after all? Her mother was still hopeful that Ted and Debra would reunite. She would not be pleased to hear that Debra had consulted a lawyer or that she planned to sell the house and buy a smaller one.

Debra couldn't talk much about Liz, either. They would have a fit if they found out she was involved in Healing Touch sessions. She didn't think that would go over well with either parent. It was not a well-understood or accepted methodology.

Her mother prepared a huge breakfast the following morning and accepted minimal help from Debra. Jonathan and Leanne played cards with their grandfather while Debra and her mother cleaned up and washed the dishes. Eileen didn't have a dishwasher and had always been adamant that they were frivolous.

Debra convinced her mother that she could pick up the cake at the local bakery. She was relieved to have some time out of the house. She took her time meandering around the old neighborhood and reminiscing about her childhood years before picking up the cake and returning to her parents' home.

While her father stayed home to have his afternoon nap, the rest of the family went over to the nearby community hall to set up the room and hang decorations. Her mother had purchased an abundant supply of banners, streamers, and novelties marking the 75th year.

Everybody from way back when would be there. Debra wondered how her father felt about reaching 75 years of age and having a huge celebration. He probably hated it, but he would go along with it because her mother expected him to.

She wasn't looking forward to the evening. Her mother always became uptight about public outings. She turned into a "regular fuss budget" as her children called her behind her back.

They returned to her parents' home to change their clothes once they were finished decorating the hall. One of Debra's brothers, Steve, meanwhile arrived from Santa Barbara. Debra and Steve had never been particularly close, but they got along. There was a five-year gap in their ages that felt like fifteen as Steve was ""old school" compared to Debra's more open-minded approach to life. Steve had never married and Debra thought it was probably because he was stuffy.

Their other two siblings, a brother and sister, lived on the East Coast with their families. They were unable to make it to the celebration, but they had contributed toward their father's gift, a beautiful gold pocket watch on a chain. Their father had always wanted one. Steve had picked it up during a recent trip to England. He had it engraved "Happy 75th Dad." Nothing profound, but the watch was beautiful. The face was surrounded by intricately carved gold filigree and each of the watch hands was set with a small diamond.

Debra retrieved the cake from the kitchen counter and they all headed for the hall in two cars. Debra sat in the back seat of

Steve's car so she could keep the huge cake box balanced on the seat beside her. Her mother held court in the front seat, which gave her a chance to get an update from Steve. The children traveled with their grandfather in his car.

As they walked up the stairs toward the hall entrance, Mrs. Cross, her parents' widowed neighbor approached them. "Hi, Debra, you look lovely. I haven't seen you in ages." She looked at both children and commented about how much they had grown before asking, "Where's Ted? It is Ted, isn't it."

Debra's mother intercepted, "Yes. Ted couldn't make it. He was called to work out of town. When you've got an important job like Ted's, you have to go wherever they need you."

Debra had been about to say they were separated, but her jaw slammed shut. So that was how it was going to be. More pretending to be the perfect family.

Mrs. Cross nodded and went on her way, oblivious to the tension that had just erupted between Debra and her mother.

Jonathan and Leanne exchanged knowing looks, but did not speak up. They had spent enough time with their grandmother to know better than to argue. Nothing raised her ire more than public embarrassment.

Debra's father had been briefly detained on the sidewalk by an old friend and caught up with them on the stairs just as her mother said, "There's no need to air your dirty laundry in public. This is not the time or the place."

"Not the time or place for what?" he asked.

"I think we should keep Ted's leaving to ourselves. I'm sure Debra will eventually come to her senses and she and the children will join him in Sacramento."

"Mom, I told you that's not an option."

"Not here, Debra. We'll talk about it later."

She just didn't listen! "Sure we will," she muttered under her breath, but she knew she and her mother never talked about anything. Rather her mother lectured and she fumed.

Many of her parents' friends recognized Debra from earlier years. They were either neighbors, members of her parents' church, or family friends. She tried to be evasive whenever discussion came up about Ted, but she was unwilling to be dishonest. She was tempted to tell the truth to teach her mother a lesson, but instead she simply said he wasn't able to make it. It made conversation difficult to say the least! Her children followed her cue. It would be up to her mother to tell her friends the truth whenever she was ready. Debra thought it would make her mother look foolish at a later date if people started putting two and two together, but who was she to decide?

Her mother spent most of the evening dizzying around the tables, making sure everybody had enough to eat and drink. Invitations had stipulated that there should be no gifts, but her father received a multitude of birthday cards and a few gifts from the people who were more determined. Some of the birthday presents were gag gifts that brought lots of laughter. Her father got a kick out of them, but he beamed with pride when he opened the last gift, the one from his wife and children. If Debra didn't know any better, she would say he looked a little choked up when he saw what was in the gift box.

Everybody was chanting, "Speech, speech!"

Her father collected himself before thanking everybody for coming. He thanked them for their well wishes and said, "Having so many of you present at my 75th birthday celebration is testimony that I have enjoyed 75 years of the 'good life'. Thank you all for helping to make my life memorable through the many years I've been on the face of this earth."

Trust her father to turn it around so that everybody else got credit. Did it even occur to him that there was something about him that made him well liked? She wished she'd had more opportunity over the years to get to know him better!

The tables were moved against the wall to clear the central floor for dancing. A Disc Jockey was set up at the end of the hall and the music started immediately following her father's speech. In no time at all, her mother was grabbing people's hands and pairing them up to dance with each other. Most of them responded with good humor, but it made Debra tired just watching her. It occurred to her that she had to give her mother some credit, though. She put a lot of effort into making sure that she and Debra's father shared an active social life. He often affectionately referred to her as his "little social butterfly."

Leanne and Jonathan were bored silly most of the evening, as there were no other young people present. Jonathan was tolerant because he was excited about seeing his father. Leanne was tolerant because that was her temperament.

Saturday was a late night by the time everybody left. They had until noon the next day to clean up, but her mother insisted they clean up the hall before leaving.

"I wouldn't be able to sleep knowing this mess was waiting for me in the morning," she declared.

They humored her enough to tidy everything up, but Debra convinced her that they should leave sweeping and washing the floor until the following day. It had been a long time since she had stayed up later than midnight and she was long past being energetic. She could get it done in next to no time after a good night's rest.

Steve had a quick coffee and left for Santa Barbara soon after everybody was up Sunday morning. Debra went over to the hall and grabbed a broom, floor mop, and pail from the storage cupboard. By the time she was done cleaning, she had just enough time to return the hall keys and have a shower before taking the children to see their father.

Debra felt anxious as she drove into the parking lot at Cattleman's Restaurant. She hadn't seen Ted in seven weeks and she wasn't sure how she would feel.

He was already waiting, leaning against a railing in front of the restaurant. Jonathan barreled out of the car to greet him and Ted gave him a welcoming hug. Leanne appeared more reserved, but Debra noticed she melted when her father finally embraced her.

Debra was surprised to see that Ted had grown a beard. It made the meeting easy. He looked like a stranger. He was, after all. She had long since come to the realization that she hardly knew the man he had become. He had changed so much during the past year.

"Hi, Debra," he said as she approached him. "So, you'll pick them up at three o'clock?"

She nodded and said goodbye to the children.

Leanne looked over to make sure her mother was all right. Debra smiled to reassure her and said, "Have a good time. See you at three."

Debra drove out of the parking lot and started to cry. She cried for what used to be and was no longer. She cried for what could have been. She cried a bit from fear that Ted would turn the children against her and finally, she cried with relief that her children were reunited with their father.

She stopped at a service station rest room to freshen herself up a little. She felt vulnerable when she returned to her parents' home without her children to deflect conversation.

Debra was hardly in the door when her mother said, "Now what is going on between you and Ted?"

She told her what Ted had said when he left.

"Rubbish "

Was it 'rubbish' because she didn't believe Debra or because she didn't believe Ted? Debra was about to get defensive when her mother said, "He's just going through a midlife crisis. He'll come around. But, you should dress in something more attractive when you pick the kids up. Quit being the frumpy wife, Debra. You've got to work to keep a man's interest."

"Why don't they have to work to keep our interest?"

"That's just the way it is, Dear."

Humph! Not in her relationship it wasn't! She shouldn't have to look her best every minute of every day like her mother did. Whatever happened to "for better or for worse?" No, she didn't think make-up and clothes would have made a difference. Ted was just tired of responsibility and commitment. She excused herself to go pack her belongings.

Conversation at lunch became stilted once they were finished talking about the previous evening. There wasn't much left that hadn't already been said. Her father retired to the livingroom for his nap. Debra and her mother cleared and washed the dishes. They spent the rest of the afternoon playing crib. Debra wasn't very good at playing cards and her mother was a shark but being skunked at cards was preferable to talking.

It only took 15 minutes to get to the restaurant in Folsom and she arrived a little early. She watched for Ted's car as she leafed through a fishing magazine left in her father's door pocket.

Leanne and Jonathan greeted her as soon as they arrived and they looked cheerful. They hugged their father goodbye before getting into their grandfather's car. Debra walked over to exchange envelopes with Ted. He gave her the signed forms for closing the bank account and she passed him the legal papers.

"What's this?" he asked.

"The divorce agreement. You can look it over and let me know whether or not it suits you." He raised his eyebrows as he looked back at her.

"If you're in agreement, you can sign it. Otherwise we can meet with my lawyer to negotiate changes or you can get your own lawyer, if you want."

"Okay." He started to walk away.

"Ted," she called. "I'd really like to have a phone number. If something happened to one of the kids, how would I contact you?"

"They've got the number. Get it from them."

Oh, good. It looked like he was going to keep in contact with Leanne and Jonathan. That encouraged her to overlook his rude behavior.

He drove away. Debra joined Leanne and Jonathan in the car and headed for her parents' home. "Did you have a good time?"

Jonathan was excited. "Mom I ate the hugest slab of prime rib. It was this thick." He demonstrated a few inches with the thumb and forefinger of his right hand. "It was the best I've ever had," he said as he rubbed his stomach in circles and made smacking noises.

"Then we walked downtown and had ice cream. I didn't think I'd be able to eat one, but I did. Tiger—that's orange and black licorice. Leanne had pina colada. I tasted it. It was good, too."

"Then we walked around the lake. Dad's living in Fair Oaks near here. He wants us to go to San Francisco for a weekend. We can go, can't we?"

"How are you going to get there?"

"Dad said he'd fly us here and then we'd drive in."

"When?"

Leanne answered, "The weekend of Jonathan's birthday."

Debra couldn't think of any reason for refusing. It would be a long, quiet weekend for her, but she was so relieved Ted was spending time with them that she gave her consent.

It would have been nice if he would have consulted her first. If she'd had other plans for them, the children would have been upset with her when she refused. She asked Leanne how the afternoon had gone for her.

"He was kind of distant, but it was nice to have him all to ourselves. He even left his cell phone turned off. It was nice."

It was amazing to Debra that they were more or less able to pick up where they left off with their father whereas she carried so much resentment. She was soon to discover, however, that her current feelings toward Ted were only the tip of the iceberg.

CHAPTER SIX

He had the gall to contact her at work to argue about the child support. "Do you think I'm made of money or something? Are you thinking of retiring?"

"No, it costs a lot to raise adolescent children and I have to think about their post-secondary education," she quoted her lawyer.

"You sending them to Harvard or what?!"

"Ted, that's not even the full percentage of your income that's allowable on the schedule for determining child support—and I'm not even asking for alimony."

"You won't need to with the amount of child support you're demanding."

"It's not for me. It's for Leanne and Jonathan."

"Yeah, well it'll be a frosty Friday in hell before I'll give you that amount. I'll see you in court first!"

"I thought you were trying to simplify your life. How is a court battle going to accomplish that?—Come on, Ted, don't do this."

"Come on, Ted, don't do this," he mimicked in a whiny voice.

That really pissed her off. She was trying to be nice. She walked around her desk, just about yanking the phone off, and used one foot to kick her office door shut before raising her voice. "Well, if we're going to do the court thing, I might as well go for the full amount and ask for alimony, too!"

"Don't threaten me!"

"Now that you mention threats, you started it. I thought we could be mature about this and settle out of court. That agreement isn't carved in stone. I told you we could negotiate."

"I'll think about it." Her ears rang as the phone receiver crashed back into the cradle.

She knew what "think about it" meant. He was going to consult with a lawyer and find out whether he stood a chance of paying less. Well he would soon discover he might end up paying more. It wasn't her idea to walk out! She wasn't going to settle for anything less than the original amount she and Barbara Cason had agreed upon!

Ted would probably let her sweat it out for a while so she didn't expect to hear from him soon. It was already a horrible day and now this on top of it all. She had been given the wrong count for one of the half-day workshops that began with a luncheon. Apparently the participants had started arriving one by one at noon and by twelve-thirty they had run out of boxed lunches. There wasn't anyone available to make a delivery until one-thirty, because the caterer was swamped. Everybody else at the workshop would be finished eating by then. What a mess!

She was unable to go to the bank at noon as planned. There wasn't time to take a break, so she would have to stop by after work. Fortunately, Leanne and Jonathan didn't have any practices or games after school and they would be able to get themselves home.

The line at the bank was atrocious at the end of the day. Debra was relieved when she was finally called over to the counter, signed the paperwork, closed the joint account, and went home. That was one less thing on her to do list.

Debra called Liz and asked whether she had time to give her Healing Touch after dinner. "My neck and back are aching— probably from tension—work has been a killer and Ted is being difficult about the child support. What can I say?"

"Good timing," Liz responded. "I don't have anything planned this evening and I'd be glad for some female company. Kurt is watching Monday Night Football and there's a little too much testosterone around here for me right now." They both laughed.

After Debra cleaned up from dinner, she made sure Leanne and Jonathan were started on their homework before she took off to Liz's. Liz decided to start with a mind clearing to help relieve the tension. She picked up her pendulum. It was new and she had just purchased it at a specialty shop. It looked like a solid wooden acorn hanging from a string. Debra really liked its appearance and told her so.

Liz held it out and said, "Clockwise is yes, counterclockwise is no. Does Debra need a pain drain?" The pendulum slowly started to go in a clockwise direction, picking up the pace and widening the circle. Liz slid it into her pocket and said, "I guess we're doing a pain drain."

"What's that?"

"It's the same technique I used when I took you through the waterfall/pond fantasy, except I'll do it without the fantasy this time. I put one hand on you to remove pain and then when that's done, I put the other hand on you to seal the area and bring in healing energy."

Debra, once again, saw colors during the session and she also felt a surge of energy where Liz's hand rested on the back of her neck. It was very pleasant. Liz grounded her afterwards by massaging her lower limbs. She then used both hands to draw an oval encompassing Debra from head to foot and said, "Please place a golden cocoon around Debra and keep negative energy out, but let positive energy in."

Debra told her later, "You strike me as one of the most unlikely people to get into spiritual stuff."

"Isn't that the truth? I couldn't believe it myself."

"How did you find out you have the ability to heal?"

"Everybody does. We don't do it alone. You, God, and the client all participate."

"Would you mind teaching me how?" Debra asked. "I really think it's wonderful."

"I'd love to. I could show you how I do it and I also have some handouts you could read to help you remember the various techniques. Maybe Kurt would be our guinea pig. He loves to receive Healing Touch and I could demonstrate for you. Actually we could do it together and you could copy what I do."

Debra thought that sounded great. She always learned best from actually doing things. They agreed Liz would call to let her know when Kurt would be available in the evening.

She went home straight from work the next day. As she drove by the bay, she noticed the sea breeze was starting to die and the water was becoming calm. She put on her swimsuit and a T-shirt as soon as she got home, grabbed a towel, and drove the few blocks to Campland on the Bay, the nearby RV Resort. Her kayak and paddle were already in the trunk of her car.

She inflated the kayak, put the pump back in the car, threw her towel and sandals into the bottom of the boat, and set off. There were lots of birds on the water. A flock of brown ducks with white on their bodies bobbed on the water. They reminded her of brown and white Mary Jane shoes with their two-toned bodies. Black colored birds with tiny white beaks also floated nearby. She didn't know what these birds were called. They were less comfortable with people than the ducks which were accustomed to being fed in the parks. The black birds quickly swam away when she paddled near them, whereas the ducks idly continued on their way.

She floated past the opening of a canal beside the Campland beach and decided she would check it out some day, but not today.

She had another mission. She wanted to paddle around De Anza Park and into the marina there. The cove always looked so inviting, but it was too far for her to paddle from Crown Point Park. Parking at Campland had helped to shorten the trip.

Debra passed alongside the manufactured homes that were situated all the way around De Anza Park. Most of them had sunrooms and decks, with beautiful flower gardens. She enjoyed looking at the orange and blue Birds of Paradise with their beaky look, the various colored Hibiscus, and the puffy blossoms of Hydrangea. Debra thought it would be incredible to wake up to a view of the bay every morning and also have it be the last thing she saw at night. She had heard the lease would soon be up on this property and all of the residents would be evicted to build a hotel and condominium complex. What a loss for the homeowners!

After she paddled around a sand bar at the corner of the park, she could see the sailboats moored at De Anza. She maneuvered her kayak through the various boats anchored in the water and read some of their names, "Last Tern", "Ship of Fools", and "Pretty Woman" were a few of the ones she noticed. How did they ever choose the names for their boats?

The water was like glass by the time she turned around to head back. A duck flew in too fast for how smooth the water was and skidded to a stop more than fifteen feet away. He even set up a mini-wake. Debra couldn't help but laugh.

She made a salad and barbecued hamburgers for dinner. Jonathan offered to flip them over half way through. He was in a great mood since his visit with his father.

Debra had called a realtor to come over the following night to give her an estimate on their house so she spent the rest of the evening making the house look presentable and asked that Leanne and Jonathan tidy their bedrooms. Regardless of whether or not Ted signed the house over to her, it would have to be sold. He clearly had no intentions of moving back to San Diego.

Debra was looking forward to seeing Elizabeth for counseling the next day. She could hardly wait to tell her about kayaking and she wanted to talk to her about Ted and her mother.

She gave Elizabeth an update of what had been happening over the past few weeks. They talked about her weekend in Sacramento and the children's visit with their father. The details of her meeting with the lawyer were discussed. She also filled her in on Ted's response to the divorce agreement. Finally, she told her a realtor would be coming to appraise the house that evening.

Elizabeth commended her for being productive and, again, asked what she had done to build in positive activities. Debra told her about purchasing the kayak and how much she was enjoying being out on the water.

"Great idea." Elizabeth said as she jotted it down. "That's a really creative one."

Debra was excited when she talked about her plan to have Liz teach her how to do Healing Touch. Elizabeth was impressed that Debra was becoming more assertive in asking for things she wants and needs.

"It sounds like you have a very trusting relationship with Liz."

"Oh, I do."

She advised Elizabeth that she was rewarding herself through reading or watching movies, or even cooking a simple meal when she completed tasks she didn't want to do. Debra reported that Leanne and Jonathan had opted to do more chores for higher allowances. Even if she didn't take that into consideration, she was surprised that she was able to build in so many new activities and still stay on top of all of her other responsibilities. "It's like I have more energy or something."

"You do. When you take care of yourself you put energy back in which helps make up for all the energy you are putting out." She then asked her, "How would you rate your life right now, on a scale of 1 to 10?

"I don't know, maybe a six."

"What would you like the rating to be?"

"Nine."

"And what would have to be different for you to give it a rating of nine?"

"I'd have my own home so I could feel more secure. That would also help me have more closure with Ted. Right now I feel like he could pull the rug out from under me, if he wanted to."

"How would he do that?"

"Well, he could decide he wants to keep the house, or something."

Elizabeth pointed out that, even if he did, the courts would probably compensate her and she would have enough money for another home.

"I guess that's true. I just feel like I'm still living under his roof or something. I don't know how to explain it. It just doesn't feel safe."

"Well at least you're already working on that. You've seen a lawyer and you're seeing a realtor tonight. What else would you need to be different to give your life a rating of nine?"

"I wish my mother and I could get along better." Debra filled her in on her mother's refusal to accept her separation from Ted and her attempts to get Debra to fix it. "I feel like she's always judging me and trying to make me more like her."

"I wonder if she feels the same way."

"What do you mean?"

"It seems both of you struggle with accepting each other as you are."

"I never thought of it that way. I guess I don't particularly approve of her behavior either. I know she's always wanted what's best for me, but she doesn't trust me to know what that is."

"Maybe that's because you become secretive or defensive. Could you experiment with not working so hard to get your mother's approval? It could be that it makes her think you lack confidence in what you're doing so she feels anxious and starts telling you what to do. When people are truly confident about their actions, they don't need anyone else's approval because they know it's right."

Debra thought that sounded reasonable.

Elizabeth asked, "Have you ever been able to change your mother?"

"No, never."

"Maybe it's time you quit trying. Your mother is who she is and so is Ted for that matter. You are trying to get Ted to show that he cares more about his children. We really can't change other people. Your energy would be better devoted to changing how you relate to them instead. I've noticed you're direct and you don't beat around the bush with me." She smiled at Debra with reassurance. "What's the worse that could happen if they don't accept you and what you're doing?"

"They could abandon me—what am I talking about? Ted already has."

"What about your mother? Do you think she would abandon you?"

Debra had to admit it wasn't likely. "So are you telling me I should just be my straightforward self?"

"Well, what you're doing isn't working for you. It might be worth a try."

"Between now and the next time we get together, I'd like you to experiment with doing things differently in your relationships with Ted and your mother. Notice what works best and we can talk about it when you come in. Meanwhile continue to build in positive activities and reward yourself for accomplishing tasks."

She asked Debra how it felt to have three weeks between sessions.

"It's a little difficult, but I have so much to accomplish. I don't want the sessions to run out too soon, so I'd prefer to wait three weeks, again." They scheduled an appointment and Debra returned to work.

Wow, that discussion sure gave her food for thought! She wished she had more time to process it, but that would have to wait until later that evening.

Jim Schwab, the realtor, was a stocky little fellow, with brown hair and a neatly tailored suit. He had a pleasant demeanor, but he stunk of aftershave that almost made Debra choke when he entered her home.

Jim went through each room making comments and writing on his notepad. A measuring tape was used to get the dimensions of each room. He seemed pleased with the appearance of the house and yard.

"Even though it's only been a year, property values have appreciated considerably since you purchased this home," he told her, as had the loan manager. He had apparently been a realtor in the area for several years and felt confident that she would have no difficulty selling her home for a good price. "The timing is good, too. Spring and summer are always our busiest seasons."

Debra shared the information provided by the loan officer regarding equity and payments. They talked about the fact that Ted hadn't signed the quitclaim deed or divorce agreement yet. He told her that, if Ted did not sign before the house was sold, the escrow officer could write a check for each of them equally sharing the proceeds.

She was very pleased with the estimate he gave her. They talked about the things she was looking for in a home and he was optimistic that she would be able to locate something acceptable in the area because her wishes were not exorbitant. Jim filled out a Listing Agreement and Debra did not hesitate to sign.

He agreed to check the current listings to see if there were any properties on the market that she might want to see. He would call her to set up a time for a viewing when he found something. Debra told him she didn't want to move into looking too soon because she wanted reassurance that her own home would sell before she became too excited about another property.

"Okay, but I don't think that will be a problem. Your home is exceptional and houses are going like hot cakes right now."

Debra's mind was reeling by the time Jim left. There was so much happening and now she was selling their home! Ted's phone rang several times before an answering machine picked up and she left a message informing him that the house was listed. She decided to ground herself and take a long bath in the Jacuzzi in the master bath. She needed time to think.

The house no longer felt like a pressing issue once she was feeling more settled. Rather, she began to think about her discussion with Elizabeth. If she wasn't so concerned about her mother's approval, what would she do differently? "Well, if it was anyone else and they lived out of town, I would send them a letter telling them what I've been up to," she thought.

H-m-m-m. Why not write her parents a letter? Her mother might think it was a bit strange that Debra had just visited and had not told her everything then, but if she wasn't doing this to gain her mother's approval, that didn't matter, did it? She should just do it!

Ted had taken his computer from the den so she would have to use Leanne's or Jonathan's. She went down to the family room where Leanne and Jonathan were watching television. "Do either of you have some time tomorrow night when I could use one of your computers to type a letter?"

Jonathan shrugged, but Leanne said, "I'm going over to Anne's to work on a group project with her and Lisa. You could use mine while I'm gone."

"When will that be?"

"I'm supposed to be there by seven o'clock and we figure it will take one and one-half to two hours. We've already done the research. We just need to put it together.

Debra thanked Leanne and went upstairs to begin thinking about what she would write. She jotted down her ideas. Visit to lawyer, listing house, counseling, and Healing Touch were all on her list. Wow! There was a lot she hadn't felt comfortable talking about with her mother. Well, she was about to throw caution to the wind.

Her stomach was churning when she sat down to write the following evening, but she eventually got on a roll. It occurred to her that she could write a letter to Terri in Chicago and then modify it to send to her mother and father. Debra had to include the information about her separation from Ted, which she would, of course, delete from her letter to her parents. Her approach was to be matter of fact about everything. She mentioned that she had seen a lawyer so she could get their financial affairs settled and was waiting for a response from Ted. She wrote that she had listed the house yesterday and was hoping to purchase a smaller, more affordable home in the neighborhood. Then she reported that she was enjoying her new friendship with Liz and they enjoyed walking together. She even indicated that she was receiving Healing Touch from Liz and was looking forward to learning how to do it herself. Finally, she wrote that she was seeing a counselor for support and finding it very helpful.

When it came time to change the letter for her parents, she started out by writing that she was sending an update as a lot was happening in her life. All of the new information she had put in Terri's letter was included, but she also thanked them for the weekend and inquired about how things were going for them. It felt good when it was all done.

Friday was the scheduled evening for her lesson in energy work. Kurt was eager to receive Healing Touch and hopped onto the table as soon as Debra arrived.

Liz handed her a tiny package. She had bought Debra her own cedar pendulum. Debra was touched and gave her a warm hug of thanks.

She showed Debra how to dangle the pendulum from its string and hold it over the various chakras. She explained that when it circles clockwise that means the chakra is open.

"Counterclockwise means the chakra is leaking energy unless it's on the leg. Back and forth, still, or quivering means energy is blocked. The goal is to have all chakras open."

Kurt's energy was blocked at the left hip.

Liz did a hand scan to feel for areas requiring extra attention. She laid her hands flat at Kurt's crown a few inches off of his body and slowly moved her hands down the length of his body. She explained that everyone is surrounded by a field of energy and that, through touching his field of energy, she could feel tingling, thickness, drafts, heat, etc.

"Not everyone can feel this, but it doesn't mean they cannot give Healing Touch." She explained that everyone has different awareness. "Some may feel energy, or see colors and visions when doing Healing Touch, but this is not indicative of them being better healers."

Liz showed Debra how to connect with the patient before starting. She placed a hand on Kurt's heart chakra on the chestbone between his nipples and held his right hand with the other. She instructed Debra to put one hand on top of hers where it was placed on Kurt's chest and to hold his left hand with her other hand.

"At this point you can do the technique I did with you where you brought up Mother Earth's red energy and combined it with God's white energy to fill your heart with pink unconditional love and let it spread into your body, mind and soul. Or if you want, you may move onto another technique."

"This is usually where I ask God to help the patient accept the energy readily and easily, to have the energy go wherever it is needed most, and to send unneeded energy back to the earth for recycling. I also welcome healing guides or teaching guides to assist. You can either say these thoughts out loud or to yourself."

She told Debra to avoid trying to control the outcome, but to trust God to know what is best. "Sometimes the patient is not ready to release whatever pain, disease, or emotions they are holding and it's up to them to let go whenever they're ready."

Liz reassured her she would not have to worry about harming anybody as long as she set a positive intent. "Even if you miss a step, God will take care of it."

She recommended Debra always move gently in and out of the patient's field and limit distractions and talking. "Sharing energy is very sacred."

"If you feel pain or energy from the patient, thank God for helping you recognize it, but ask that it be drained off of your elbows or body so you won't carry it around with you after your work is done."

Liz told her they would do a magnetic unruffling together where they would sweep his magnetic field to remove stale energy and Debra could copy her. They both held their hands with their fingers pointing down a few inches off of Kurt's body and raked down from above his crown to past his toes. They then shook off their hands toward the floor.

"The only other thing we'll cover today is a pain drain. I don't want to give you too much to remember and what you're learning today is really all you need to be able to help somebody."

She asked Kurt whether he had any pain. He said his lower back and left shoulder were sore so Liz instructed Debra to put her left hand on Kurt's shoulder and point her right hand downward and away from her body, as if signaling to slow down a bicycle. Liz did the same, but with her left hand on Kurt's lower back. She asked Kurt to send his pain to where their hands rested and advised Debra to close her eyes and ask God to send the pain up her left arm, across her shoulders, and off her right hand.

They reversed hands after a while, putting their right hands on the area that was painful and holding their left hands upward in the air with palms facing upwards.

"Now think about bringing healing energy into your left hand, down your arm, across your chest, and through your right hand to Kurt." Liz explained that they were bringing in healing energy from the universal energy field to replace the void that had occurred from the draining action. She recommended that Debra open her eyes to check to see if Kurt's eyes were flickering, as this would let her know whether or not he was in a deep state of relaxation.

"It's important to ground the patient afterwards so they don't feel dizzy or unbalanced." They each massaged a leg three times from the knee, down the calf and foot, and off the toes. "Kurt, slowly come back to the room and think feet, feet, feet."

"Do I have to?" Kurt looked blissful. "That was wonderful. Thanks you two."

Liz wrung her hands together as if wiping them clean and told Debra to do the same to end the healing session.

Kurt rose slowly. They all went toward the back of the house where Liz gave them each a glass of water and they settled in the family room.

"As I've mentioned before, it's important that both you and the patient drink lots of water over the next few days. The patient will process things for a few days. Sometimes they feel worse before they feel better as their body works through changes and releases."

Debra stayed and visited for a while. Liz gave her some handouts that summarized the techniques they had done and also explained the various chakras, their focus, and associated colors and emotions.

Debra hugged them both goodbye and thanked them for helping her learn Healing Touch. It felt special even when she was not the patient!

CHAPTER SEVEN

Debra woke Saturday morning to fog and drizzle. There was a For Sale sign already posted in the front yard, but she didn't think this weather would motivate anybody to go shopping for a house. She called Liz and they cancelled their walk. Debra made herself a cup of tea and curled up on the sofa with a quilt. O-o-h, she loved rainy mornings. They were a perfect excuse to be lazy. It rarely rained in San Diego, whereas it had been much more common when she lived in Sacramento.

"Well, if you were honest with yourself you'd admit you rarely gave yourself permission to lounge around even when the weather was lousy!" She must have been out of her mind back then. She was learning to enjoy life so much more now. She must remember to thank Elizabeth.

Debra emptied the dishwasher and tidied the house in case there was a showing. Leanne had a volleyball tournament at her school. Debra was going to watch the games with some of the other parents. Jonathan would be there with a few of his friends as their siblings were also playing in the tournament. Debra thought about packing some lunches, but remembered there would be a concession booth with hot dogs, beverages, and snacks. They didn't always have to eat healthy!

Leanne went to school early to practice before the tournament. Debra took her time going through her morning routine and arrived at the school about twenty minutes before the first game. She was greeted by some of the other parents who moved over so she could join them on the gym bleachers. Jonathan and his buddies grabbed seats beside the second string on the bottom bench just before the first whistle.

Debra liked volleyball. The rules were simple and it was an easy game to follow. The parents in her section demonstrated good sportsmanship and she was pleased to be included in their conversations between games. Leanne's team was playing well. They had won all of their games so far that day. Jonathan and his friends had started a comic cheering section that helped to keep the players upbeat. They had even made pom-poms by shredding flyers they had found left at the door! A couple of the boys were in gymnastics and gave a demonstration during one of the breaks. It was an entertaining day on the whole.

Leanne's team had to sit out and watch a game, the winner of which would play the championship game against them.

Observing intently, they tried to see if they could pick up any hints that would help when it was their turn. Some of the players chewed their nails or tapped their feet, and others sat frozen to their seats. All of them appeared stressed and there was a minimum of chatter. Debra actually thought Leanne could be far too serious. Debra realized she was a late bloomer when it came to learning to live life to the fullest and she hoped it wasn't too late to model the importance of enjoying life.

Amid screams and acrobatics from their cheering section, Leanne's team won the championship. They all shook hands with the members of the opposing team and were beaming with pride when the team captain accepted the championship trophy on their behalf. The coach bought Slurpees for the team at 7-11 afterwards. Debra decided to take Jonathan and his cheering section for Slurpees to thank them for their contribution. They thought that was a hoot!

Saturday night was quiet. Jonathan and Debra rented a movie while Leanne spent the evening celebrating at Lisa's.

Debra woke early Sunday morning. The conditions were perfect for kayaking. She left the children a note before driving to Crown Point Park. The water was so smooth she decided to paddle across to Fiesta Island. There were a few other kayakers out on the water, in addition to several rowing skulls. She could see cars on the distant freeway and the occasional jogger on the walkway. It otherwise looked like the rest of San Diego was still sleeping.

The kayak slipped into the water when she gave it a gentle shove. There was hardly a ripple in the water. The splashing of the paddle as she dipped it in and out was the only sound she heard as she crossed the bay.

She eventually paddled alongside the beach at Fiesta Island and stuck out her hand to touch the sand. "There, I made it."

A water-skier sped by at a distance. Debra took a rest from paddling and her boat rocked gently when the wake eventually reached her. It would have been hard work to cross to Fiesta Island if it were later in the day because the water would have been choppy due to wind, motorboats, and jet skis. A breeze was just starting and she decided she'd better paddle back before the water became rough.

She returned home and had showered and dressed by the time Jonathan was up. Leanne followed quite some time later.

Debra cooked waffles for brunch, which were everybody's favorite. She told them she was hoping they could get their chores done early in case the realtor wanted to bring somebody through the house. Leanne was going to Balboa Park for the afternoon and said she would get them done before she left. Jonathan was more reluctant, but agreed anyway.

Jim called later that morning to say he wanted to bring a couple through at two o'clock, if that was acceptable. Debra agreed and told Jonathan she would take him to Pacific Beach to watch the surfers. Jim called, again, around one o'clock and asked if another realtor could show the house at four thirty. A lock box for the house key had been installed so the realtors would have easy access. At least they were getting some bites. She felt kind of anxious and excited. What if one of these people wanted their house?

They left the house almost spotless before going out for the afternoon. Debra and Jonathan wandered down Crystal Pier after she finally found a parking spot on the street. It was a beautiful sunny day and people were out in droves.

Jonathan loved watching the surfers and Debra also found it fascinating. Every time they thought they'd move on, another surfer or two would set out to ride a wave and they would end up staying to watch. Debra and Jonathan finally managed to pull themselves away and walked to the nearby Dairy Queen for chocolate dipped ice cream cones.

They decided to drive into La Jolla nearby to see the seals at La Jolla Cove. Debra had to find parking, again. The seals could be heard as soon as they walked down the stairs to the walkway.

"Oh! Gross! I'd forgotten how much seals stink!' Jonathan exclaimed, holding his nose. People were lined up all along the railing of the break wall. Every once in a while a group of them would shriek because they were splashed by the waves pounding off of the break wall. Jonathan, of course, wanted to be one of them, but Debra was trying to avoid standing on the areas of the walkway that were already wet in the hope of being missed by the spray.

Some of the seals were fat and lazy, basking in the sun on the beach and rocks. The dry ones looked yellowish brown and furry, but once they became too hot, they would drag themselves into one of the small pools that had collected on the huge rock platform and would roll around until they looked dark and shiny. There were also a few seals frolicking in and out of the foam waves in the cove. Debra and Jonathan wound their way through the crowded walkway when they became bored with looking at the seals. It was getting late and the air was chilly so they headed for home. If the realtor's car was still parked in the driveway, they could always park around the block for a while.

Leanne came in the door shortly after Debra began cooking dinner. Debra usually cooked a big meal on Sundays, but that was difficult to do when she had been out all afternoon so she put together a tuna fish casserole. She added steamed baby peas to make it more nutritious. That brought on lots of complaining from Jonathan, but he ate it anyway.

The following week was relatively uneventful, with the exception that their house was shown a few times and one offer was made. The offer was ridiculously low and she and Jim decided the buyer was not serious enough, so Debra turned it down without making a counter offer. She might have considered, but she didn't even have Ted's fax number for sending real estate offers to him.

It was enough hassle having to keep the house tidy and the beds made in case the house was shown. This would be further complicated once an offer was made that required Ted's involvement. She decided to call Ted to get his work and home fax numbers. She didn't want to risk losing a sale, because she was unprepared. Ted was uncommunicative and only begrudgingly gave her the information.

Barbara Cason called Friday to say Ted's solicitor in Sacramento had contacted her. They were in the process of exchanging financial information and she would keep Debra posted regarding any developments. It would have been nice if Ted would have mentioned he had hired a lawyer when she talked to him a couple of days ago. She was losing more and more respect for him as time went on.

Debra continued to ground herself every day and she was trying to build in relaxation whenever possible, but she still felt a little stressed as she and Liz started out on their Saturday morning walk. She wondered what would happen with the divorce agreement and she was worried about selling the house.

It was fairly windy on the bay that day so they decided to leave the path and walk back through the neighborhood. They made comments about the various homes and types of landscaping as they walked. They shared similar ideas for what they would like to do to the properties they passed.

Liz was the first to notice a For Sale sign in the yard of one of the houses just around the corner from their block. "Debra, look at this home. Isn't it cute?"

Debra had to agree.

"This house must have just been listed. I don't remember seeing a For Sale sign on Wednesday when we walked by. Why don't you get one of the brochures?"

Debra walked over to get a brochure and kept her fingers crossed as she perused the sheet looking for the listing price. Liz looked over her shoulder and they both saw it at once.

"H-m-m-m, not bad." Liz said.

Debra felt a twinge of excitement as her eyes scanned the house and yard. "It needs some yard work, but the stucco's been recently painted." The walls had been painted a pleasant pastel peach shade. The white latticework on the windows gave it a classy look.

"I like the brick work on the bottom half," Liz said.

"Me, too. It's a nice contrast to the stucco." She added, "That deep red color won't show the dirt that gets splashed on the walls when you water the plants around the outside of the house. I really like the porch on the front, too. I've always wanted to have a front porch with a swing. I wonder what the house is like inside."

"Why don't we see if we could look at it this weekend?" Liz said, and then caught herself, "That is, if you don't mind if I look at it with you."

"I'd really like that. A second opinion would be great."

"Kurt's away at a conference in San Francisco all weekend so I've got lots of spare time to do whatever I want to do. Do you have time later today?"

"I've got all the time in the world. As long as I do some housework and get some laundry done this weekend, I'm set."

They agreed Debra would call her realtor and try to arrange a time that afternoon or sometime the following day. Neither one had a pen nor paper so Debra was glad the address was on the brochure. Liz wondered why Debra's realtor had not contacted her about the new listing, but Debra told her it was her fault because she had told him she wanted to wait. She still felt that way, but the location of this house was too good to pass up.

She made the call the moment she stepped in the door. There would be time later to have a shower. She paged Jim Schwab and left him a message about wanting to see the property. Jim returned her call soon afterwards. He told her he'd called the other realtor. The home was vacant and there had been tenants so the back yard needed a little work, but there had been some recent renovations and the house was apparently clean and presentable. "I was told it's a decent little home," he said. He could set it up for that day provided she was available in the early afternoon. They agreed on one o'clock and Debra called Liz to let her know.

Debra's stomach felt like it was full of butterflies. Decisions, decisions, decisions. She almost wished she had a tranquilizer. She decided to tackle her share of the housework. There was a viewing of their home scheduled for later that afternoon. She threw in a load of laundry and tidied up before hauling out the vacuum cleaner. Debra buzzed through the house. Anxiety was great for getting chores done!

Leanne and Jonathan were also busy completing their chores. Jonathan wanted his allowance so he could go to a movie and Leanne was going shopping with some friends.

They all took turns using the necessary cleaning solutions and apparatus. Debra had just enough time to grab a quick sandwich and shower before the realtor arrived. She didn't feel much like eating, but she managed to force herself to finish her lunch.

Liz came over and they waited for the realtor. Debra wanted to meet him there, but he insisted on picking them up. Liz started to cough as they climbed into Jim's newly washed SUV. She didn't like his aftershave any more than Debra did. Fortunately the drive was short.

Once inside the house, Jim went on ahead to turn on lights even though it was daylight. The entryway was small, but functional with an average-sized coat closet. It had two framed glass doors that opened into an L-shaped living room and dining room. The main feature of this room was a gas fireplace on the end wall with built-in shelves for a television on one side and books or ornaments on the other. A huge mirror over the fireplace added depth to the room.

Debra noticed there were hardwood floors throughout which had recently been refinished. The walls were newly painted in a neutral off white shade, with a slight hint of peach.

"I like it when a house is vacant. There's no furniture or wall hangings to hide imperfections," Liz said.

Debra agreed, "It's easier to imagine your own belongings in it, too. I'd add some color to the walls if I bought the house.

They wandered into the kitchen and Debra gasped. She hadn't expected it to be so roomy. It had lots of cupboards and an eating area had been added to make the room spacious. The cabinets were extremely old-fashioned with dark stain, but there were lots of them.

Liz said, "The cupboards are nothing to write home to mother about and the flooring is in bad shape, but you could replace them someday."

Debra laughed as her eyes scanned the room. "No kidding. I would definitely want to do that." She looked out of the window over the kitchen sink and noticed the back yard was completely fenced with a small patio. "Oh, nice."

"Would you like to see the yard before we see the rest of the house?" Jim asked. Debra nodded. He led them through a small coatroom and out the back door.

Once outside Debra was already imagining the types of trees, shrubs, and plants she would like to add. Liz commented, "I can see your mind already churning. I know you love gardening. This project could really be fun!"

Debra could not help but agree as they went back into the house. The three bedrooms were lined along the hallway. All were a decent size. Here, again, there were hardwood floors. There were only one and one-half baths, which would be an adjustment, but one Debra thought she and the children could survive. H-m-m that would leave her with no bathrooms to clean if the children each did one! At least the bathroom fixtures were all in good shape, although, the linoleum needed replacing.

Jim pointed out features and opened closet doors as they stepped into each room. There was no lack of closet space. Whoever had planned this house was using his head.

She decided to take another look at the kitchen. "Some nice light maple cabinets would be heavenly in this room…with a walk-in pantry in the corner. I could have the lino replaced at the same time."

Liz agreed. "And you could get a nice etched glass door for the pantry."

"Definitely." She turned to Jim, "The thing is, the owner is going to want early possession being as it's vacant. What if I can't sell my house fast enough?"

"You could make an offer conditional to the sale of your own home and also conditional to obtaining financing," Jim told her. He expressed concern that, although the property needed some work, the selling price reflected that and he didn't think it would be on the market long.

They estimated the amount she might get this property for and compared it to the estimated equity in her current home. Payments on this house would be extremely affordable. They decided to go back to Debra's house to write an offer.

They chose a price that was unlikely to offend the owner, set the possession date for two months away, and made the sale conditional to her selling her home. Debra was so excited she could hardly breathe.

Liz and Debra decided to spend the afternoon together and Liz gave Jim her cell phone number in case he needed to contact Debra about the offer while she was out. Debra preferred to leave her house during viewings because she thought it encouraged prospective buyers to take their time looking.

Jim left with the offer in his briefcase. Liz suggested they go for a drive or walk back to her place and experiment with doing Healing Touch. Debra chose going to Liz's because she thought that might do a better job of calming her.

She retrieved her pendulum from her bedroom and they walked to Liz's. "Liz, let's walk around the corner and take another look, okay?"

Liz laughed, "Oh, boy, you've got it bad. You know, I'm almost as excited as you are. Wouldn't it be wonderful for you to get a house that close?" Debra nodded in agreement and they both slid an arm around the other's back and gave each other a brief squeeze before heading down the street.

They stood outside the listed property and chatted about renovations Debra could make and things she could do to the yard. They shared ideas about arranging her furniture and then talked about decorating the walls and windows.

Liz and Debra pulled themselves away to walk to Liz's home. Liz said, "We're so buzzed about the house. Let's do a grounding ritual before we get started."

They grounded themselves and afterwards Debra did all of the things Liz had shown her. She stumbled a bit in the beginning. She almost forgot to pendulum Liz and she had to ask Liz which hand took the pain away and which one received healing energy, but other than that she felt good about her first solo session.

Liz made a pot of tea and put out a plate of homemade chocolate chip cookies. Her cell phone rang at three-thirty and they both just about jumped out of their skins. It was Jim with a counter offer. He would meet them at Liz's so they could go over it together.

The owner had raised the price somewhat, but more significantly he had moved the possession date up to a few days before the end of the following month. Debra panicked a bit at that. She wanted the house so much! She could afford it. She could keep her promise to the children to keep them in the neighborhood. And, she would live just around the corner from Liz. Those were all things to be considered.

"It only takes one buyer who wants your house for you to be able to sell it. It will probably go fast, but I can't guarantee that you'd get a possession date that soon. Would you be able to afford to make both mortgage payments for a month, if you had to?"

Debra thought about it briefly. "The location, price, and size of this house are perfect. How can I afford not to? If I had to, I could get an interim loan, until the money comes through on my house."

As soon as Jim left, Debra said, "Wow, that was speedy. Do you realize we only first saw the house this morning? I sure hope I can sell my house fast enough."

She and Liz parted company. Debra was exhausted and decided to go home for a nap.

She felt rested by the time both Leanne and Jonathan were home. She took them past the house. Jonathan was disgusted at how much smaller the house was compared to the one they lived in. Leanne was so happy it was in the same neighborhood that she wouldn't have cared if it was a hovel. Besides, as she pointed out, it would be much less work to keep clean. That helped to bring Jonathan around to their point of view.

There were three more showings at their house the next day. Liz invited her over to teach her how to do a mind clearing. She used a teddy bear as an example. Then they drove to Sunset Cliffs to walk along the cliffs for the rest of the afternoon. Both Leanne and Jonathan made plans so they would be out of the house for the entire afternoon. Liz carried her cell phone with her in case there was an offer on Debra's house, but it didn't ring.

Debra received a call from her lawyer on Monday afternoon. Ted and his solicitor had made some changes to the divorce agreement. When could Debra come in to discuss them? Debra wished they could get together right away, but Barbara's schedule was full until Wednesday.

Barbara appeared optimistic as she met with Debra to share the information about Ted's income and assets. She said she didn't know why Ted was wasting money on another lawyer because the only change he had made was with respect to the amount of child support. His income was higher than Debra had anticipated. She could considerably reduce the amount of child support requested and still receive the minimum amount she had previously told Barbara she would be willing to accept before they inflated it for bargaining. Debra agreed with Barbara when she recommended that Debra counter with that amount. Barbara would call with Ted's response as soon as she heard back from his lawyer.

It was only a day later when Barbara advised her that Ted had agreed to sign the revised divorce agreement. She only had a verbal agreement, but she would have the papers typed and immediately sent to Ted's lawyer by courier service. The amount of the equity in their home was deducted from Debra's share of their other assets and Ted would need to sign over the remainder. Barbara agreed to ask Ted's solicitor to forward the signed quitclaim deed by courier and she would register it immediately to facilitate Debra selling the house. Once both Ted and Debra had signed the Dissolution of Marriage Agreement, she would submit it to court records. Barbara congratulated Debra and told her the rest of her legal costs would be deducted before a check would be sent to her.

It wasn't until the following week that Jim called Debra at home one evening. "I've got an offer on your house. Are you going to be home so I can bring it over?"

Of course, she was.

It looked pretty good. She would have liked an earlier possession date and the price was a bit lower than she was willing to accept, but at least the buyers had a pre-approved mortgage. Jim wrote up a counter offer. The quitclaim deed had finally been registered so Debra did not require Ted's signature.

The prospective buyer was apparently as eager to have this settled as Debra because Ted returned only a couple of hours later with a revised counter offer. It was late when Debra accepted the counter offer and finally went to bed for the night.

The house sold for what she felt was a decent price and helped to compensate for the fact that she would have to pay mortgage payments on both properties for one month. That would at least give her a chance to get some renovations done on the other property before they moved in, although things would be financially tight until everything came through. Debra had so much on her mind, she was surprised she fell asleep immediately and did not hear a thing until the alarm went off the next morning.

Debra was soon preoccupied with obtaining financing for their new home and gathering information for getting renovations done. In the midst of everything, she came home from work one day to find a letter from her mother in the mailbox. She placed it unopened on her dresser. She would deal with it later.

CHAPTER EIGHT

Debra remembered her mother's letter as soon as she woke the next morning. She was dreading reading it.

"What's the worse that can happen?" she remembered Elizabeth asking. "You get another lecture," she told herself. "Big deal! You've had hundreds of those." She marched over to the dresser and ripped open the envelope.

It started out fine. Her mother wrote that it was nice to receive a letter instead of a bill in her mailbox. Her father was enjoying his new watch. She included an update of how each of Debra's siblings and their families were doing. She and Debra's father were disappointed that Debra and Ted were not working things out, but it looked like Debra was getting on with her life. Her mother hoped Debra wasn't being too hasty in visiting a lawyer. That got Debra's back up a little bit. She started to skim read at this point. She was impatient to see how the rest of the letter would read.

The kayaking sounded relaxing, the new house seemed charming, and it was good that she was enjoying her friendship with Liz. She went on to talk about the failing health of a couple of their friends…Eleanor Schiffer, a family friend, was extremely ill and …Whoa!… Eleanor was finding Healing Touch to be very helpful. Her mother did not know much about Healing Touch, but she was glad Eleanor had found some relief somewhere. The letter ended with good wishes for Debra and her children.

Debra felt like crying. She remembered Eleanor as a cheerful and energetic person, who loved to help others. It was sad in itself that someone like Eleanor was so ill but, she did not know her well and what really made her tearful was relief that her mother had not blasted her for any of the changes she was making in her life. She could hardly believe how much it meant to her.

Ted called that night to confirm arrangements for Leanne and Jonathan's weekend visit a couple of weeks away. Debra answered the call. Leanne was usually the first to get the phone, but she was in the shower. Ted, again, announced his name, but Debra just smiled to herself this time. She thanked him for signing the quitclaim deed and divorce agreement.

He seemed a little taken back and hesitated before saying, "You're welcome—about the kids' visit—I wanted to confirm they can go before I book the flights. Uh-h-h, they can go right?"

"They can go, but would you please discuss it with me first next time in case I already have other plans. I want you to be able to see them whenever you want, but I don't want to be the bad guy either."

"Oh—sure."

"Do you want to talk to Jonathan? Leanne is just getting out of the shower. I'll have her pick up the extension."

Jonathan jumped to the phone when she told him his father was on the line. Debra went upstairs to let Leanne know about the call. She made sure she gave them privacy while they chatted with their father. Leanne came off briefly to ask about a ride to and from the airport. Debra would drive them provided he booked the flights outside of her work hours and emailed their flight itinerary.

A whole weekend to herself. It sounded a bit overwhelming. It was the first time she would not be with Jonathan for his birthday. She couldn't miss a birthday. They would just have to celebrate early.

She made arrangements with the realtor so she could take Leanne and Jonathan to see their new home. Jonathan was dragging his feet as they entered the house. He sure didn't like change in his life. Leanne gave him a tiny shove to get him moving and he stumbled into the entryway. He started to protest, but Debra commented, "If you want, you can walk back home without seeing your new bedroom. It's up to you." That shut him up.

They toured the house. Debra showed them their bedrooms and told them they could each choose new bedding and paint colors for their rooms. "I'm hoping to decorate the house in shades of green and peach. The wall color has a touch of peach in it and our family room furniture is teal green so I think that would be a good choice."

Jonathan piped up, "I want dark green on two walls and deep orangish on the other two. Tim's dad has that in his den and it looks really cool."

"I think I could live with that as long as the orange has a peach tint to it."

Leanne said, "I would like to pick out my comforter first and then choose a color that goes with it."

"Good idea. I thought maybe we could go to J C Penny's. They have a nice selection of bedding."

She explained to them that she would be replacing the kitchen cabinets and flooring, in addition to the bathroom flooring. She took some measurements so she could place the orders. Jonathan soon became preoccupied making noises and listening to them echo against the bare walls and floors. It got Debra thinking that she would have to pick up some area rugs to make the house quieter.

Leanne was a little horrified that there were only one and one-half bathrooms, but otherwise seemed to think the house was nice enough. Jonathan even said it looked bigger from the inside than it did on the outside. Debra took that as acceptance from him. She would check with Ted to see if he wanted any of the extra furniture before she got rid of anything. She sure had lots to do.

Debra sighed as she dropped into the chair in Elizabeth's office the next day.

Elizabeth smiled and said, "Why the heavy sigh?"

"Things are moving along at epic speed and it gets overwhelming, at times."

"What's happening?"

"Well, Ted signed the divorce agreement and I will officially be divorced in three months. I bought a house and I sold our house." She filled Elizabeth in on the details.

"Things are definitely moving along, aren't they?" They both smiled. "How are you holding up?"

"Pretty good, actually. I hope to slow things down soon. Sometimes I miss my old rut."

"That's understandable. It was comfortable and familiar." She smiled. "How did you do with your homework?" She looked down at her notes. "What did you experiment with doing differently in your relationships with Ted and your mother?"

"I'm not really sure what I did with Ted, but he certainly was different."

"How's that?"

"I left a message when I listed the house and I called to get his fax number, but I didn't notice much change until our last phone conversation."

"What happened then?"

"Well, first off, I thanked him for signing the paperwork and that seemed to catch him off guard or something. I guess he doesn't expect me to be nice to him."

"No?"

"He probably expects me to attack him and maybe that's what else I did differently. I told him I would prefer that he let me know about visits with the children before telling them. I was assertive, but I was also nice about it."

"How did he respond?"

"He was more agreeable than usual."

Elizabeth asked if she had noticed anything else, as she jotted down some notes.

"Not with Ted, but I sure got an unexpected response from my mother." She told Elizabeth about the letter she wrote and how she had written as if she was sending it to someone else.

"What response did you get from your mother?"

"She didn't criticize me or give advice. Well, except for one comment that she hoped I wasn't being too hasty in seeing a lawyer. But, I think I can excuse her for that. The thing that was most surprising, though, is that not only did she not jump on the bandwagon about me becoming involved in Healing Touch, but she told me one of her friends is ill and is finding Healing Touch very helpful."

"That must have been a pleasant surprise."

"Actually, it just about brought me to tears. I guess I do care an awful lot about her approval."

"That's okay, as long as you don't communicate that to her. It's important that you don't let it interfere with you being yourself and doing the things that are important to you." She then asked Debra, "What breaks did you build in for yourself since we last met?"

Debra gave her a summary of the past three weeks and was amazed that she had managed to build in as many positive activities as she had. She told Elizabeth about watching the volleyball tournament, kayaking, learning and doing Healing Touch, and walking along the Sunset Cliffs. All that and reading and grounding rituals too!

"You know, I'm actually doing fairly well. I've been meaning to thank you for helping me to make life so much more enjoyable."

"You're welcome. But, you're the one who did all the work. It was you who made it happen."

Elizabeth was pleased that Debra was doing so well. She told Debra she was impressed with the determination Debra showed in tackling new things to get her life on track.

Debra thanked her and asked, "Could we wait to get together until after I move into the new house? That'll be my next big step plus Leanne and Jonathan will have had their first weekend visit with Ted by then, too. I'll be interested to see how I'll feel after that."

Elizabeth suggested that she plan her time well to make it easier the weekend the children would be gone. She recommended that Debra continue to do the things that were working well for her and they scheduled an appointment for just over one month away.

Debra stopped in at a floor and tile business suggested to her by a couple of her co-workers and ordered flooring for the bathrooms and kitchen. She also visited a cabinet-making shop that had come highly recommended and, after perusing the various selections, ordered the cabinets, countertop, ceramic tile backsplash, and kitchen sink for their new home. The cost was fairly expensive, but she had made arrangements to hold back some of the equity from their house and planned to put it toward renovations for the new house.

The kitchen floor had to be installed before the cabinets. It would be a few weeks before the cabinets arrived and could be installed. If there were any delays with the flooring, it would be dicey as to whether that occurred before or after their move, but at least they were ordered and a tentative installation date was arranged.

A large workshop was scheduled at San Diego Convention Center the following week. Eight of the consultants in Debra's organization would be presenting and they had developed some innovative new material. Debra and her staff had spent several days preparing the new information for handouts and typing several revisions before finally having the last draft copied and overheads made. Due to the many changes being implemented, Debra and her boss had decided she would spend the day at the Convention Center to ensure that everything ran smoothly.

Debra and her staff met at the loading dock at six fifteen in the morning. Debra thought that was a horrible hour to start work, but they had lots to do before the start of the workshop. They used two dollies to transport boxes containing handouts, supplies, table decorations, and treats to the various conference rooms. The staff laid out pads of paper, pens with their advertising logo, and appropriate literature on the tables of each of the conference rooms. They then distributed small flowered plants as table decorations and put candy bags on each table.

Everybody convened in the registration area once the rooms were ready. Each of the staff was assigned to a section of three registration tables where participants signed the roster before being given a workshop folder.

The two hundred and sixty participants started arriving soon after the registration area was ready. Everything was organized alphabetically and registration ran smoothly. The Convention Center staff responsible for catering, bookings, and events meanwhile came through the lobby and introduced themselves to Debra. They also let her know how they could be contacted, if needed. It was nice to finally be able to put faces to the voices. She had spent so much time talking to them on the phone.

There was a continental breakfast set up on the outside wall of the lobby where registrants hung out before wandering off to their assigned conference rooms. It was with relief that Debra finally sat down to enjoy a cup of tea and a muffin after the last registrants had gone to their rooms. The rest of the staff joined her for refreshments before returning to the office.

Debra later stopped by each of the workshop rooms to make sure none of the presenters required any assistance. In case additional copies were required, she had a contract set up at Mailboxes, Etc. on the Mezzanine level of the Convention Center. She peeked inside each of the rooms and made eye contact with the presenters so they could signal if they needed anything. One of the presenters gave her a thumb down signal indicating that the temperature of the room needed to be lowered. Another indicated that her room was too cold. Debra contacted the Events Manager using the in-house phone and he agreed to take care of it.

Debra returned to the registration area. She could hear a bird chirping. A sparrow was flying around and landed on the floor near some glass doors. The poor little thing was trapped inside the building! Debra inched toward one of the doors and opened it in the hope that he would find his way out, but he took off as soon as she approached him.

Debra decided to prop one of the doors open on the chance that the sparrow would return. As she opened the door, she noticed it was a beautiful sunny day. She walked out onto the cement concourse behind the building. The view was incredible! She wandered past an intriguing metal sculpture and leaned against the retaining wall so she could look out onto the bay.

A marina filled with sailboats and motorboats was located immediately behind the concourse and beside it was a park with green grass. It never ceased to amaze Debra that the parks had such green grass and yet San Diego rarely had rain. The lawn was dotted with tables, lamps, and white tent canopies set up for a celebration of some kind. Debra remembered noticing a pamphlet in the lobby advertising the Cesar E. Chavez Community Breakfast.

The majestic Coronado Hotel, with its multiple red tiled peaked roofs could be seen directly across the bay. She could also see several huge ocean-faring boats in the harbor to the south and the span of the Coronado Bridge was impressive in the distance. It made her feel like San Diego was just a small civilization on the edge of the whole world.

She went back inside and pulled out some work she had brought to keep her occupied. As she set up her lap top computer, she saw movement out of the corner of her eye. The sparrow had a companion, a pretty orange-breasted sparrow. She decided to open another door hoping that a cross breeze would attract them. Much as she enjoyed their cheerful chirping, she wanted to set them free. Sure enough, after a few minutes of flying around, the sparrow flew out the open door and was soon followed by the other.

Debra waited a while before, again, checking the presenters' rooms. The doors into the hallway were now all standing open. She went in and quietly checked with a participant in each room. All of the rooms were stifling hot so she contacted the Events Manager to have the temperature lowered.

Debra returned to her laptop. Noon was approaching and there was no food set out on the tables. She kept working, meanwhile checking her watch every few moments. Debra started to panic when eleven-forty-five arrived and the tables remained bare. She hurried down the hallway and opened a door marked "pantry". Several staff members were standing and chatting beside trolleys of large bowls of salads and trays of deli meats, etc. wrapped in cellophane.

"I'm concerned that the food has not been put out yet." She told a smartly dressed Hispanic man in a chef's uniform.

"We have lots of time. Lunch is not until twelve-thirty."

"No," she corrected him. "Lunch is at noon."

The catering staff hustled about placing the various dishes in an attractive display on the tables. The last dish of food was unwrapped just as the first workshop participant came around the corner from the conference rooms.

Debra realized it had been her mistake. She had requested the same lunch arrangement as for previous workshops at the Convention Center and had forgotten that the most recent workshop's lunch break had been scheduled at twelve-thirty instead of noon. Debra made sure she apologized to the head caterer and thanked him and his staff for their quick action in resolving the problem.

Lunch went by without a hitch. Buffet tables were set outside as well as in the lobby and she helped direct the participants to reduce lineups at the tables. The rest of the day ran smoothly. Debra's staff arrived at four o'clock to retrieve workshop supplies from the conference rooms and pack them up to be returned to the office. They worked in teams and tackled each room as soon as the presentation was completed and participants started to leave. It was five o'clock by the time they left the Convention Center. It had been a long day for all of the staff.

The rest of the week was less demanding. She went to Liz's after their walk on Saturday and had the opportunity to, again, do Healing Touch on Liz. This time Liz gave her the chance to stumble through the mind clearing technique. Debra kept a sheet of illustrated instructions nearby for easy reference. It would take some practice before she would be able to remember where and in which sequence to place her hands, as this technique was not as simple as the others she had learned.

Debra took Jonathan and Leanne out for lunch on Sunday followed by a trip to J C Penney to scout out new bedding. Leanne chose a comforter with a blend of peach and green. Debra purchased all of the accessories, including bedskirt, pillow shams, and pouf valances. Jonathan's choice was a forest green plaid with orange and gold threads running through it. The matching valance was pleated as was the bedskirt. Debra chose a light duvet with a cover of two-toned sage green foliage print. The shams, bed skirt, and valances were dyed the deeper of the sage colors. She picked up peach accent pillows for the top of the bed in addition to a peach colored table skirt. All three of them were excited as they carried their shopping bags out to the car.

Debra had not minded putting their purchases on her charge card because she wanted to make their new house feel like home and she knew she could pay off the balance once the house transactions were finalized.

They drove to Home Depot next to look at paint chips. It took them a while, but they found paint colors to match their bedding. Leanne chose to paint one wall a deeper peach and leave the remaining walls with the hint of peach. Jonathan would have two walls painted forest green and the other two in a deep peachy orange.

Debra consulted with the paint expert and also asked about wallpaper. It was suggested she consider rag painting the bedroom wall across from her bed so it would look like two-toned wallpaper. The sales rep showed her which supplies she would need, a small pail, a bag of white rags, and a tin of faux paint lacquer. He also had a ten-dollar videotape demonstrating faux painting techniques. It sounded enticing so she picked out two shades of sage green matching her duvet cover and planned to rag paint the darker shade over the lighter one. They would wait until after the possession date to purchase the paint, so they could take it directly to the new house.

Both Leanne and Jonathan hurried off to spend the rest of the afternoon with their friends and, no doubt, tell them about their shopping spree. Debra went home to enjoy a quiet hour by herself before preparing dinner. She had chicken breasts marinating in the fridge along with cabbage and pineapple coleslaw made earlier in the day. Miniature colored marshmallows had made this particular recipe of coleslaw her children's favorite since they were small.

There was no school the following week due to Spring Break. Jonathan was signed up for a soccer camp during the day and Leanne was registered for tennis lessons. They would still have lots of idle time on their hands and Debra suggested they go through their belongings to get rid of anything they no longer needed in preparation for the move. She ended up having to go through Jonathan's belongings with him one evening as he tended to be a pack rat and had hardly gotten rid of anything when he sorted them on his own.

Debra was excited about moving into a smaller home. It would be a great opportunity to organize things and get rid of a lot of clutter. She planned to tackle the garage while the children were away on the weekend. Both children had been instructed to place the items they valued in a certain corner of the garage or they might be gone when they returned. She would eventually have to purchase a shed for the yard as the new house did not have a garage and they would need somewhere to put tools, bikes, and other sporting equipment.

They celebrated Jonathan's birthday on Thursday evening. Debra took Jonathan and a few of his friends to Burger King. Leanne joined them at home later when they ate birthday cake with ice cream and Jonathan opened his gifts.

A whole week of hanging out with their friends left both Leanne and Jonathan ready for a weekend away by the time Friday arrived. Jonathan and Tim were starting to get into little tiffs and Leanne was extremely bored. It felt strange when Debra left them at the airport. This was whole new territory for her. She had never been without both children for an entire weekend since they had been born.

Debra slumped onto the couch as soon as she got home. So much for planning her weekend! She didn't feel like doing anything but moping. Debra sat for a while, but eventually talked herself into getting up. She made a salad and reheated some leftover chili. There was nobody around to have to be sociable with. She could read her Eileen Goudge novel while she ate and listened to music, her kind of music. Debra hadn't read more than a couple of chapters before she began to feel drowsy. She slithered down onto the couch, pulled a fleece throw over herself, and fell asleep.

It was dark by the time she woke. She reached up to turn on a lamp so she could read the time on her watch. Eight-forty p.m. "It's a little too early to go to bed for the night," she chuckled. She reached for the *TV Guide*. There was just enough time to have a bathroom break and get a snack before watching a re-run of *Six Days and Seven Nights*.

She could do whatever she wanted. She could watch whatever she wanted. This wasn't so bad.

Debra spread some nachos on a plate and sprinkled them with grated cheddar cheese. She heated them in the microwave and added chopped fresh tomatoes. Then she poured herself a Snapple drink and added ice. She was soon enjoying the chemistry and witty repartee between Harrison Ford and Anne Heche. She tidied up the kitchen during the commercials and when she finally went to bed for the night, she slept soundly.

Liz was quick to ask how her weekend by herself was going when Debra joined her the next morning.

"It has its moments, but I'm doing okay. It helps that I know they'll be back in less than two days. I'm going to start sorting through what to keep and what to get rid of before the move so that should help keep me busy."

"Do you have any plans for tonight or would you like to come over and have dinner and watch a movie with Kurt and I? I'm not making anything fancy, but we'd like the company."

"That interferes with my plans of eating dinner and watching a movie by myself." Before Liz could think she was serious, she laughed, "No, actually I'd love to do that. Do you want me to bring anything?"

"Just yourself."

They talked about which rental movies they had already seen and which ones they would like to see. Liz thought that gave her a few to choose between and said she would pick one up later that morning.

Debra showered when she got home even though she knew she would soon be out in the garage. There was something about starting out fresh that appealed to her.

She opened the garage doors and made three piles, one to keep, the second to throw out, and the other to take to the Salvation Army. It was astounding how much junk there was considering that they had moved less than one year ago! Of course, because it was a transfer they had hired a moving company. Movers packed everything! Her sister had told her the movers had even packed the contents of her garbage can when she moved out to New York!

She was filthy and sweaty by the time she went back into the house for lunch. She washed up the best she could before making herself a plate of fresh veggies and fruit, with a large glass of iced tea.

"If I had my new home, I could sit in my swing on my front porch and eat my lunch," Debra told herself. She sure was looking forward to the move. She would have to look into getting a swing soon.

By the end of the afternoon, everything she wasn't keeping was bundled up in garbage bags. She loaded her car and drove to the Salvation Army depot to deposit the items to be recycled. Then, she boxed some of the things that wouldn't be needed until after the move and labeled them clearly. The rest of their belongings were stacked in a corner separate from the piled up garbage bags that were waiting to be taken out to the curb for trash pick up. Debra went in for her second shower of the day and laid down for a nap before going over to Liz's.

Kurt was barbecuing chicken breasts marinated in bourbon and peach juice, accompanied by zucchini, mushrooms and onions. It smelled delicious. Liz had prepared a green salad topped with sliced kiwi, strawberries, and rose petals.

They were complimented when they sat down to eat and Debra commented, "If this isn't 'anything fancy', I would hate to see extravagant! This is delicious!"

Liz had rented *K-Pax*. Kevin Spacey was one of Debra's favorite actors and Liz and Kurt apparently shared her view. They just about rolled on the floor laughing during a scene when Kevin Spacey ate a banana, peel and all. Kurt told them that, on his way back from his latest conference, he viewed a special about *K-Pax* on the plane. Kevin Spacey was interviewed and said he had eaten several bananas including their peels, in order to shoot that clip. He apparently said he had a "potassium high" for a few days afterwards.

Kurt re-wound that section of the tape and re-played it. They laughed even harder during the following clip when Kevin Spacey turned around and looked longingly at the bowl of fruit in the hope that he would be offered another banana, because they now knew that he had eaten several bananas beforehand.

Debra returned home at the end of the evening feeling cheerful and relaxed. She and Ted hadn't socialized with anybody following their move to San Diego and she had forgotten how pleasant it was to share an evening with friends.

She spent most of Sunday going through the contents of all of the hallway, linen, and bedroom closets. This left her with more garbage bags to drag out to the garage and several more to take to the Salvation Army. She was really enjoying getting organized.

Leanne and Jonathan gave their mother huge welcoming hugs when she met them at the arrival gate. They looked bushed and apparently enjoyed a "terrific" weekend. They ate fish and chips at

Fisherman's Wharf and toured Union Square where they were entertained by several buskers. Jonathan's favorite was a tall, thin man who folded himself up into a tiny plexi-glass cube. They both thought the Golden Gate Bridge was impressive.

Jonathan was quick to shove his birthday present into his mother's hands as soon as they returned to the car. "Look, Mom. Dad gave me a new Game Boy!"

Her gift of a new soccer ball and pants could hardly measure up, but she knew she had better get used to it. Their father would be able to spare no expense in purchasing gifts and he would be spending nothing but quality time with them, without the interference of normal everyday life. On the other hand, she reminded herself, she had the opportunity to live with them day in and day out and was able to spend much more time with them.

CHAPTER NINE

Debra was thrilled when the realtor handed her the house keys Friday night. There was so much she wanted to do before they moved in and she could hardly wait to get started. She had even skipped her morning walk so she could get an early start. The supplies she would need were already loaded into her car when she drove over to her new house.

The first thing she did was open some windows to get rid of the stale air from the house having been closed up so long. Debra then wandered through the house and took another look, meanwhile fantasizing about the decorating she had planned. She had never bought a house on her own before. She was so excited.

First off, she wanted to remove the kitchen cabinets. She retrieved the proper screwdriver from her toolbox, hopped up onto the chair, and started removing the screws that fastened the cupboards to the wall. It was tricky to take out the last screw of each cabinet, without having it fall down on her, but she got up on the countertop and used her legs to help brace the woodwork against the wall until finished.

The bottom cupboards were easier because she didn't have to balance the cabinets while she unscrewed them, but she ended up laying on the floor, half in and half out of the cupboard to reach the screws. Talk about uncomfortable!

Debra was sore and tired by the time she had detached all of the cupboards, but there was no way she was going to pay the cabinet installers to remove cabinets when she could do it herself. She also wanted to paint the wall behind the cabinets before the new ones were installed. The previous owner had fortunately left behind a pail of the leftover wall paint for touch ups. She didn't know whether there was enough, but at least she knew which brand and color to get if she needed more.

Debra washed up and then went out onto the front step to eat her lunch while she waited for Kurt and Liz to arrive. Debra had commandeered Kurt to come over that afternoon to unhook the plumbing on the kitchen sink and the dishwasher. She had told Kurt and Liz that the only thing she knew about plumbing was how to replace washers.

Then she had remembered that she actually also knew how to take the trap apart. She had explained that she had dropped one of the diamond earrings Ted had given her for their tenth anniversary. It had fallen into the drain and she couldn't bare waiting until Ted got home to see if it was there, so she had used a plumbing wrench to remove the trap and look for herself. All three of them had groaned with disgust when she described extracting the tiny earring from the grimy sludge that had poured into the pail underneath the sink when she removed the trap.

Kurt would be taking some of the kitchen cabinets to hang in his garage in exchange for his plumbing assistance. He had also offered to take the rest to the dump for her.

Debra appreciated the opportunity to survey the front yard while she waited for Liz and Kurt to arrive. There were two large trees, but other than that it was mostly grass, with unkempt dirt beds intended for flowers. She was looking forward to remedying the situation.

Kurt and Liz soon drove up. She hugged them in greeting before going inside. Kurt nodded his approval as he walked through each of the rooms and she told him about her plans for renovations. "Debra, ya' done good!" he said when they were finished their tour. They all laughed at his intentional use of poor language.

He went out to his truck to get the tools he needed to dismantle the plumbing while Debra fetched a pail and some rags for under the sink. Kurt looked inside the cupboard when he returned, "You're lucky. Somebody installed shut off valves right here so you won't have to keep the water turned off in the rest of the house while you're waiting for the new sink to be installed."

Debra had not even thought to look. That was good news! She and Liz stood and chatted as he went to work on the plumbing. Kurt seemed to know what he was doing and he soon started pulling the dishwasher out from under the counter. The three of them carried the cupboards outside and placed them in the back of Kurt's pick up. There were so many cupboards that it took them several trips. They were all panting by the time they were done.

Kurt and Liz were pleasantly surprised when Debra produced chilled sodas from a cooler she had brought. "You thought of everything, didn't you?" Liz said as she popped the cap on her soda.

"I really appreciate your help. I couldn't have done this myself. I hope you'll both come for dinner, when we get moved in."

"Once you're all settled we will, but don't go stressing yourself about it." Liz replied.

As they finished their drinks, Kurt said, "Well, we'd better get going if I'm going to drop some of these cabinets off at home and deliver the rest of the them to the dump before it closes."

Debra asked whether he needed her help to unload them, but Liz said she could help him when they got home and Kurt thought he could push the rest off of the truck when he got to the landfill site.

"In that case, I'm going to pull off the boards that supported the cabinets and crack fill this wall so it'll be dry when I come back to paint in the morning."

"You are such a glutton for punishment," Liz told her laughing, "but, I know I would do the same thing."

Debra was humming as she opened the container of putty and started to mix it with her putty knife. She realized that she hadn't even moved in and yet it already felt like home. "Life is good," she told herself, "life is good."

She finished up and plopped herself into a hot Jacuzzi as soon as she got home. She ached everywhere, but the day had been so productive and rewarding that she didn't care. Debra cooked dinner in her robe. Leanne and Jonathan were a little surprised when she came to the dinner table still dressed in her robe, but they could see that their mother was in a wonderful mood as she told them about what she had accomplished at the new house, so they didn't ask questions. It wasn't long after dinner before she dragged herself up to bed and fell into a blissful sleep.

She awoke bright and early Sunday morning. Leanne and Jonathan were still sleeping when she left for the other house.

Debra donned one of Ted's old shirts from a bag of rags she had saved and tied a rag over her hair before tackling the walls with a sanding block. She was soon covered with fine, white dust. She didn't stop sanding until the plastered holes were so smooth that she couldn't tell where they were even if she rubbed her hand over the walls with her eyes closed. Debra dusted the walls off and let things settle before opening the tin of paint. There was more than enough paint to cover the two walls where the cupboards had been.

Debra was going to crack fill the bedroom walls in preparation for painting when it occurred to her that they had just been professionally painted so there was no crack-filling to be done. What a treat! That was her least favorite part about painting.

Debra planned to purchase vertical blinds for all of the windows, with the exception of the living room window. It already had an attractive beige/peach tweed vertical blind. She went around the house and measured the windows before applying the second coat of paint in the kitchen. She then went home to have lunch with her children.

"What are you doing here?" Leanne looked surprised when Debra came into the kitchen.

Debra laughed as she said, "Nice greeting! I came home to have lunch with you two."

"We could manage on our own. You don't have to interrupt your day to take care of us, right Jonathan?"

"Yeah, we know you're having fun getting the house ready— Mom, can I help paint my bedroom?"

She hesitated, but then remembered there was no wall-to-wall carpeting to worry about. "I guess so. One of us could use the paintbrush while the other rolls. Which would you rather do?"

"I want to use that roller thingamajig."

"I thought you might. What about you Leanne, do you want to help paint your bedroom?"

"Yeah, but it's only one wall so could I do it myself? It would be cool to say I painted it."

Debra nodded. "Both bedrooms are ready. When do you want to paint? I was thinking of starting this afternoon after I stop by Home Depot and pick up the paint and some blinds."

They had not made plans for the day yet and decided painting might be fun. They collected some old clothes and shoes to change into at the house. There was no way either one of them would go into Home Depot dressed in painting clothes!

Debra retrieved the paint chips and they headed off to the store. She picked up extra paint brushes, trays, and rollers and also purchased the supplies she would need to rag paint her bedroom wall. Leanne and Jonathan helped her find the various sized blinds she needed.

Debra started with Jonathan's bedroom because there was more to do and it also gave her a chance to show them both how to paint a wall before Leanne went off to do her own room. Debra peeked in on her a couple of times to see if she needed any help, but Leanne was doing a good job.

Leanne called her mother into her bedroom to take a look when it was all done. "It's pretty Mom, isn't it?"

Debra walked over, put her arm around Leanne and kissed the top of her head, "It sure is, honey."

Leanne had always been a perfectionist. She hadn't missed any spots and she had been careful not to leave any of the new paint on the ceiling or adjoining walls. The darker peach shade was attractive next to the pale peach and it was a nice contrast.

"You did a wonderful job of choosing the color and a great job of painting it." Debra told her.

Jonathan, on the other hand, had to be supervised closely to make sure he covered the wall well enough, but with the two of them working together, she knew they could make it look good. They painted the two green walls first and Debra painted all of the edges at the ceiling. Jonathan was disenchanted with painting by the time they were done the second coat on both walls so Debra reassured him that she appreciated his help, but she could do the other color herself.

Debra went to Jonathan's soccer game Monday evening, although she was itching to return to the other house. She put the first coat of paint on Jonathan's other two walls on Tuesday and finished it up the following evening. Debra was impressed! The forest green did look striking next to the deep peach and it was very rich looking. She could imagine a lawyer's study painted these colors.

She took Jonathan to see his bedroom the next day and he was tickled pink. "Mom, I can hardly wait to move in. This is so cool!"

That was just the response she was hoping for when she decided they would redecorate the bedrooms. She wanted Leanne and Jonathan to be as pleased about the move as she was.

Debra could hardly wait to paint her bedroom. She sighed with satisfaction when she finally pried open the tin to the light sage paint. It was such a warm color! She soon discovered that, if she applied it carefully, it covered in only one coat. When she was all done she sat on the floor and looked around. It was wonderful! It was also great that there was no wall-to-wall carpeting, it took away the stress of worrying about paint spills and made clean up easy.

She decided to wait to do the rag painting in her bedroom until after the move. It wouldn't be difficult to move the furniture away from one wall and she wanted to be patient and rested when she tried out the new technique. It's not as if the room didn't look wonderful already. The faux painting would be a finishing touch.

Debra was chatting a mile a minute about what had been done as she and Liz walked around the bay Saturday morning.

"Whoa, whoa, whoa! I can hardly keep up with you." Liz said laughing. "How about we stop by the house on the way back and you can show me."

Debra said she was hoping they would.

"But until then, let's slow it down a little. I'm too young to die right this minute," Liz said, meanwhile exaggeratedly gasping for breath.

Debra laughed, she hadn't realized she was walking about as fast as she was talking until Liz pointed it out.

They slowed their pace and by the time they arrived at Debra's new house, Debra was feeling much more relaxed.

Leanne's bedroom was in the front. Liz thought the peach contrasting wall was a nice touch and very pretty. Jonathan's bedroom was next and Liz gasped when she entered the room. "This is really sharp! It's not me, but it'll be perfect for your son."

She almost hummed when she saw Debra's room. "Oh, Debra this is so warm. It's beautiful." Debra told her about how she planned to rag paint one wall with a deeper shade and Liz thought that was a great idea. "I've seen that done in show homes. It's very attractive."

Debra vacuumed the house and washed the floors over the weekend. The new flooring had been put down and it was beautiful, but she wanted to scrub off the spots of excess glue. She also cleaned the windows and installed the blinds, before hanging the valance rods. She was glad she still had an electric drill and a toolbox. She was only slightly surprised that Ted hadn't taken them with him when he left. She guessed that house repairs were not a part of his definition of a simple lifestyle!

Debra had to shorten the blinds, which was a pain, but they hung so much nicer once she removed the extra slats. Then she took the iron and ironing board over so she could iron the valances and hang them right away before they became wrinkled. She stuffed Leanne's pouf valance with tissue paper so it would look puffy.

Each time she visited the house, she took over a carload of packed boxes. She had hired movers to move the furniture, but she planned to move the boxes herself to keep the cost down. The kitchen cabinets would be installed soon and Debra wanted to have as much done as possible before the actual move in date.

Debra realized she was overdoing it. It was exciting and rewarding, but it was also taking its toll on her body. If she wasn't packing to get ready for the move, she was over at the other house. Not only that, but her job was as demanding as ever. She and Liz had been together a couple of times to exchange Healing Touch, but Debra knew she wasn't taking care of herself as well as she should. She thought she'd better build in some relaxation so she decided to go kayaking after work one day.

It was late afternoon and the tide was getting low. Debra had to walk further than usual into wet sand before getting in her kayak. The bay was fairly breezy so she decided to paddle past Campland on the Bay and check out the canal around the corner. It would be calmer there.

The waves disappeared as she paddled up the canal. She noticed there was a variety of wildlife on the canal and more than she typically saw on the bay. Debra attributed it to the fact that this area was more secluded.

She spotted a blue stork walking along the water's edge. It looked elegant as it strode by. She'd never seen one before and it occurred to her that having a kayak gave her the opportunity to view wildlife she wouldn't otherwise see.

Further on she saw a white egret. It looked like a ballerina. Then she noticed a gray one that looked like a wizened old man. Both took flight as she paddled nearby. Wow! It was like they were in slow motion. They were so graceful!

She decided to drift after a while and just float along the canal. She eventually looked down and noticed that the water had become so shallow that she was in less than two feet. All of a sudden it occurred to her that, if she didn't get busy paddling, the tide would go out completely and she'd be walking. So much for relaxing!

She drove her paddle in, left—right—left—right—left—right. She thought she'd never get to the canal opening. By the time she did, her paddle was hitting the bottom. It was with relief that she headed back out into the bay. Dumb, dumb, dumb! She had to laugh. She would have been up to her knees in mud if she'd got stuck in that canal! She was really tired now, but it was a pleasant tiredness. This called for a relaxing evening at home. "No packing, no nothing," she told herself.

Leanne and Jonathan were both shocked when their mother plopped herself down on the couch after cleaning up from dinner and declared, "I'm not moving for the rest of the night!" They watched television together for the rest of the evening, meanwhile chatting about the various programs and then Debra went up to bed and read for twenty minutes before falling asleep.

Debra could hardly wait to get off work the day the cabinets were installed. She stopped by the house and was tickled pink when she walked into the kitchen. The light maple woodwork was even more beautiful than she had remembered and the raised panels were classy. The walk-in pantry was incredible with a beautiful etched glass door and brass leading. It was huge with white metal shelving from ceiling to floor. She had chosen a white Swanstone double sink and two-toned teal green arborite for the countertop that set the cabinets off nicely. The kitchen was the most important room in the house as far as she was concerned and this one was going to be blissful to work in.

Everything took place on schedule. The ceramic tile backsplash was installed. An electrician came in to install lighting under the base of the cabinets and to add some track lights to the kitchen ceiling. Once the kitchen was complete, Debra picked out valances for the bay window in the eating area, with one to match over the kitchen sink window.

The linoleum she had chosen was also two-toned teal, but was a lighter shade than the countertop. Debra made sure there was no white in it because it would show dirt too easily. The valances were decorated with splashes of peach, plum and teal green. Debra had decided on the plum to add a dash of color. A border strip design of teal green and plum on a white background set off the ceramic backsplash over the countertop.

Moving day was only one day away! Debra started bringing over boxes from the kitchen and enjoyed unpacking for the first time in her life. She had ordered two sets of pots and pans drawers. The space they provided, combined with the huge pantry, made unpacking a pleasure.

The movers were due to arrive early Saturday morning, but Debra awoke hours before. She was surprised when Leanne came around the corner of the kitchen as she was wiping down the inside of the refrigerator. "What are you doing up so early? I thought I would have to haul you out of bed before the movers arrived."

"I'm looking forward to setting up my new bedroom. When do you think they'll unload my bedroom furniture?"

"We could ask them to try to put it in last so they take it out first," Debra told her.

"Would you, Mom. That would be great!"

The movers didn't seem to mind when she approached them, although they warned her that the larger pieces went in first and then the smaller pieces, so she would have to wait a little while before they got to the mattresses and box springs.

Jonathan got himself up on his own, too. He was also excited about the move.

The three of them were very busy arranging furniture in their new home once the movers left. This was by far the easiest move Debra had ever had because almost everything was unpacked before she even moved in. She helped Leanne and Jonathan set up their bedrooms. Everything looked picture perfect once the bedding was on their beds and they had unpacked their belongings into their closets and drawers.

After a while, Debra made a cup of tea and hid herself away in her own bedroom. She sat in a wicker chair in the corner and looked around. She wanted to sit and appreciate how good it felt to be in her own home. Her bedroom was incredibly warm and cozy. When she finally left her bedroom, both Leanne and Jonathan were napping on their beds. She smiled to herself as she went into the kitchen to finish unpacking some of the last minute things she had brought over from the old house that day.

It was a drag the next day when Debra had to go back to the old house to clean up. It was one of the last places she wanted to be. She finished quickly so she could return home. That house represented nothing but sad memories for Debra. It was with relief that she dropped the house keys off for the realtor to give to the new owners.

She spent the rest of the day getting everything organized and tidy. Leanne and Jonathan wandered in and out all day and even brought a couple of friends by to show them their new home.

Debra had Monday off as a paid "moving day". What a lark! She was already moved! It was a great opportunity to enjoy a peaceful day alone at home, finish up a few things and maybe clean up the yard a bit. She had definitely earned it!

When she got up, Debra enjoyed a leisurely cup of tea on the front porch. She did her grounding ritual outdoors before strolling back into the house to have her morning shower. Once she was dressed she went into the coatroom at the back door. It was loaded to the hilt with the items that had been in the garage because Debra had yet to pick up a shed. She contemplated whether to look into buying a shed before getting on with her yard work, but opted in favor of the gardening. This was supposed to be her special day, after all.

She gathered up the gardening tools she would need and decided to start with the front yard. It was pleasant listening to the birds sing and chirp in the trees overhead as she dug through the dirt and cleared the weeds. The flowerbeds were obviously neglected, but Debra didn't mind. It would just be that much more rewarding when she was done.

She was humming to herself when she heard a voice say "Good morning."

She looked up to see a woman leaning over the fence from the next yard. Her hair appeared to be naturally gray and her shoulders were stooped. Debra estimated her age to be somewhere over eighty.

Her face was creased with many wrinkles, but her eyes lit up and her smile was warm as she held out her hand to Debra, "You must be my new neighbor."

"That I am." Debra rose from the ground, pulled off one of her gardening gloves, and gently shook her hand. "Good morning, I'm Debra Logan."

"Edna Harris. Lived in this very house for more than 35 years. It's good to see a young family move in next door. We need some young blood around here. I see you've got children."

Debra smiled, "Yes, two." She told Edna their names and ages.

"What about a husband? I haven't seen a man around."

"I'm divorced."

"There seems to be a lot of that going around lately."

Debra grimaced and nodded in agreement. She looked over at Edna's yard. "You have a lovely garden."

"Why thank you, Dear. I don't get around like I used to, my arthritis bothers me, but I like to putter. You fancy yourself to be a bit of a gardener?"

Debra said she did and that she hoped to make her yard something to be proud of some day, too.

"Well, you're off to a good start. It looks better already."

Debra thanked her.

"Looks like you need to get yourself some peat moss, though. That'll loosen the soil for you.

"I think this yard needs a lot of things. It hasn't been taken care of at all."

"No, the tenants didn't seem to care much about gardening. It'll be a pleasure to see you take a stab at turning things around."

"I'm sure going to give it a try."

"I'll let you get back at it." Edna was wearing a sleeveless seersucker blouse and Bermuda length shorts. Debra noticed she had a wiry little frame and knobby knees. Edna hobbled a bit as she turned and walked away.

Debra finished cleaning out the flowerbeds and raked the lawn. There were a lot of leaves and it looked as if the grass hadn't been raked since before winter. She filled several garbage bags and then went into the house to prepare lunch.

A sandwich would have to do. Groceries were limited, as she hadn't wanted to move anymore from the old house than she had to. That was one thing she would have to take care of before the day ended.

She ate her lunch on the front door step, which, again, reminded her of the need to get a porch swing. She decided to abandon the idea of cleaning up the back yard. There was always the weekend. She would, instead look into buying a swing and pick up some groceries. The swing could be her reward for getting groceries. Ha! She liked that idea.

Debra remembered seeing a warehouse for playground equipment just off of Interstate 5. She checked the yellow pages and sure enough, there it was, "Playground Warehouse" on Santa Fe. It was less than ten minutes away.

The selection of playground equipment was incredible. It took her a while to track down the swings. She had to choose between one that screwed into the ceiling of the porch with eyehooks and one that came with a stand. The stand looked like a lot of work to put together and took more space, but it could be moved around. She decided on the other swing because it looked like less hassle. Ted wasn't the only one trying to simplify his life!

By the time she bought groceries, put them away, and hauled the dismantled swing onto the porch, she was almost too tired to put it together. On the other hand, if she put it together, she could relax on the swing. That sounded like a plan!

She was peacefully enjoying rocking back and forth when Leanne returned home from school. Leanne joined her and they chatted about how good it felt to be in the new house.

"Mom, I'm really proud of you for not falling apart when Dad left. Thanks."

Debra hugged her close, "Oh, Leanne, I almost did. It was touch and go for a while there."

"I know. But, you didn't. I really appreciate the fact that you didn't make us move out of the neighborhood, too."

"It was the least I could do. I'm pretty lucky to have such wonderful kids as you and Jonathan. It's been a tough time for you two, too."

Jonathan made fun of them when he arrived home. "Aren't you two a little too old for swings?"

"You're never too old for swings. I'm going to enjoy my retirement in a porch swing some day."

After a while, she went in to make dinner. She toured the house while dinner was cooking and breathed a sigh of contentment as she walked around. No, the new house wasn't as impressive or regal as the other house, but it was theirs and it sure was warm and cozy, just like she had hoped it would be.

CHAPTER TEN

Mrs. Harris was already out in her yard when Debra left for work the next day.

"Good morning."

"Good morning, Dear. It looks like we might get some rain later today. Have you got your umbrella?"

"No, I don't. That's a good idea." She was already running late, because she had, at the last minute, decided to grab shams from each of the beds in case she ended up carpet shopping after work, but she turned around and hurried back into the house anyway. She was soon hustling down the sidewalk with an umbrella in her hand. "Thank you! Hope you enjoy your day!" Debra hollered as she got into the car.

Debra was soon caught up in her workday. The usual places they used for bookings were unavailable for one of their workshop dates and she was struggling to find an alternate site. She called around until she found one. Catamaran Village had several rooms available, but she would have to drive over to take a look and check their suitability. She would have liked to stop by on her way home from work as it was just barely off of her route, but she needed to get this settled right away.

Debra nodded appreciatively once she parked and walked into the hotel entrance at the Catamaran. The floor was lined with shale rock and there was a waterfall and pond in the middle of the lobby. The pond was filled with huge gold and white Koi fish. Beautiful flowered tropical plants were supported by several jut-outs in the shale wall above the water. It was like being in an outdoor tropical setting. There was even a colorful parrot on a tree nearby. Debra wondered whether it was real or not.

"Scr-e-e-e-ch". Debra jumped as the parrot's call echoed throughout the lobby. It was definitely alive. He started to climb up the tree using his beak to pull himself up. He let out another squawk as soon as he reached an upper branch. Debra was startled, again, as the sound rang out. She grinned as she made her way to the lobby desk and asked for the Events Manager.

He soon arrived and took Debra up the stairs that overlooked the lobby. There was a full-sized handmade rustic canoe hanging from the ceiling near the stairwell. She wondered how they managed to find something that rare. He led her down a carpeted corridor and out double glass doors to a long promenade balcony. All of the rooms were located off of the balcony and overlooked the bay.

Debra gasped, "This is beautiful!"

"It is lovely, isn't it?"

She was hoping the rooms would be a decent size as they were unlocked for her to view. The first three were large enough.

As they entered the fourth room, which was a little smaller than the other three, Debra told him, "It looks good. This one room may be a little tight, but I think we could manage."

They discussed equipment needs and Debra agreed to fax room set up diagrams. He gave her the contact information for the Catering Manager before Debra returned to her office. Rain started to pour down just as she parked her car.

"Thank you Mrs. Harris," she said to herself as she opened up her umbrella and ran toward the office building.

Jonathan's soccer game was cancelled due to the rain so Debra stopped by IKEA on her way home from work to look at some area rugs. She brought in the shams to match colors. She found two rugs that were perfect for Leanne and Jonathan's bedrooms, but her favorite find was a sage green carpet with a sculptured border of large peach flowers and green leaves for her own bedroom. Debra was drenched by the time she tied the plastic wrapped carpet rolls to the top of her car, but she didn't care. It was all she could do not to speed home. She could hardly wait to put them down.

She hauled the rolls into the house. Jonathan had offered to help her carry them in once he found out what she had bought, but she had told him there was no point in him getting wet, too. She instead let him help her get them into the bedrooms.

"Mom, this is so cool!" Jonathan exclaimed as they opened his carpet. His was forest green/orange tweed with a raised border of more forest green.

Leanne's rug was the same shade of green as her comforter, with tiny peach flecks. She came home just as they were laying it out.

She stopped dead in the doorway, "Mom, how did you find such a perfect color?"

"I took one of the shams from your bed."

Leanne came over, gave her a hug, and thanked her.

All three of them went into Debra's bedroom to open her plastic roll. Debra got tears in her eyes as they unrolled her carpet. It was too beautiful for words. Leanne noticed and slipped her arm around her mother, "You're sure getting weepy in your old age!" They both laughed.

Debra had ironically been unable to find a carpet she liked for the living room. She would have thought it would be the easiest to locate because she would be looking for colors that were more neutral, but that had not been the case. She would have to check some other stores.

She thought about hanging some pictures once they were finished dinner and the dishwasher was turned on, but when she briefly thought about how much she appreciated having a dishwasher, it made her think of her mother and her opposition to using one. It was about time she gave her mother a call to let her know how the move went.

Her mother answered on the second ring. She seemed to be in a cheerful mood as Debra told her all about their move and the decorating they had done so far.

"Your father and I are thinking about replacing the living room carpet. It's getting worn and dirty. We saw one we liked, but it would mean we would have to have your father's easy chair re-upholstered so we have to look into the cost of that first. Interesting, you're just getting into peach and we're getting rid of it."

Debra didn't know whether that was an insult or not, but she decided not to get defensive. She instead changed the topic and asked how their health was.

"Your father has been a little tired lately, but we've been very busy. He'll be fine once we slow things down a little. He's napping right now." She asked about Leanne and Jonathan. Debra filled her in on their latest sports triumphs and told her they were doing well at school. They ended the call on a positive note.

Debra retrieved a hammer and small level from the coatroom so she could hang pictures. Some of the pictures had colors in them that looked like they had been chosen for her new living room whereas some of the others were unsuitable. She had less wall space than previously so she planned to get rid of some of the wall coverings anyway. They were hung in next to no time once she sorted them according to where she wanted them. She didn't have anything suitable for over the couch so she left that wall bare.

Leanne and Jonathan helped her hang the pictures in their bedrooms and then she finished up in the bathrooms and kitchen. She would wait to do her bedroom until after she rag painted the wall. The rest of their home looked homier and it was pleasant to no longer have pictures stacked on the floors of every room. She was soon engrossed in a novel until bedtime.

The following evening she assisted Jonathan's soccer coach by calling some of the team members to let them know about the time and location of their rescheduled soccer game. She left messages at a few of the homes, but some of the other parents took the time to chat with her. Debra enjoyed it so much that it occurred to her that she really needed to get out more. She was ready to socialize.

Ted called that evening to see if the children could spend Memorial Day weekend with him at Lake Tahoe. He had a friend with a boat who was going to teach them how to water-ski. Debra agreed and handed the phone back to Leanne. Both children were excited about spending a weekend with their father in Lake Tahoe.

Her fifth counseling appointment was scheduled with Elizabeth for the next day. Debra was amazed at how well she was doing. She didn't even feel like she needed the sixth appointment!

She provided Elizabeth with an update and told her how wonderful it felt to be in her own home. She even told Elizabeth she was ready to become more sociable now that she was no longer depressed.

Elizabeth, again, congratulated her for all of her hard work. She asked Debra how she would rate her life now on a scale from one to ten.

"I'd say an eight. I think it'll be a nine once I get out there and meet some new people. I'm still a little lonely, but I've decided to sign up for a book discussion group and I'm hoping that will help." She told Elizabeth she didn't really feel like she needed counseling anymore and Elizabeth agreed that this could be their last session.

Elizabeth asked Debra what challenges she anticipated in the future. Debra thought it might be a small challenge if Ted asked to have the children stay with him for a whole month, but she thought the biggest challenge would be if he became involved in a serious relationship and that woman became involved in her children's lives.

They talked about the importance of Debra supporting her children in accepting a new partner in their father's life. Elizabeth explained that loyalty binds are difficult enough for children in blended family situations without their parents placing pressure on them.

"Would it bother you personally, if Ted was involved with another woman."

"I'm not sure, but I don't think so. I guess I might feel offended that he could have a positive relationship with someone else when I feel like he didn't give me a fair chance."

"Would you ever take him back, if he asked you?"

"Definitely not! I'd rather be alone and be lonely than be with Ted and be lonely. It makes more sense to me. If things became difficult for him, I don't think I could trust him not to become too self-absorbed, again." Then she added, "If I were seriously involved with another man, that would be another challenge. It would be extremely difficult if the children didn't accept him."

"Your children will accept another man in your life, provided they are confident that you are happy with him and provided he treats them well. It will also help if Ted gives them permission to have another male figure in their lives."

Debra nodded, "At any rate, that's a long way off because I'm not interested in a serious relationship with a man right now. But, how will I know when I'm ready?"

"One thing I know is that it's when people least feel they need a relationship that they make the best choices about relationships. For example, it's important that you feel extremely self-confident and that you also feel your life is whole even without a man."

"That makes sense. I'm not looking forward to dating. I was young when I met Ted and I know nothing about the dating scene in the adult world, especially nowadays."

Elizabeth asked how the children were coping and Debra was pleased to say that she thought they were doing fine now that Ted was arranging visits with them.

"The work you have put into giving them stability in their lives has helped, too. The other thing you need to commend yourself for is the fact that you didn't put pressure on them to quit loving their father just because he left you."

"I couldn't do that. Their relationship with their father is very important."

Elizabeth asked, "What would you have to do to make things go back to the way they were when you first came in for counseling?"

"I'd have to quit building in breaks for myself and live a hectic life of running around and doing chores. I would no longer do special things for myself. And I'd be insecure and defensive in my relationships with Ted and my mother." Then she added, "But, I know that's not going to happen. It feels too good now to back track. I really appreciate your support in helping me turn my life around."

"It was a pleasure. I'm really impressed with how hard you worked to get your life on track. You know how to reach me, if you need counseling at some later date."

They wished each other well and said goodbye.

Debra felt kind of sad to end their relationship, but on the other hand, she was beaming. She really did have her life on track and it felt so good!

She returned to the office and the first thing she did was book an appointment with Kim, her hair stylist. It was time to get a new hairstyle now that she was feeling better about herself. She also decided to call one of the community libraries to inquire about a book discussion group. She deliberately chose not to contact Pacific Beach Library as Liz attended that group and she wanted to do this independently. She stopped by the other library to pick up a copy of *Galileo's Daughter*, the book the group had selected. There were several copies on hold for members of the group. It wasn't the type of book Debra normally read, but she was willing to be open-minded. She had three weeks to read it before their next scheduled meeting.

Debra arrived early for her hair appointment when the time came so she could look through the magazines and choose a style. She showed her selection to Kim and Kim agreed that it would work well with the texture and thickness of Debra's hair.

Kim kept her own hair styled in the latest cuts and was constantly changing her own hair color. Some of her choices were a bit extreme, but Debra trusted her. "Surprise me with the color. I give you carte blanche."

She was anxious about how it would turn out, but she became distracted while chatting with Kim and a few of the other customers in the salon. The unveiling time arrived soon enough. Kim turned her chair around and let her look in the mirror. Debra gasped. Her hair had been colored a slightly deeper shade so it would shine more and then Kim had added attractive highlights. It was short and sassy and she loved it!

Kim showed her that all she had to do to style it was add some mousse and mess it up with her hands. "You have just enough natural curl on top to make it feminine."

She arrived home feeling extremely pleased. Leanne noticed her first, "Mom, your hair looks great!"

Jonathan turned around to take a look, "Cool!"

Debra's co-workers were quick to notice her new hairstyle and she received lots of compliments. It was great for her ego.

Liz said she almost didn't recognize Debra the next time they met for their walk. "You've got a new attitude to go with that new do. I love it!"

"Thanks, it sure is easy to take care of. Even a bad hair day with this new hair style is better than a good hair day with the old one."

They talked about their plans for the rest of the weekend. Kurt and Liz were attending a mystery dinner theatre that evening. Debra planned to rag paint her bedroom wall and shop for a living room carpet.

"What are you doing next weekend?" Debra asked. "The kids are going to be with their father and I wondered if you and Kurt would like to come over for dinner Saturday evening."

"We don't have any plans that I know of. We thought we'd hang around home and work on the yard. I'll check with Kurt, but it sounds good to me." She asked if Debra wanted her to bring anything.

"Just yourselves. You wouldn't let me bring anything!"

Jonathan was at a soccer practice and Leanne was still sleeping, so the house was quiet when she returned home. Debra collected her painting supplies. She was anxious, but excited as she laid everything out. She had already watched the brief clip of the rag painting instructional video a few times and figured she knew what to do. It looked like the most important thing to remember was to avoid too much overlapping when painting one section beside another one or the color would be too dark in that area.

She haphazardly slapped the paint on from various directions on a small area of the wall just as had been shown in the video. Then she crumpled up a rag in her hand and dabbed at it, turning her wrist back and forth between each touch on the wall. She stepped back to take a look. It looked good to her.

Debra kept repeating the process, being careful to avoid getting paint on the ceiling, adjoining walls, or baseboards. She was impressed with the overall effect when the entire wall was finished. It was classy and it sure didn't take very long.

She cleaned up, meanwhile stopping several times to admire her handiwork. "Darn, I'm good." She chuckled to herself.

Leanne had roused herself from bed and came in to see what she was up to. "Mom, that looks incredible! Who would have dreamed you'd be so talented?"

"Thanks a lot," Debra said as she took an affectionate swipe at Leanne's head.

They had a late breakfast together before Debra left to go shopping. She found the carpet she was looking for at Home Depot. It was woven in various shades of beige with peach intermingled throughout the design. She decided to pick up some throw pillows for the couch to tie it into the rest of the room and drove to IKEA to purchase a few.

Debra stopped in the print section while she was there in case there was something suitable for over the couch. She became excited as she was leafing through the display and noticed a print by Monet. It was a beautiful scene with boats on a canal that reflected a European village. Many of the building walls were beige stucco and there were also a multitude of eye-pleasing colors throughout the painting, two of which included small amounts of teal green and peach. All she needed to do was choose a frame and mat that would compliment the scene. She selected a steel blue metal frame as she recalled how much she had liked it on the print in Elizabeth's office. It would also be attractive with this picture because of the blue of the water. She would finish it off with a peach mat to draw out the peach in the print.

Debra went home and carried in her purchases, with the exception of the carpet. Leanne was lounging on the couch watching Much Music. Debra hated to disturb her, but the carpet was too heavy for her to carry in and the picture was too large for her to hang by herself.

"Leanne, I know you're relaxing, but I would really appreciate your help carrying in the carpet and hanging this print. They're both too large for me to handle on my own."

"A-w-w-w Mom!" Then she saw her mother's look of disappointment. "Okay, but give me time to get some clothes on, okay?"

"Sure. Thanks. I have to put this print in the frame before I can hang it anyway."

She put it all together and just before she finished, Leanne went to her bedroom to change. Debra noticed the next-door neighbors, a well dressed middle aged couple, getting out of their car as she and Leanne struggled with the roll of carpet. They lived on the opposite side from Edna and she hadn't met them yet. Debra said, "Good morning," but their only response was to turn and walk into their house.

"Friendly," Leanne commented.

Debra shrugged, "Maybe they didn't hear me."

They eventually managed to get the carpet inside. It added warmth to the room once it was laid out.

The print was difficult to hang as it was awkward for Leanne to hold against the wall and it kept slipping while Debra stepped back to decide how high to hang it. They ended up with a few gray marks on the wall. Debra pencilled in the location for the screws, hammered in a couple of plaster screws, and washed the marks off from when the picture had slipped. Once the print was hung and centered they both stepped back to take a look.

It was breathtaking! The Monet did an excellent job of bringing the whole room together as it picked up the teal green from her couch, the peach from the walls, and the beige of the carpet and blinds. Debra tossed a few pillows onto the couch, and one into a chair. The room was complete.

Just then Jonathan returned from his soccer practice, "Wow, this looks awesome!" He hesitated, "Hey, it doesn't echo in here anymore! Bummer!"

The rest of the day was spent completing chores. Debra sat out in her swing during the early evening. It had been a warm day and it was still balmy. She wanted to take time out to appreciate how well everything was pulling together. It really was incredible and she felt blessed.

After a while, she noticed Edna sitting on her front doorstep. She greeted her and asked how she was doing.

"Fine, Dear. I'm just having a cup of tea. Why don't you come over and join me?"

The children were off visiting their friends and she could use some company. Debra, again, complimented Edna on her beautiful yard as she walked down the sidewalk toward her. There were blossoms galore, including a wide variety of beautiful roses, with just the right amount of foliage to set them off.

Edna took her inside the house and down the hallway to the kitchen in the back. As Debra passed the living room, it reminded her of her grandmother's house. The overstuffed couch and chairs were covered in floral prints with large doilies placed over their backs. There were two-tiered dark wooden end tables at each end of the couch with a coffee table to match. Each of the tables was decorated with a lacy doily and one of many potted African violets that were spread throughout the room.

The kitchen also reminded her of her grandmother's home. It smelled of freshly baked peanut butter cookies and waxed linoleum. The kitchen table was a once popular imitation gray marble with leaves at both ends and chrome legs. She even had lace curtains like her grandmother had had on the windows! The tablecloth was hand embroidered and there were a few opened mail items on it, with a grocery list scrawled onto a ripped piece of used envelope beside a crystal sugar bowl—one of those once popular antique ones, with a crystal lid and a hole on one side so the spoon handle could stick out. Debra felt so nostalgic remembering the special times with her grandmother, she felt like hugging her.

"Mrs. Harris, your home is so warm and delightful!"

"Edna, Dear, call me Edna, and thank you. Now have yourself a cup of tea and perhaps you'd like some peanut butter cookies. I just baked them today."

She placed a teacup and saucer on the table followed by a teapot covered with an old-fashioned quilted cozy to keep it warm. Edna ended up pouring the tea as Debra was preoccupied tripping down memory lane. Her grandmother had had a quilted cozy just like it, with a hole for the spout and one for the handle. Edna topped up her own tea and added a generous serving of milk from a crystal creamer that matched the sugar bowl. The tea had brewed longer than Debra liked, but that also reminded her of her grandmother so she didn't mind.

Debra was definitely going to indulge in the cookies. They smelled delicious. Edna loaded up a tray for Debra to carry and they returned to the front step.

"I bet you've seen a lot of changes in this neighborhood since you first moved in," Debra said.

"Yes, there were only a few houses here when Mr. Harris and I built this home. We had a double lot at one time with a large garden and yard for the children to play in, but Mr. Harris sold it off. That's where your house is now. I guess it's just as well, because he passed away six years ago and he's no longer here to help me tend the yard."

Debra expressed her condolences and asked whether she had any grown up children living nearby.

"My youngest child, David, lives in Encinitas. He stops by for dinner and does the odd repair job for me. I have a daughter, Katherine, in Connecticut. She's the eldest. I don't see her much. Too far away. My other daughter, Patsy, lives in Japan. Her husband works for the Consulate over there. They come home once every few years."

"You must get lonely sometimes."

"Ah, but I have my bridge group Wednesday afternoons and I go to church on Sunday mornings. And, Rueben is a good companion."

"Rueben?"

Edna called out, "Here kitty, kitty. Here puss, puss. Come on Rueben."

Just then Rueben showed himself. He had been lounging in the sun in the dirt beside the house wall.

Rueben stretched and stuck out each of his front legs one at a time before strolling over. He arched his back and rubbed against Edna's legs as she bent over to stroke his fur. He was a huge silver Himalayan tomcat.

"Scrub him behind the ears, if you want to make friends with him. He's a sucker for that."

Debra reached over to scratch behind his ears and sure enough, he came over to rub against her legs. Before she knew it, he was purring. "He sure is a handsome cat. How old is he?"

"Your guess is as good as mine. He was a stray we picked up so we don't know how old he was when we got him, but he's pretty old."

Debra noticed, with relief, that he wore a bell. "Does he ever catch birds wearing that thing?"

"If he does, he doesn't bring them home to me, so I think not."

"That's good, because I'm thinking of getting a bird feeder. I would hate to lure them to my yard only to have Rueben devour them."

"No, that wouldn't do."

She asked Debra about her job. Mrs. Harris had never worked outside of the home. "I can never quite figure how the women of

121

today keep up with their homes and families when they have jobs."

Debra laughed. "I'm not sure we do. We just do our best and hope it all works out. We have more time-saving appliances and I think we tend to buy more ready-made things instead of baking or sewing from scratch all the time."

"That's true. The wringer washer worked just fine in my day, but it was very time-consuming and I certainly never had a dishwasher."

"Most families are smaller nowadays, too." Debra commented.

"I don't know whether that's a Godsend or not because the eldest children tended to help with the younger ones."

Debra couldn't argue with that.

"Mind you. Speaking of eldest children taking care of the younger ones, that makes me think of a funny story about when the children were little."

"Katherine was supposed to be watching the two youngest. Anyway, they decided to play with the wringer washer. David was just a little guy. He climbed in to sit on the gyrator and Patsy turned it on." She shook her head back and forth.

"David was having a gay old time twisting back and forth inside the washer. Anyway, David noticed a thread on the wringer and he started to pluck at it." She grinned. "Unfortunately, he didn't pull his hand back in time and his arm was pulled into the wringer all the way up to the armpit."

Debra gasped.

"He hollered and screamed and set up such a commotion that Katherine came running. Instead of pushing the release on the wringer, she simply put the roller in reverse and wrung his arm out to teach him a lesson for playing with the washer!" Edna started to chuckle and said, "He wasn't hurt at all, well not until I tanned his hide."

Debra couldn't help but laugh out loud just imagining his arm being wrung out backwards.

"David could be a little imp and the two eldest had lots of fun tormenting him. They used to dress him in doll clothes and parade him up and down the sidewalk in a baby buggy. They even tied him to the clothesline like a dog and made him eat mud pies."

Debra really laughed at that.

They returned to chatting about the differences between the generations. Debra helped Edna carry the dishes back into the kitchen and thanked her for the tea and cookies before returning home.

Jonathan was in the living room playing Play Station with Tim. "We decided to come home and play Crash Bandicott. Tim doesn't have a Play Station." Debra was so preoccupied chatting with Edna that she hadn't even noticed them.

Debra asked if they would like some snacks. They decided on nachos and salsa and Debra offered to get them some before retiring to her bedroom. She planned to spend a quiet evening reading in her new bedroom. Debra pulled out her copy of *Galileo's Daughter*. She soon discovered it was a great cure for insomnia. She was asleep half way through the first chapter.

CHAPTER ELEVEN

Debra woke Sunday morning impatient to tackle the back yard, but she had to get some chores done first. She threw laundry into the washer, changed the sheets on her bed, and unloaded the dishwasher. Then she put the wash in the dryer, threw another load into the washer, and went to Vons for groceries. The morning gloom had disappeared by the time she put the groceries away and it was getting warmer outside.

She collected her gardening tools and went into the back yard. It would take more than the rest of the morning to dig around the trees and clear out the flowerbeds. She stopped briefly for lunch, once again taking care of some of the laundry. There was a pleasant sea breeze by early afternoon so Debra donned a wide-brimmed straw hat and continued clearing the dirt beds. Rueben stopped by and she removed a gardening glove so she could scratch behind his ears. He eventually meandered on his way and she resumed gardening. She raked the lawn and filled several garbage bags by the time she was finished the back yard. It sure felt good afterwards when she finally got into the shower.

Debra planned to barbecue salmon for dinner. She lit the barbecue and put rice in the electric steamer before washing the salmon, stuffing it with chopped onion and mustard, and wrapping it in tin foil. She made a tossed salad, set the table, and went out to sit in the porch swing for a few minutes.

Jonathan had already returned from playing baseball in the school playground and Leanne was just coming up the sidewalk.

"Mom, Lisa is going to get her drivers' license now that's she's sixteen. Would you be willing to teach me how to drive so I could get my license?"

Debra hesitated.

"A-w-w, come on Mom. Dad's not here to complain. You know I'll be responsible."

"I guess so, but I want you to take driver's education. You might as well learn how to drive properly and I've also heard insurance costs less when you have driver's education."

Leanne grabbed her mother and hugged her. "Thanks, Mom. I'll be careful, I promise!"

Debra laughed as Leanne just about bowled her over with her hug, "I'm sure you will."

It was such a nice day that they decided to take their dinner outside on the porch to eat. Jonathan grabbed a lawn chair from the back and Debra and Leanne shared the swing.

Debra related the story Edna told about her children playing with the wringer washer. Debra had to go into elaborate detail to describe a wringer washer to her children, but once they got the picture, they laughed when she finished the story. Jonathan was horrified when she told them about David being dressed up in baby clothes and toted around the neighborhood, but Leanne thought it was hilarious. Debra figured it was all a matter of perspective.

The next door neighbors arrived home and, although Debra waved in greeting, they, again, did not respond. Leanne whispered, "I know they saw you this time. They're just plain unfriendly." Maybe so, but Debra wasn't the type to give up easily. She considered it a personal challenge to win over unapproachable people.

Liz and Debra continued to walk Wednesday mornings. Debra was giving her an update regarding the progress she had made on the house and yard when she mentioned that she had yet to decide how she was going to get a shed.

"I bet Kurt wouldn't mind picking up a shed in his truck and I bet he'd pick up a couple of small trees for you, too," Liz offered.

"I really don't want to take advantage of him. He's so kind."

"Just offer to give him a healing touch session and he'll think that's a fair trade."

"You sure?"

"Wouldn't you?"

"Good point. I'll call him tonight and say I'm offering my personal services to him." They chuckled at the double innuendo. Kurt would get a kick out of that.

She called Kurt and he was quick to ask her what her definition of "personal services" was.

He laughed when she told him and he said, "That's an offer I can't refuse. It's not really a fair deal for you, though. We were already planning to go to Home Depot on Saturday."

"In that case, how about you also pick up a couple of large bags of peat moss?" Debra teased.

"Does your offer include a mind clearing?"

"It might, if you help me get the shed into my back yard."

"Sure, do you want to come with us so you can pick out the trees and shed you want?"

It sounded good to her.

Debra was less anxious this time when she dropped Leanne and Jonathan off at the airport for their visit with their father. She knew she could enjoy the time alone. Leanne and Jonathan were also less anxious as they had a better idea what to expect from a visit with their father.

Debra drove to Wal-Mart that evening. It was time to get her long awaited bird feeder. She had hung one years ago, but she had had to abandon the idea because Ted found the little sparrows' incessant chirping irritating. She threw a huge bag of wild birdseed into her cart and, while she was there, she noticed the hummingbird feeders. Debra couldn't resist. She didn't know whether she could get a hummingbird to come to her feeder, but she sure hoped so. Another woman was in the aisle and noticed Debra looking at the feeders.

"I'd recommend you get a large one so you don't have to keep refilling it."

"Oh, do hummingbirds really eat out of these things?"

The other customer chuckled. "Yes, and they're thirsty little varmints."

"Thanks for the tip. I also noticed there's a package here for deterring ants, does that work, too?"

"I don't know, I've never seen that before. It's worth a try because they sure are attracted to the hummingbird nectar. I think I'll get some, too."

Debra, immediately upon her return home, hung the birdfeeders in a large tree in the back yard. She positioned them so the birds could be easily viewed from her kitchen window, but would not be easily startled by her working at the sink.

She remembered that Terri had given her a beautiful set of wind chimes as a going away gift when she moved to San Diego. Ted had found them annoying also so they had been relegated to a shelf in the garage, but she had brought them with her to the new house. She retrieved the chimes from the coatroom and hung them on the front porch. A gentle breeze caused them to tinkle merrily. She felt like a child as she rubbed her hands together in glee. This was exactly what she wanted!

She would make dinner and sit in her swing with a good book. Debra found herself dreading reading the book group selection so she instead picked up the Anita Shreve novel she had also chosen at the library. She opened a can of black beans and rinsed and drained them before adding sliced olives, shredded cheddar cheese, and chopped cilantro, tomatoes, and green onion tops. She tossed in minced garlic, lime juice, and cumin and spooned some of the mixture onto a leaf of lettuce. Then she toasted some pita bread in the toaster oven, sliced it into triangles with a pizza cutter, and headed outside with a plate of food.

Debra was enjoying her novel, but she put it aside. She wanted to look around and appreciate things. It was so pleasant to live in a home that wasn't marred by memories of Ted, somewhere she could hang wind chimes and bird feeders without complaint or criticism. She had really enjoyed decorating it, too.

Now that both the front and the back yards were cleaned up, it was time to think about plants and shrubs. There was a lot to do to get the yard the way she wanted it. It was a work in progress, but it was enjoyable and rewarding.

Liz and Debra piled into the truck with Kurt immediately following their walk the next morning. They wanted to go to Home Depot before the cashier line-ups became too long.

Debra chose an aluminum shed. There were an overwhelming number of screws, but here again, she wasn't willing to pay the labor costs to have it assembled. At least she had an electric drill. It would take forever to assemble with an ordinary screwdriver.

Debra picked out a Flowering Plum with purple leaves and rose-pink blossoms and a Golden Ninebark with striking yellow leaves to add some color to the yard. Kurt hefted them onto the dolly, with two large bags of peat moss. They would pick up the shed at the loading dock.

Kurt wandered off to get some hardware he needed for minor repairs while Liz and Debra meandered through the perennial plant section. Debra picked up a variety of perennials for her flowerbeds. She also chose some pansies and petunias. Edna would probably give her tips on growing roses, if she asked, so she wanted to leave room for them.

Liz came up beside her, "The previous home owner was really into annuals. I'm eventually going to replace everything with perennials, but I'm going to do it a bit at a time so I can see what grows well here. The soil and climate are so different from Colorado. I rarely see plants here that we had in Colorado." She looked over into Debra's cart. "What are you getting?"

"Well," Debra said and then began to imitate the voice of the announcer for *Lifestyles of the Rich and Famous*. "I've got colorful Impatiens and attractive rose-pink Cyclamen for the shady areas. The deep purple climbing Clematis will invitingly trail up the trellis on the side of the porch. Masses of rich orange Canna will be dramatic along the fence, with some spectacular blue Hydrangea." She pointed inside her cart. "Two-toned deep pink geraniums and colorful pansies and petunias will complete the effect by filling in the spaces until the perennials spread. Finally, I chose a kaleidoscope of lilies because they add a natural quality and will multiply each year."

They both started to giggle and Liz asked, "Seriously, what would you suggest for my yard?"

Debra asked Liz what her favorite colors were and whether she preferred short plants, taller ones, or a combination. Then she made some suggestions and Liz loaded up her cart. Kurt soon joined them and they made their way to the checkout.

It was tricky loading the boxed shed so that it didn't crush their plants, but they eventually found a way to wedge it in the back of the truck. They stopped at Debra's home first. They pretty much had to drag the shed into the back yard. Debra would assemble it sometime later. While Debra and Liz unloaded the plants, Kurt carried in the trees.

Debra thanked them and gave them each a hug. "See you later for dinner."

Debra placed the plants around the yard and meanwhile thought about what else she would need to complete the effect she wanted. She planned to go to Armstrong Garden Centers to get some shrubs. She thought they would have a better selection and she could put them in the trunk of her car, if she tied the hood open.

She picked up a variety of azalea bushes, some bougainvillea, and a variegated Weigela because its blossoms would attract birds. She included a flowery hibiscus, a gardenia because of its fragrant blossoms, and an oleander because it was colorful and hardy. She also chose variegated Euonymus groundcover for against the fence before wandering over to look at the roses. There were too many roses to choose between. She would wait until she spoke to Edna.

Debra ate lunch and then planted the trees. She added ample peat moss and water into each hole before dropping the tree in, covering it with soil, and tamping it down before watering it, again. She then used a wheelbarrow to dump the rest of the peat moss into the remaining dirt beds and mixed it in with the soil so it wouldn't blow away, if it became windy. She was returning the wheelbarrow to the back yard when she noticed a bird at her new feeder. She stopping moving so she wouldn't scare it away. It was a pretty little sparrow with an orange breast and crown. His head quickly darted back and forth between each nibble. He ate so fast, it looked as if he thought it was his last meal. A car door slammed out on the street and he flew away. She hoped he'd tell other birds about his find.

It was time to quit gardening for the day so she could shower and prepare dinner. She baked a graham wafer crust to allow time for it to cool while she was in the shower. She later filled the shell with strawberry parfait, a mixture of frozen strawberries, strawberry Jell-O, and vanilla ice cream and put it in the fridge to set. It was only supposed to require twenty minutes, but Debra preferred to allow extra time to be sure.

Debra was making baked homemade vegetable lasagna with zucchini, mushrooms, and spinach and zesty garlic flavored tomato sauce. It was a great deal of work to prepare because so many of the ingredients had to be cooked before going into the lasagna pan, but, it was a good recipe for company because everything could be cleaned up before they arrived. She would serve it with Caesar salad and her favorite homemade garlicky Caesar dressing.

Debra went out to the porch to sit on her swing. She picked up her Shreve novel to distract her from thinking about gardening. It was time to relax. She had long since abandoned the idea of reading *Galileo's Daughter*. It was a tolerance test for her. She would, at some time in the future, check out the book group's next selection to see if it was more appealing. Debra eventually nodded off, but she, fortunately, woke in time to put the lasagna in the oven and set the table.

Both Liz and Kurt looked like they had had too much sun when they arrived at her door. They weren't moving as quickly as usual either.

"Have you two been overdoing it?" Debra asked them.

"Just a little bit," Kurt responded. "I think the slave driver here has forgotten we have a whole weekend to get everything done."

Liz gave him a light shove. "Ha! It was you who wouldn't leave it."

"How about I give you both Healing Touch after dinner? Maybe that would revive you."

"Why wait until after dinner?" Kurt asked, laughing. "No, really, I can wait, but that sounds great."

Liz handed her a wrapped box. "It's a housewarming gift."

How thoughtful! As she opened the gift-wrap, a box for a water fountain was revealed. It included a large ceramic bowl, a pump, a couple of handfuls of smooth multi-colored rocks, a few baubles, and several flat shale-type pieces. There was even a cute little ceramic green frog.

"It's wonderful!" Debra was so touched, it brought tears to her eyes. "Thanks you two."

With instruction from Liz, Debra placed the pump in first and surrounded it with the smaller, smooth rocks and baubles. She stacked the shale and larger flat rocks in the center. Then she perched the little green frog on one of the ledges. It was delightful!

She hugged them both. "You're always doing such kind things for me. I don't know how to repay you!"

Liz and Kurt said in unison, "Healing Touch!" and everybody laughed.

Kurt helped her fill the fountain with water and she plugged it in.

"I'm thinking about converting the dining room area into a place to do energy work. I wouldn't have a massage table or anything, but I've got a recliner chair and a CD player—and now I've got a water fountain."

They thought it was a great idea. Debra took them for a quick tour of the house to show them the decorating she had done. They were both impressed and Kurt wanted to know how she had rag painted the bedroom wall.

"Liz, this would look great on that wall in the spare bedroom. You know the one where the previous owners did a poor job of crack filling and then painted over it. I don't think we'll ever get it smooth, short of replacing the Gyproc. If I rag painted the wall, though, it would look like it was intentionally textured."

Liz agreed that it would be worth trying. "That wall couldn't look any worse than it does now."

"It's very easy to do and fast, too," Debra told them. "I was really surprised."

Debra poured them each a glass of wine. The oven timer started to buzz shortly afterwards. Debra put the lasagna on a hotplate on the counter to allow it to set while they ate their salad. They shared lots of laughter and joking while they ate dinner. Then they relaxed for a while before cleaning up the kitchen and retiring to the living room.

"Who's my first victim?" Debra asked.

Kurt and Liz laughed. Kurt said, "Liz, you can go first, if you want."

"What the heck! We'll probably have to haul Kurt out of the chair when you're done with him anyway. This way we can just leave him there."

Debra put in a *Forest Dreams* CD, dimmed the lights, and lit a few candles. She proceeded with the session. She and Liz would, every once in a while, quietly tell each other the colors they were seeing. They almost always saw the same colors simultaneously or shortly after one another.

Kurt didn't see colors and never had, but he tended to feel heat and vibrations, which was something Debra rarely felt. When Debra was finished administering Healing Touch to both of them, they talked about people's different experiences. Liz reassured them that everybody's experience tends to be different and that it is not indicative of the healer's ability, but rather the patient's level of sensitivity.

Kurt said, "Hey! Are you trying to say, I'm not sensitive?"

"No, people are just sensitive to different things."

"Well, I may not see colors, but it still feels wonderful to me. Thank you, Debra."

Liz also thanked her and commented that Debra was becoming very confident in doing energy work. They chatted a while before heading for home. Debra felt tired, but content as she climbed into bed. It had been a lovely evening.

Debra enjoyed the treat of doing her grounding and cleansing ritual the next morning while listening to the trickle of her new fountain. She spent the majority of the day gardening between rest breaks. She had what she called a "heart attack lunch" which consisted of avocado wedges sprinkled with salt and pepper, served with sliced cheddar cheese, tomato wedges, whole black olives, and nachos on a large plate that she balanced on her lap while she read a book on her swing. She allowed herself to read another chapter before returning to planting the shrubs and plants that were scattered around the yard.

Debra was bent over placing one of the shrubs into its hole when she noticed the women of the still unmet next door couple getting out of her car. She stood up and called out, "Good afternoon." The woman continued up the sidewalk and into her house as if she had not heard. Debra shrugged and resumed gardening.

She felt proud when she was finally able to go into the house to clean up at the end of the afternoon. With the exception of the spaces left for roses, her yard was taking shape and it looked pretty good.

As Debra ate leftover lasagna for dinner, she was aware that a long evening stretched ahead of her. She really wanted to be around some people. She racked her brain to think about what she used to do for entertainment in the evening. When things were better between her and Ted, they occasionally visited the movie theatre. But, she had never been to a movie theatre by herself before.

Debra tried to imagine what that would be like. Once she got through the line-up it wouldn't be bad. Theatres were dark and probably nobody would even notice she was there alone.

She looked through the theatre section in the newspaper. There were several movies that looked enticing, but the one that held the most appeal was *The Importance of Being Earnest* with Reese Witherspoon. What the heck, she could do it! She made herself look presentable and coaxed herself to drive to the movie theatre. She felt self-conscious in the line-up even though nobody seemed to notice her. Once she got inside, she treated herself to some popcorn and a soda. She could not believe how much the prices had gone up since the last time she had been to the theatre! It was easy to find a seat as most of the people were coupled or in groups so there were lots of single seats left. Once the movie started, she soon forgot she was there alone and it was pleasant having other people around enjoying the humor at the same time.

Debra set out for Fiesta Island Monday morning with her kayak and paddle stowed in the trunk. It was only a brief drive away and she was ready for a change of scenery. She noticed the Hilton Hotel flag was limp as she drove by, which was a good indicator for pleasant kayaking. She passed several groups of cyclists as she drove along the Island road. Fortunately, it was early. The wind was calm so the kiteboarders hadn't arrived yet. They wouldn't enjoy having to maneuver around her kayak in Enchantment Cove where she planned to set in.

Debra pulled over onto the sand at the side of the road and went about inflating her kayak. Dogs were permitted off leash on the beach and every once in a while a dog would lumber by. She watched as a man put his kayak in the water and two golden retrievers followed him in. One swam on each side of his kayak as he paddled around. The water looked cold to her, but at least they were getting lots of good exercise.

Debra waded in up to her knees to get into her kayak. The kiteboarders had coined this cove "Stinky's" because the water tended to be stagnant. It was chilly, but Debra didn't think it smelled or looked dirty. She paddled to the other side where there was a scout camp. Vanloads of children were in the process of arriving. She paddled along the edge and around the corner until she could see the Hilton Hotel beach where she let herself simply float. It was so peaceful there. After a while, she noticed the Hilton flag was starting to pick up so she decided to paddle back before it got too choppy. She let her kayak dry and then packed up and drove home.

Debra changed her clothes and went over to knock on Edna's door. It took Edna a while to come to the door. They exchanged greetings and Debra asked Edna whether she would like to come over for tea. "I want to pick your brain about rose growing."

"I beg your pardon?"

"I want to pick your brain about rose growing." Edna looked puzzled until Debra explained, "I need to know what roses to buy."

"Oh, my, my." Edna laughed. "Yes, Dear I could certainly help you with that. Just wait until I get my cane. I'm a little stiff and sore today. Too much gardening, I fear."

Once Debra saw how difficult walking was for Edna, she regretted that she hadn't simply visited with her at Edna's home. She helped Edna up the stairs of her front porch. Debra told her, "Wait here a second, I'll get you something more comfortable to sit on. Don't take another step. She fetched the padded wicker chair from her bedroom and set it down for Edna. "You sit here and I'll get the tea."

Debra came back and chatted with Edna while she waited for the kettle to boil. She went back inside and soon returned with a tray of tea and muffins.

Edna told her, "I've just been admiring your garden, Dear. It's looking like there's lot of promise, now. You've done a fine job of selecting your plants. It'll be beautiful when it all fills in."

Debra thanked Edna, poured her a cup of tea, added some cream, and offered her a muffin with butter. She even ripped open the muffin and buttered it for her.

Edna laughed, "It's such fun to be fussed over. Even it my arthritis weren't acting up, I'd be tempted to pretend it was just so I could have the service," she winked at Debra.

Debra asked her where she had arthritis.

"Pretty much everywhere, but my knees are the worst…too much kneeling to scrub floors and do gardening over the years, I suspect."

Debra wanted to bring up the topic of Healing Touch, but she felt apprehensive. She didn't want Edna to think she was strange. Instead she asked her what her favorite roses were.

"My favorite are the Double Delights. Those are the ones that are red with white centers. They're very fragrant, you know. I'm kind of partial to Peace roses, too. They're yellow, with pink edges. Very pretty. Then, of course, there's Pristine and Angel Face. Couldn't go wrong if you decide on those either."

"What's your secret to growing such beautiful roses? I notice you're out there bright and early almost every morning."

"Well, you don't want the aphids and white flies to kill all the buds. I make my own detergent bug spray, hook it up to the hose, and spray them hard in the morning to knock the bugs off. You have to get out before the sun gets hot, though, while there's still dew on the rosebuds."

"H-m-m-m, sounds like a lot of work."

"It is Dear, but I love my roses. I make my own compost. It's good and smelly, too. I put real honest to goodness garbage in it." She sounded proud.

Debra couldn't help but smile at that. She didn't think she was going to get that carried away, but the other information sounded helpful.

They visited for a while and then Debra gave Edna her arm and helped her back to her house. Debra was going to try to assemble the shed.

She used a knife to cut the box open. The first thing she did was find the instructions and check to make sure all of the parts were there. The number of screws enclosed was very intimidating.

"This is one 'Rome' that is definitely not going to be built in one day!" she told herself.

She only stopped once for a brief lunch and tackled one wall at a time until it was finally a freestanding structure. She was glad it didn't get very windy in San Diego. The shed wouldn't become stable until she attached the roof. Debra took a break and read another chapter in her book before starting to assemble the roof. She screwed a couple of roof sections together before deciding to call it a day. It would soon be time to pick up Leanne and Jonathan at the airport.

Both children looked exhausted, but content when she met them at the arrivals gate. They had had a wonderful time in Lake Tahoe. Leanne had managed to pull herself out of the water on skis on her second try, whereas Jonathan had made four attempts before being successful. Jonathan was still at the age where he was all legs and arms so he was working on becoming more coordinated.

They had stayed in a luxurious hotel and, if Jonathan reports were to be taken seriously, they had almost eaten themselves into oblivion.

CHAPTER TWELVE

The following week was a short one due to the long weekend and it felt like it, too. Debra, as usual, was involved in coordinating several upcoming conferences simultaneously with other workshops already in progress. There never seemed to be a gap so she could get caught up and short weeks only meant she had one less day to get the work done. At least the workshops at Catamaran Village had gone well and she was relieved that she would have another option when booking sites. Debra kicked off her shoes and flopped onto the couch when she arrived home from work Friday evening. Friday had not arrived a day too soon!

Jonathan came home soon afterwards. He threw himself into an armchair and swung his legs up over the arm. "Why do short weeks always seem so long?" he asked.

"Maybe because you expect them to be shorter than they really are."

"Right, Mom. Very funny!"

Debra wasn't trying to be funny. She thought there was some reality in that statement. Just then, Leanne came through the door. Her head was hung low and her backpack just barely hung off of one arm.

"What's the matter, Honey?"

"I need to talk to you." She glanced over at Jonathan, "Alone."

"We could go out on the porch."

Debra picked up the remote for the television and gave it to Jonathan, "Give us some privacy, okay?"

They went outside and Leanne immediately became tearful, "Mom, I'm sorry. I know it was really stupid of us, but Lisa borrowed her mother's car. We were just going to go around the block so she could show us how she could drive. But, she hit the fence on the side of the driveway and that scared her so she drove back into the garage and we never went anywhere. Lisa's father is going to call you and he said we all had to tell our parents. I'm really sorry, Mom."

Debra sat quietly for a while before speaking, "Debra do you realize that someone could have been hurt or killed?"

"I know, I don't know what we were thinking. We just sort of piled into the car without thinking, I guess."

"This is so unlike you, Leanne. I don't know what to say." She eventually added, "If something major had happened, there wouldn't have been any insurance coverage because Lisa doesn't have her license yet. Her parents could have had their lives sued right out from underneath them."

"I never thought of that."

"I need some time to think about what your discipline is. I'll let you know when I've decided."

Leanne went inside the house. Debra remembered watching a psychologist on television who said the discipline should match the behavior. She couldn't exactly withdraw car privileges when Leanne didn't have any yet! She wasn't willing to have her postpone going for driving lessons because Leanne was already registered and she would have to forfeit the fee.

She also remembered that the psychologist said she did not believe in grounding children or adolescents because one of their most important developmental tasks involves developing healthy peer relationships. Making them stay home interfered with that process. Debra racked her brain to think about what discipline would be fitting with Leanne's behavior.

As Leanne had done something irresponsible, she would have to do something to demonstrate responsibility. Debra supposed it would be best if it was something that would give Leanne some time to think about what she had done. She eventually came up with the idea that Leanne could clean all of the house windows. That would involve responsible behavior and it would definitely give her time to think!

"H-m-m-m, not bad," she told herself. She went into the house to tell Leanne.

Leanne didn't complain in the least when Debra told her she would have to clean the windows that weekend. She seemed to realize the enormity of what she had done and was relieved that the outcome was only a slight dent in the car and a broken fence.

While walking the following day, Debra told Liz what had happened and how she had responded.

"That's a good idea." Liz said. "I used to ground my daughters. It was more of a discipline to me than it was to them because they would spend the time trying to make my life miserable." She laughed, "I think they enjoyed that part of it a little too much!"

"I know what you mean. My sister used to terrorize me when she had to stay home!"

They both laughed.

"This is off the topic, but, I have a proposition for you. I'm wondering if you would help me teach Healing Touch to a group of eight to twelve women."

Debra said, "You're kidding, right?"

"Actually, I'm not. One of the women I work with knows I do energy work and she asked me if I would be willing to teach it to her Bible Study Group. I haven't accepted, yet, but I will if you'll assist me. They're apparently all very interested in checking it out."

"What would we have to do?"

"We'd keep it elementary and just stick to the basics. We could do a demonstration of connecting with the patient, followed by a pain drain, and grounding. If we had a few tables, we could have two people working on each patient. That way everybody would get to be a patient and each person would also get the chance to do Healing Touch at least once. You and I could rotate around the tables to give feedback. What do you think?"

"I guess so, but when?"

"The group is two hours long and they meet on Thursday evenings. They're actually hoping we can do it next Thursday."

Debra asked why they were in such a hurry.

"One of the members of their congregation has recently become extremely ill and is benefiting from Healing Touch so it has all of a sudden become a big topic and they're eager to learn it right away. They're just over in Clairemont so it's not far to drive."

"Well, as I told my counselor, I'm ready to start getting out there. The book discussion group didn't work out, so I guess I'm game to try something else."

"That's great, but what do you mean the book discussion group didn't work out?"

"I planned to attend one group, but I couldn't stand to read the books they selected. The first one was *Galileo's Daughter* and it was full of scientific data. It bored me to tears. The next one was a historical war novel. I checked their list over the past year. They tend to choose books that don't interest me so I decided not to join their group."

"Why don't you come to my group? I love it and the book selections are fun. Last month we read Judy Blume's *Summer*

Sisters and did that ever provoke a controversial debate! It was great fun!"

"It's just I'd rather find something on my own so that I have to socialize rather than rely on you. If you were there, I wouldn't have to talk to other people."

"Okay. That makes sense, but if you change your mind, let me know."

Liz was thrilled that Debra was receptive to teaching Healing Touch to the Bible Study Group. They went back to her house to go over their ideas and plan what they would do. Liz asked Debra whether she would be willing to do a meditation exercise to get them all centered. Debra felt a little anxious when Liz explained that Debra could take everybody through the pond/waterfall fantasy.

"That's like reading out loud in public without anything to read!"

"That's okay," Liz reassured her. "You've been there, you just take yourself there, again, and talk out loud about it while you're doing it."

Liz agreed to have her co-worker ask the ladies in the group to bring foam mattresses, blankets, and pillows for the tables. Debra would bring Jonathan's ghetto blaster and some taped music. Liz would provide handouts summarizing the techniques they demonstrated.

Leanne was already up and ready to clean windows by the time Debra returned home. Debra agreed to use a chair to stand on while she finished assembling the roof of the shed and Leanne took the stepladder. It turned out the chair was more convenient to use than the ladder anyway. Every once in a while she would look over at her bird feeder. The birds in the neighborhood were now aware of its existence and there were several chickadees and sparrows feeding at it off and on throughout the day.

One of the little sparrows looked like he had a nervous twitch or something. His wings constantly flickered back and forth. Debra named him "Twitchy". Debra later noticed Twitchy on the ground. Another sparrow was collecting birdseed from the grass. It would eat a seed, pick up another one, hop over to Twitchy, and drop it into his opened mouth. It must have been his mother. She kept hopping back and forth between feeding herself and feeding Twitchy. Debra thought they were adorable.

Debra finished assembling the shed by lunchtime. The door had been a hassle to hang, but she had finally managed to get the rollers in the right place on the runner over the doorway. She was looking forward to cleaning out the coatroom and getting things put away in the shed.

She and the children ate lunch together on the front porch which was shaded by the time noon arrived. Debra had made a pasta salad they all liked with cucumber, cubed cheese, and dill. Jonathan called it "cold Kraft Dinner ala cucumber".

The next-door neighbors drove into their driveway and got out of their car. Debra had since found out from Edna that they were George and Nancy Berger, but Leanne had nicknamed them "The Unsociables". Leanne whispered to Debra, "I bet you ten dollars you can't get them to say hello to you before the year is over."

Debra couldn't resist. "You're on." She called out to her neighbors, "Hello, Mr. and Mrs. Berger, how are you today?" No response. Leanne and Debra grinned at each other, while Jonathan just shook his head.

Debra drove to the garden center to get roses. She picked up some of the ones that were Edna's favorites. "I guess the worse that can happen is that I kill them all," she told herself as she added a few extras that appealed to her. She also bought some plant food recommended by Edna.

When she returned home, she looked out of the kitchen window to find Rueben intently watching the birds at the feeder, as he crouched behind one of the bushes. She watched him to see whether she needed to get rid of the feeder. His eyelids became heavier and heavier until his eyes became slits and eventually closed completely. His head started to droop and he ended up napping while the birds continued to feed. No, it didn't look like he was going to be much of a threat to the birds.

Leanne had finished the windows and was off visiting her friends. Debra felt disappointed as she had enjoyed Leanne's company while she was working in the yard. It reminded her that she definitely needed to start mixing more with people.

She planted her roses, cleaned up, and spent the rest of the afternoon sitting in her porch swing. She was wondering which social activity she could join. It was a poor time to be looking at starting something new. Most group activities wound down for the summer months.

The next morning, Debra bought a newspaper and scanned the Lifestyle section. It usually included write-ups on current events and courses. The one that caught her eye was a review of a dance program. It was about an introductory ballroom dance course that was held weekly at a local university.

The article indicated that couples could sign up, but that all participants would be classed as singles and had to change partners several times throughout each lesson to ensure that they learned to lead or follow with a multitude of partners. It offered lessons on the foxtrot, waltz, rhumba, and cha cha. Debra had always wanted to learn to ballroom dance, but Ted had not enjoyed dancing of any type so they had never gone. She decided she would register when the time came the following week.

Debra felt increasingly anxious as Thursday evening approached and she thought about speaking in front of a group of strangers at the Bible Study Group.

Liz reassured her during their early morning Wednesday walk, "You're not really public speaking. You're telling a story...a story that you know really well. Why don't you do a rehearsal on one of the kids? You can't do Jonathan, he'd laugh." She knew Jonathan only too well through her conversations with Debra.

"Maybe Leanne would be willing to let you do Healing Touch on her tonight."

Leanne was reluctant when Debra spoke to her. "Mom, I've got a really important exam tomorrow morning. I can't take the time for that. As it is, I'll probably be awake all night worrying!"

"Tell you what, then. If you let me do the fantasy with you, I'll give you a mind clearing. We'll wait until you're ready for bed and then, I promise you, you'll be so relaxed, you'll be much more able to sleep tonight. Okay?"

"Okay, but it'd better work. I can't afford to waste any time."

They got together in the space Debra now called her "sanctuary". Debra had added a few candles, some crystals in a bowl, and a stained glass hummingbird in the window. She had hung an appealing angel mobile and an angel calendar. She also had an attractive fleece blanket hung over the back of the recliner chair so she could cover people and help them feel cozy when she was treating them. She hadn't had a chance to use it yet, but she planned to. She had even picked up some peppermint lotion at the Body Shop.

She took Leanne through the fantasy and, in no time at all, she noticed Leanne was relaxed enough that her eyelids were no longer flickering. She went through the mind clearing technique and then treated Leanne to a foot massage with peppermint lotion to ground her.

Leanne was slow to waken and she looked drowsy when Debra finally told her to open her eyes.

"That was heavenly. How come you've never done this with me before?"

"I don't know. I thought you wouldn't be interested."

"Maybe not, but only because I didn't know what I was missing." Then she added, "Oh, by the way, I just about drowned when you took me through the tunnel and into the cave. I think you'd better step that up a little bit if you don't want to panic the old people. They can't hold their breath as long underwater as I can."

"Okay, thanks, I'll keep that in mind." She told Leanne what the gifts represented, but didn't ask her what they were because she thought Leanne was at an age where she needed lots of privacy.

Debra's stomach was churning Thursday evening as she, Liz, and some of the participants got a room in the church ready for the session. There was lots of chatter and the ladies had brought Afghans, foam, and pillows to make the tables more comfortable. One of the younger women had even brought a stepping stool to assist them in getting up on the tables.

They set chairs around in a circle and waited for everybody to arrive. The chairperson knew who was coming and, once the last person arrived, she introduced Liz and Debra. She then led the group in a prayer as they all joined hands.

Liz asked each of the participants what their experience was with Healing Touch. One woman had been to a weekend workshop, but the rest either knew someone who had been given Healing Touch or they did not know anything about it. Liz provided a brief explanation of the benefits of Healing Touch, but it was when she referred to the use of God's energy that Debra noticed a change in the group. They seemed more receptive and attentive.

Debra turned on the *Songbirds at Sunrise* tape so there was quiet music with bird sounds playing. She then led them through the waterfall fantasy. It took her a while to relax and she stumbled a bit in the beginning. Debra remembered to tell them to come up in the cave whenever they were ready, but also made sure she gave them enough time to open their gifts. She explained the meaning of the gifts, but again, she did not ask what they received in case they did not feel comfortable sharing in a group.

Liz asked for a volunteer so she and Debra could provide a demonstration. They did a hand/heart connection and then proceeded with a magnetic unruffling and pain drain as they had done when Debra first learned Healing Touch with Kurt. They finished up by massaging the woman's calves and all the way down including her feet and toes.

Each member of the group then took turns being the patient or the giver, with three people at each of three tables. Nine people were in attendance so the women in each group changed places three times. Debra and Liz walked around and provided instructions where needed. Debra found the experience to be impactful. She could feel tremendous healing energy in the room with so many people participating.

Once everyone had received treatment they, again, sat around in a circle so they could debrief. Several of the women had felt heat or pulsing when receiving treatment and one of the younger members had started to see colors. They were all in agreement that the experience had been pleasant and relaxing.

One woman reported that she had experienced back problems during the past few months. She commented that her back had been so sore at the beginning of the meeting that she had almost decided to leave, but she was glad she had stayed for her healing session because the pain had gone away. "I have to admit, that I was skeptical that there would be any benefit to Healing Touch, but my back hasn't hurt since the treatment."

Another participant said her headache had disappeared and another reported her arthritic hand felt less painful. They talked a while about the people they would like to help with Healing Touch and they, again, shared a prayer.

The women worked together to pack up the tables and prepare tea. A few of the women had brought muffins and cookies. There was lots of chatter and laughter as they all sat around a table and enjoyed the snacks.

Liz and Debra distributed the handouts, packed up their belongings, and made sure they said goodbye to everybody before leaving.

"Well, what did you think?" Liz asked as they got into her car.

"I wouldn't have missed that for the world. That was an incredible experience. Thank you."

"Thank you. I don't know what I would have done without you there to help out. There's no way I could have kept that many people on track at one time. It was a great experience though, wasn't it?"

They chatted about where they thought things went well and what they would do differently, if they taught another group.

Debra spent the weekend catching up on household chores and gardening. She was on her way to Vons to get groceries when she noticed a yard sale a few blocks from her home. She didn't usually pay any attention to them, but this one had a lovely set of wicker furniture sitting on the lawn next to a "House For Sale" sign. It would be wonderful to have some wicker furniture on her front porch.

She parked the car and wandered over. There was a loveseat and chair and both were in good condition. Debra asked the price and it was reasonable. She gave the woman money to hold it in exchange for a receipt, while she went to the ATM to get more cash, but she didn't know how she was going to get it home.

The woman told her, "Look I need to get rid of it because there's nowhere to put it where we're moving to. I'm sure my husband will drive it over for you when you get back with the cash." Then she yelled, "Bob!"

A stocky little fellow came right over. He agreed to move it in the back of his truck. Debra soon returned with the rest of the money. Bob followed her to her home and helped her move the furniture onto her porch.

"Thank you so much. It looks perfect!"

"No problem," Bob said as he turned to leave. "Hope you enjoy it."

Debra could pick up some cushions and then she would have somewhere comfortable for Edna to sit while they were visiting. The porch looked much homier, now. She went to Target to get some cushions and also decided to get another birdfeeder for the front porch so she could enjoy watching and listening to the birds while she was in her swing. The one in the backyard was nice, but she didn't spend as much time there as she did in the front because the front porch was shaded in the afternoon and evening.

The Bergers showed up just as she was hanging her birdfeeder. "Good afternoon," she said cheerily as they looked her way. She grimaced as they, according to form, ignored her.

When it came time to register for ballroom dance lessons Tuesday evening, Debra was a bundle of nerves. She found the building easy enough, but as she walked up the steps to the second floor where registration was held, her steps became slower and slower. "This is a stupid idea. I don't really want to learn to ballroom dance," she told herself. Her other voice said to her, "You need to get out and meet some people, you can't spend the rest of your life at home talking to yourself." Her comeback to that was, "Yeah, but what if I can't dance? What if I look stupid?" Unfortunately, she had a response to that, too, "Then you give it a try and if it doesn't work out, you can always quit." Debra, of course, knew she never quit anything, but she proceeded toward the registration desk anyway.

"Oh, my gosh!"

When she went around the corner she could see people lined up all the way down the hallway. She never dreamed ballroom dancing lessons would be so popular. There was a mixture of men and women, with many of them still dressed in their business clothes. One man was dressed in jeans, cowboy boots, and a hat which she thought was a little out of place, but it showed her that she'd be meeting all kinds of people in the course. The registrants' ages were anywhere from early twenties to late fifties, but the majority seemed to fall in the thirty to forty something range.

Her anxiety made her more talkative and she soon became involved chatting with a petite redhead standing behind her in the line up. They eventually introduced themselves.

"Hi, I'm Jean. For all I know I have two left feet, but I'm bound and determined to learn to dance." Jean's auburn curls bounced as she talked.

"Me, too. My name's Debra." They shook hands. "I can't believe I'm doing this. I must be going through a mid-life crisis or something. Every time I turn around, I'm doing something I've never done before."

Jean laughed. "You, too? I swear I'm cracking up in my old age. Ever since my husband left, my whole life has been turned upside down."

"That makes two of us," Debra told her.

"Now, how could my husband's leaving have possibly turned your life upside down?"

Debra initially looked puzzled, then she realized what they had said. They both burst into laughter, probably more from anxiety than hilarity. When Debra finally collected herself, she said, "You know what I meant."

"I know, but I couldn't resist. It struck me as funny."

The line moved quickly and they were soon filling out registration forms. As Debra was completing hers, she heard the woman at the desk tell the next woman in the line up that registration was full and she would have to wait until the next session.

Debra turned to Jean, "If I'd walked any slower up those stairs, I wouldn't have gotten in."

"Right back at ya'. That's the woman who was standing behind me. I guess it was meant to be, huh?"

Debra grimaced in response. She finished her paperwork the same time as Jean. They handed them in and walked out to the parking lot together.

As they went their separate ways to their cars, Debra told her. "Bye, see you next week."

"I'll be there with bells on my toes!" Jean responded.

Jonathan greeted her as soon as she got in the door to their house. "Dad called. He's going to be in San Diego for a conference and he wants to know if he can see us Friday night before he goes back to Sacramento."

"I guess so." So much for checking with her first. But, the children were at an age where they could make those decisions for themselves and it's not as if he was taking them out of town or anything.

"May I call him and let him know?"

She agreed and told him not to forget to get a time.

Jonathan soon hollered, "Mom, is it okay if Dad comes to the house to pick us up? I want to show him my new bedroom."

That caught Debra a little off-guard. This was their home and she didn't particularly want to share it with Ted. On the other hand, she could understand Jonathan wanting to share this part of his life with his father.

"Sure."

"Thanks, Mom," he yelled back at her and returned to talking with his father.

Debra wondered how it would feel to have Ted in their home. She also wondered what he would think. She had to remind herself that his opinion didn't matter. Nonetheless, she found herself tidying up before his arrival on Friday evening, not only the house, but her own appearance, also.

It was awkward when he first entered their house. There was a look of surprise on his face when he saw Debra. He looked her up and down as he appraised her new hairstyle, tanned face, and limbs.

"You sure look fit and healthy."

"Thank you. I'm spending lots of time enjoying the outdoors."

"It shows."

Debra thought he needed to lose the beard or, at the least, complicate his life enough to keep it trimmed. Even though he was cleanly dressed, he looked dreadful.

Jonathan took his father to see his newly decorated bedroom. Leanne joined them so she could show him hers. Jonathan insisted on dragging his father through the rest of the house. Debra was standing in the hallway and she couldn't help but notice that Ted glanced into her bedroom.

"It looks like you're doing really well," he said as Jonathan led him back to the front door.

"Thanks, we are." She felt like adding, "No thanks to you," but she refrained. "How's the new job?" she asked him.

"It's working out well. I bought a small property in the hills in Fair Oaks. It's only a twenty-minute drive to work in Sacramento. It's nice enough." He made it sound like it wasn't. "I'd like to have Leanne and Jonathan out sometime this summer."

"Just call Leanne and Jonathan when you decide. I've thought it over and you don't have to let me know first. The kids are old enough to make those decisions for themselves and it's not as if I would make plans without including them, so they'd know when they're available."

Ted looked surprised, "Okay, thanks."

He looked over at Jonathan and Leanne, "Are you ready to go?"

They were, so they said goodbye to their mother and headed out the door. Ted was taking them to dinner and a movie.

Another quiet evening at home. Debra welcomed this one less than any of them. Even though it had been a stressful week, she didn't feel like being alone.

"I guess I could always see what Edna's up to," she said to herself. She went over and knocked on the door.

Edna invited her in. "Your timing is perfect. Would you be so kind as to help me wind up some wool?—Then we could have tea."

Debra followed her into the livingroom where Edna was in the process of tearing apart a sweater she had knit. It was an attractive pattern with lots of cables and a delightful popcorn stitch.

"What's the matter, wrong size?"

"Oh, no, Dear. I just want to make a different sweater."

Debra was a little puzzled, but she didn't ask questions. Instead she wound the wool in large balls while Edna unraveled the knitting, row by row.

"Now be careful not to wind it too tight or it loses its elasticity," Edna told her.

"Is this alright?" she asked as she held the ball out for Edna to see.

Edna looked over the rim of her eyeglasses, "Looks fine."

Edna ripped, Debra wound, and they talked. Once the wool was completely wound into several balls, they went into the kitchen to get tea. The evening passed pleasantly and she felt content when she returned home. Debra fell asleep in bed while reading, but woke when the children returned home and she got up to ask them about their evening.

"Dad took us to see *About A Boy*, you know, that new movie with Hugh Grant. It was hilarious!" Jonathan exclaimed.

"I'm glad you had a good time. What about you, Leanne? How was dinner?"

"We had baby back ribs at Chili's. They were to die for. Oh, but, Dad and Jonathan ate this huge onion blossom. It was disgusting!"

Debra grinned. She thought they were disgusting, too.

Next thing she knew Jonathan was gesturing with his hands and trying to draw its size. "It was so cool! I ate so much I won't need any food tomorrow."

"Yeah, right." Leanne said. "This from the human garburetor."

Jonathan grinned as he realized she was right. They all knew he couldn't ever seem to get enough to eat.

The weekend passed uneventfully. Debra walked with Liz and went to one of Jonathan's soccer games, but, other than that, she spent the weekend doing household chores, gardening, and relaxing.

Debra received a response to her letter to Terri. Terri wrote that she was enjoying Chicago although she missed Sacramento weather. She was fascinated that Debra was getting into energy work and she wanted to hear more as she was considering taking a course. She wrote that it seemed that every time she turned around, she was hearing about Healing Touch and she was, finally, going to find out what it was all about.

Debra was pleased to hear from her. They had been such good friends, it would have been a crime not to stay in touch. She was pleased that Terri was interested in learning about Healing Touch. Terri had sent her email address so it would be more convenient for Debra to respond. She would ask Liz to email her handouts, so she could forward them to Terri.

Debra remained in her office clothes Tuesday after work. She had been told that she should wear comfortable dress shoes instead of sneakers for her ballroom dance lessons to make it easier to "glide" on the parquet flooring. Debra couldn't imagine being able to glide when dancing no matter what type the flooring was, so she would wear anything that might help.

It didn't take her and Jean long to spot each other. It was as if they both had honing devices. Neither one of them wanted to be alone. Debra could feel the anxiety and excitement in the room as she looked around.

Jean told her, "I was afraid you wouldn't come."

Debra laughed. "I was afraid I wouldn't come. I'm sure glad you're here. This whole thing is scaring me to death."

"Join the club. Look at all the people. I didn't realize there were so many insane people in San Diego!" They both laughed.

An attractive blonde in a red dress looked over at them. Her nose was wrinkled in distaste and she looked as if she was going to tell them to settle down. Not easily deterred, Jean kept right on talking. "This is the one time in my life, I wish someone would go around the room and ask each person what brought them here. I'd love to know."

Debra asked her, "What brought you?"

"I was tired of sitting at home by myself. I enjoyed it sometimes, but it was getting to be overkill. How about you?"

"The same. I only moved to San Diego one year ago and I haven't yet got around to making any friends. I have one now, but I can't live in her back pocket."

"I don't know what my excuse is then because I've lived in San Diego all my life. It seems that since my divorce, all of the couples that were our friends either continue to see my ex or they act like divorce is contagious or something and they don't want to spend time with me anymore."

Debra noticed the blonde woman give them a disdainful look and then move away out of earshot. Jean commented, "I guess she doesn't want to be associated with us."

They commiserated with each other about their new single lives until a man in the center of the room used a microphone to call for everyone's attention. He was tall and fit and was dressed in an attractive suit with polished black shoes. He welcomed everybody and then introduced his "Teaching Assistants," a female partner and three other couples, who were also attractively dressed.

"I'm Frank. Tonight we'll be introducing you to the foxtrot. We'll demonstrate for you and then I'll walk you through the steps. I want all of the women on this side of the room and all the men on the other," he said, as he pointed to each side of the room.

There was chatter all around while everybody got sorted. Debra and Jean stuck to each other like glue and kept exchanging nervous glances. They decided to stay in the front row, as they both agreed that, if they were going to be there to learn how to dance, they might as well know what was going on.

Music began to play and Debra watched the four teaching couples effortlessly glide and circle around in the middle of the room.

"They make it look so easy," Jean whispered to her.

Debra nodded. Now she really wanted to go home. "I'll never be able to look like that."

Just then the music stopped and the four couples in the center row quit dancing.

Frank explained that the tempo for the basic foxtrot step was "Slow, slow, quick, quick." He and his assistants demonstrated by walking through the steps. "We'll start with the females, first. Men, you can watch and then we'll give you a chance to practice. You'll be doing the reverse." Frank and the female instructors turned their backs toward the females and walked them through, meanwhile saying, "Slow, slow, quick, quick," with each four steps and showing them how to slide the last step across so that one foot ended up beside the other.

The women all copied and there was lots of laughter when some of the women became confused and went the wrong direction so that there were minor collisions. After a while, they were all following the steps in harmony, so Frank turned around and he and the other male instructors demonstrated for the men. The women meanwhile continued to practice while watching the female assistants demonstrate for them in the center of the room.

Frank walked the men through until they were all doing the steps at the same time.

"Now it's time for the men and women to try it together. I'd like the women to cross the room and choose a partner. Quickly, so we have lots of time to practice."

Debra and Jean exchanged horrified glances before crossing the room. There was really no time to be choosy, everybody scrambled to get somebody. Frank and the rest of his group demonstrated the stance and hold. There were two females left without partners, as the class was short two men, so two of the male teaching assistants paired up with them. The rest of the instructors walked around the room and assisted those whose hands and arms were not placed properly.

There was lots of chatter and laughter as people proceeded to bump into each other and step on each other's toes. Debra's partner had an incredible sense of humor and he almost kept her in stitches with his sarcasm and self-degrading remarks. Frank eventually got everybody moving around the room in the same direction. They all panicked when they heard music start to play.

"You've got to be kidding! We're going to do this to music?" Debra overheard Jean remark to her partner. She, somehow or other, had ended up nearby.

The blonde in the red dress, who was also close by, raised her eyebrows and shook her head back and forth in disgust. "Most people do dance to music," she said in a haughty voice.

Debra heard Jean mutter under her breath, "Well, pardon me."

They were soon trying to match their steps to music with Frank saying, "slow, slow, quick, quick," over the microphone. What a lark! Debra could hear laughter, muttered apologies, and smart cracks all over the room, but everybody seemed to be having so much fun.

They all became more synchronized and the room became quieter the longer they stepped around the room. Debra didn't think you could call it dancing, they weren't graceful enough for that, but they were starting to catch on.

Frank interrupted them and sent the women and men back to opposite sides of the room. He was going to teach them additional steps! She and Jean grabbed each other's arm when they were reunited.

"What a scream!" Jean said.

"It is, isn't it?" Debra responded.

The next step was even more difficult, but it was demonstrated and practiced using the same methods and the men were eventually sent to choose a female partner on the other side of the room.

Debra's new partner was particularly clumsy, but she had to commend him for the effort he put into trying to get it right. She was fortunate in that, just before Frank asked them to practice with music, he requested another partner change. The next fellow was quiet and extremely studious about his steps. She could hear him counting under his breath. They looked a little stiff as they danced around the room, but they, at least, weren't stepping on each other or bumping into anybody.

When the class was over, Debra and Jean, again, accompanied each other to the parking lot.

"Can you believe that blonde?" Jean asked her. Debra just shook her head. They talked about their partners, commenting on their strengths and weaknesses. Both Debra and Jean were in agreement that they were glad they had come.

CHAPTER THIRTEEN

Work remained hectic, but now that her garden and home were set up the way she wanted them, Debra's life took on a pleasant rhythm. She got up a little earlier most mornings so she could tend to her garden. Edna was usually out at the same time and they would chat over the fence. Debra continued to walk with Liz two mornings each week and they occasionally got together to exchange Healing Touch. Kayaking, reading, visiting with Edna, and gardening provided a respite from household chores. Debra continued to go to Jonathan's soccer games and to drive him and Leanne to and from games or practices when needed, but with the exception of her weekly ballroom dance lesson and occasional dinners shared with Liz and Kurt, she otherwise enjoyed quiet evenings at home.

Debra looked forward to her ballroom dance classes. They had covered the basic steps for the waltz and the cha cha during previous lessons and were going to learn the rhumba next. Jean was excited. She thought this particular Latin American dance was "sexy". It made Debra worry that she wouldn't look sexy.

They changed partners approximately every ten minutes during the lessons and were therefore meeting a lot of people. Debra and Jean always filled each other in on who they enjoyed dancing with most and which men they wanted to avoid. Most of the people were friendly and they were relieved that the disapproving blonde had not returned to classes after the first lesson.

Debra quickly caught on to the rhumba. She was flexible and found it natural to swivel her hips with each step as was typical of the Latin American dances. "I agree with you, Jean. The rhumba is definitely my favorite."

"It's just plain sexy! Look at Tom." Her eyes sparkled as she looked over at Tom. "He's really doing well. I hope he chooses me next."

Debra laughed. She was sure Tom would grab Jean, if he got a chance. There was definitely something cooking between the two of them.

There were practice sessions for one-half hour before the lessons where the participants had the opportunity to become more adept at the dance steps learned in the previous lesson. Debra was surprised when one of the male teaching assistants asked her to dance the rhumba at the practice session the following week.

"You sure you want to dance with me? I'm only a beginner."

"We're all beginners at one time or another. You'll be fine."

His frame was excellent and she soon discovered that a good lead could make a world of difference. He had her turning and swiveling all over the dance floor. Every once in a while he would instruct her to seductively swing her arm out as she stepped out to the side or raise her hand in the air as he tilted her back. They did rhumba dance steps she had never even seen before!

When she reunited with Jean, all Jean said was, "Holy shit! I couldn't believe that was you. You looked like a million bucks!"

"It felt incredible, too! Now, I'm really motivated to keep practicing."

"You and me both. I thought it would take years to look like that!"

The evening's lesson was directed at teaching more advanced fox trot steps. They learned to change direction and do slow twirls. It certainly made the fox trot look more inviting.

Leanne was arriving home just as Debra drove up. Leanne had been working at Petsmart since the beginning of summer vacation so she could earn some extra money. Jonathan, who had more time on his hands since summer vacation had started, had taken over some of her household chores so he could also earn more money. They both seemed to be enjoying their summer.

"How was your day?" Debra asked her.

"Pretty good. We got some new puppies in the store today. They are so cute!"

"You can't have one," Debra said, laughing.

"I know. It's actually kind of nice, I can play with them at the store every day, but they're not solely my responsibility."

"Good!" Debra responded as she put her arm around Leanne's shoulders and they strolled up the walk together.

"Mom, would it be okay if I borrowed the car tomorrow night so a group of us could go to a movie?" Leanne had passed her driver's test immediately following her driver's education and she occasionally borrowed her mother's car. Lisa's father had never called about their "joy ride". The threat in itself had been successful in getting all of the kids to talk to their parents.

"An early movie, or a late one?" Debra asked.

"An early one. Most of us have to get up in the morning to work."

"That should be okay. I'll be staying in tomorrow evening, anyway."

Leanne thanked her and went to her bedroom to change out of her Petsmart uniform.

When Jonathan arrived home later from shooting hoops with some of his buddies, he said, "Dad called. He wants us to spend the first weekend in August at his place."

"There's no way I can get a whole weekend off. Besides, Scott's birthday is on that Sunday," Leanne responded. Leanne and Scott had been dating for a couple of weeks. "Would you be okay going by yourself?"

"Sure, but I don't think Dad will be happy."

"It's not my fault he moved back to Sacramento. I can't put my whole life on hold for him."

"Well, you'll have to call and tell him. I'm not going to take the heat for you." Jonathan told her.

Ted asked to speak with Debra after he heard the news. "Debra, why is Leanne working? It's not as if I'm not providing enough child support."

"I know, and I appreciate that, but it's natural for someone her age to want to earn their own money. It's also good experience for her."

"Well, I don't know how we're going to get together if she's working every weekend."

"Maybe she could get time off, if she had more notice. Otherwise, you may have to come to San Diego to visit."

He was not impressed, but it wasn't something that Debra was willing to get into an argument about. She handed the phone back to Leanne so she could try to work something out with her father. Jonathan ended up going to Sacramento without Leanne and he and his father enjoyed a weekend fishing. Ted traveled to San Diego one weekend in August and gave Leanne enough advance notice that she was able to get a day off to spend with him.

The rest of the summer sped by quickly. Liz's daughters traveled to San Diego to visit their parents and Debra had a chance to meet them. She found the eldest a little slow to warm up to her, but the other one was spontaneous and friendly. Jonathan and Leanne were soon back at school and the days became shorter. Debra had finished the beginner ballroom dance lessons. She and

Jean had immediately signed up for the intermediate lessons that would be starting at the end of September. Four more dances would be added to the repertoire, including the Tango, West Coast Swing, Two Step, and Slow Foxtrot.

Debra had not seen Edna for a few days. She was surprised because Edna was usually out tending to her roses by the time Debra left for work in the morning. She had noticed people coming and going into Edna's house that she had never seen before. One of them, an attractive dark-haired man had been at the house a couple of evenings. Debra had wondered if it was Edna's son, but then it had occurred to her that he looked like he was around Debra's own age and he was probably too young to be Edna's son.

She called over to a female visitor the next day after work, introduced herself, and asked whether Edna was okay.

"Well, actually, she's fallen and she's in a bad way. She's got a hairline crack in her pelvis and her entire right side is badly bruised."

"Oh, I'm sorry to hear that. I wish I'd known. Is there anything I can do to help?"

"She has lots of in-home care so I think everything's taken care of." She wore one of those modern day smocks over matching pants and Debra assumed she was one of the home care nurses. "She's stubborn and refuses to be hospitalized although that would be the best place for her for the next few days."

"Would it be okay if I visit her?"

"Let me check. What did you say your name was?" Debra told her and she went inside. She soon returned and motioned for Debra to come over. She led Debra into a bedroom where Edna lay in bed. There was a pained expression on Edna's face and she looked pale and listless.

"Hi, Edna. I hear you're under the weather."

"Feels more like I'm under a slab of cement. I ache all over." She smiled wanly.

She hadn't lost her sense of humor. Debra went over and patted her hand. She hesitated but decided to stick her neck out before she changed her mind. "I do energy work. Would you like me to give you Healing Touch? It might help you feel better."

"Can't say I know what that is, but I'm desperate enough to try anything."

"Is it okay if I put my hand on your chest?"

"You do whatever you need to do."

Debra placed her left hand on Edna's chestbone and held Edna's right hand with her other hand to connect with her. She wasn't able to pendulum Edna because her pendulum was at home and she did a body scan even though she had yet to feel anything through that method.

Edna asked her, "Do you need to uncover me?"

"No," Debra reassured her, "You're fine just the way you are. Now, close your eyes and relax."

She did a magnetic unruffle, which was a little difficult because of trying to reach over the bed to Edna's other side, but she managed. Edna's breathing was already less labored. Debra placed her left hand on Edna's shoulder and started to talk about the fantasy meadow while she did a pain drain. Edna was snoring before Debra even had a chance to suggest she dive into the pool beneath the waterfall. Debra continued with the treatment, sealing the area, and restoring energy before gently placing her hands on Edna's shoulders to ground her. She was reluctant to massage her lower limbs in case they were too bruised.

Hoping not to disturb Edna, she crept out of the room. She found the nurse in the kitchen making tea. "I'm leaving now. She's sleeping. I'd like to come back tomorrow, if that's okay."

"I'll be on shift the same time tomorrow, if you want to come back then. You'd otherwise have to check with whoever's on duty."

"This time works fine...thanks."

Debra hoped that Edna would sleep for a while. She was becoming very fond of her.

Debra returned to see Edna the following day. "How are you feeling, today?"

"I've been better. I sure slept well after you left yesterday. I don't know what you did, but thank you."

"You're welcome. I'd like to do energy work, again today, if that's okay."

"Be my guest. I'm not going anywhere soon." Debra noticed a slight smile, although it looked like it took considerable effort.

"I've brought my pendulum today so I'm going to use it to check energy flow on various areas of your body."

Edna paid only scant attention as Debra dangled the pendulum over the various chakras. Energy flow was restricted at the right knee, hip, and shoulder, in addition to the sacral chakra, just below her navel.

"I've got a stomach ache and I don't mind telling you."

Debra glanced over at the bottles of medication on the table. "Are you taking pain killers?"

Edna nodded.

"They can be really hard on the stomach." Debra said before, again, asking her to close her eyes and try to relax.

Debra proceeded with the treatment. Edna soon appeared to be sleeping. Rueben wandered into the room and jumped onto the bed. He curled up on the corner and, every once in a while, he opened one eye to peek at Debra. Debra later figured he probably thought she was insane as she stood there beside the bed with one hand held up in the air.

She joined the nurse in the kitchen, who said, "I guess I should introduce myself. I'm Pam."

Debra shook her hand and reminded Pam that her name was Debra.

"Edna told me you did Healing Touch on her yesterday. What is that, anyway?"

Debra explained that it was the transfer of energy. She told her that some people consider the energy to come from the universe through the planets, stars, and moon, whereas other people believe it is God's energy.

"Well, whatever you did, Edna said it sure helped her feel better. Are you coming over tomorrow?"

"Yes, but it won't be until later in the evening because my son has a soccer game."

"I'll have gone home by then. I'll tell her son to expect you. He'll be here tomorrow evening. He's been stopping by a few evenings each week."

They said goodbye and Debra went home to make dinner. She was surprised, but impressed that Edna's son visited so often. She knew she wouldn't be that dedicated if it were her mother who was ill. Of course, her mother wouldn't be anywhere near as pleasant to care for as Edna either. Her mother was like a bear with a sore head any time she was laid up.

When Debra tapped on Edna's door next evening, she was surprised that the man who answered the door was the same one she had previously observed coming and going. He couldn't possibly be Edna's son!

"Hi, you must be Debra. Come on in. My mother is looking forward to your visit."

Debra laughed, "How could that be, she usually sleeps through most of it."

He chuckled, "Maybe that's why. At any rate, I'm David, her son," he said as he held out his hand. "I've heard a lot about you from my mother. Even the nurse was singing your praises."

Debra blushed. As she placed her hand in his, she noticed that David had a pleasant smile that reached all the way to his blue eyes. He gave her hand a light squeeze before following her into his mother's bedroom.

Edna's eyes lit up when she saw Debra, "Hi, Dear."

Debra took one of her hands, "How's it feel today?"

"Like I fell off the roof of a barn and I was too old to be on it in the first place!" Debra and David both laughed. "Actually, I feel a little bit better today. I was sick as a dog last night, but my stomach's more settled now."

"That's good. Is it okay if I do Healing Touch on you today, or would you rather visit with your son?"

"Heck, no. David's probably tired of talking with his old mother, anyway. I'd rather have the whatchamacallit," she said as she waved her hand around in the air.

David asked, "Would it disturb things if I stayed? I'd like to see you work your magic."

Now Debra was really blushing! She wasn't used to being observed, but also his eyes were the deepest blue she had ever seen and there was something about his close proximity in Edna's small bedroom that was disturbing.

"No, you can stay as long as you're quiet." She collected her bearings as she pendulumed Edna and told David what she was doing.

She did a magnetic unruffling and explained that the technique was for the purpose of removing negative and stale energy. She then began a pain drain. It was disconcerting to know that he was sitting there with his eyes open watching her while she had hers closed. She was tempted to ask him to close his eyes, too.

One thing she discovered was that, even though she was less focused than usual, the treatment seemed to have the same effect on Edna. Edna was asleep within minutes.

When she was finished, she and David went into the kitchen. "So, tell me. What were you doing in there? Why did you change hands?"

Debra explained the differences between the pain drain versus sealing the area and bringing in healing energy. She also explained about grounding Edna at the end.

"Fascinating," he said as he looked at her. Debra wasn't sure whether he was referring to the techniques or her and she ended up blushing, again.

Just then, there was a knock at the door.

"The night time coverage," he said as he walked to the door and let the nurse in. They exchanged greetings and the nurse immediately headed back to the kitchen.

"I only stay until the night nurse arrives and gets Mom settled for the evening. I don't stay overnight because it's a long drive into work in the morning and I can't stay tonight, even though it's Friday, because I've got an appointment to get the car transmission overhauled first thing tomorrow."

"I'm impressed that you make it here as often as you do," Debra said. "Well, I'd better get going. It was nice meeting you."

"I enjoyed meeting you, too." He thanked her for helping his mother. They said goodnight and Debra returned home.

As she walked down Edna's sidewalk, she noticed that Edna's roses did not look as healthy as usual. She decided that she would take care of Edna's garden when she did her own.

Debra made sure she sprayed the roses in both yards before she joined Liz the following morning.

"I asked Mary if any of the women in the Bible Study Group had followed through with what they had learned in Healing Touch. She told me that the eldest woman in the group, the one who had the ongoing back problems, hasn't had back pain since the session," said Liz.

"No kidding."

"The Healing Touch must have released something. A couple of the other women have been experimenting with energy work and one other is treating her husband who is in the hospital."

"It's nice to hear that there's been some follow through."

"I was pleased to hear it, too. You just never know."

Debra told her about Edna's fall and let her know she was giving Edna Healing Touch.

"Good for you. I'm sure it will make a big difference in her recovery."

It was an exceptionally pleasant morning and they decided to extend their walk by going through the residential section and along Pacific Beach. The waves crashed against the shore and several sea gulls and terns walked along the water's edge through the wash. Debra couldn't help but comment that it never ceased to amaze her how beautiful the ocean was and yet she so rarely took the time to see it. As they headed for home, they agreed they would include Pacific Beach in their walks more often.

Debra noticed the Bergers out in their front yard. Mrs. Berger was digging around her plants and Mr. Berger was watering a tree. "Good morning," she said smiling. Neither one of them so much as looked over. "Well at least they're predictable," she muttered under her breath.

Edna became more cheerful and looked better as each day passed. She was soon getting out of bed for brief periods. The walker was awkward for her to manage, but she was determined.

Debra continued to stop by in the evening to help Edna fall asleep comfortably. Now that Edna was feeling somewhat better, she and Debra would chat for a while before Debra did Healing Touch.

"I'm all tuckered out, but it was nice to sit in the big chair for a while and look out the window. The nurses tell me that you've been tending to my roses. I don't know how to thank you, Dear."

Debra leaned over and hugged her. "You just get better soon. That'll be thanks enough. The mornings aren't the same without you on the other side of the fence talking to your roses and me."

Edna smiled and took Debra's hand, "You remind me of my daughters. I'm so glad you're my neighbor."

"You're very special to me, too," Debra responded.

Debra commented that it was nice that David came by throughout the week.

"He's a good boy. For someone who was a mistake, he's turned out to be anything but," Edna told her.

"What do you mean 'mistake'?"

"Mr. Harris and I hadn't intended to have more children. I was getting on in years when David came along, so we jokingly refer to him as our mistake. But, he knows we don't mean it and it's turned into more of an endearment than anything else."

Just then Rueben came bounding across the bed. Edna had received a helium filled Mylar balloon with get well wishes. It had since deflated somewhat and been untied from the bedpost. Rueben would, every once in a while, attack it by jumping at the ribbon strings dangling from the balloon.

They both laughed when he took another leap through the ribbons and thumped to the floor as the balloon bounced across the ceiling. He batted the ribbons around for a while before jumping onto the bed and plunking his heavy body down.

Debra helped Edna get settled for the evening after she did Healing Touch. Just as she was leaving, there was a light tap on the door. It was Leanne.

"Is something wrong?"

"Jonathan's not feeling well."

Debra said, "I'll be right home." She said goodbye to the nurse.

Jonathan was lying on the couch looking flushed. "What's the matter, Jonathan?"

"I've got a horrible headache and my stomach doesn't feel very good."

Debra offered to do Healing Touch.

"I don't care what you do, just please make it go away."

"Let's get you settled in bed, first, so you don't have to get up afterwards."

Jonathan got himself ready for bed and climbed in under the covers. "Okay, Mom, I'm ready."

Debra went in and administered Healing Touch. She stroked Jonathan's face for a while afterwards and he was soon fast asleep. It was nice to have a chance to share some closeness. It seemed that the older the children got, the less opportunity there was to do things for them or share physical affection and she, at times, missed it.

David opened the door for Debra when she arrived at Edna's house the following evening. His hand lightly brushed her back as he closed the door behind her and it didn't go unnoticed by either one of them.

They visited with Edna for a while. Edna mentioned how pleasant it was to waken every morning to the sounds of birds chirping and singing. "I enjoy singing and I like to listen to the birds sing. But, you know, David can't carry a tune in a paper bag."

David interrupted her, "Mom, I'm sure Debra doesn't want to hear this story."

"Oh, sure she does, Dear." She continued on as if he hadn't spoken, "When David was in third grade, they were practicing for a concert and he was so off key that the music teacher asked if he would mind mouthing the words. He was so rebellious that he became disruptive and had to be sent out of the room!"

Debra laughed as David defended himself, "I was only nine years old. I didn't think my singing was any worse than the fellow standing beside me and she didn't ask him to lip sync."

"That's because he was a quiet little thing, whereas you could really bellow!" Edna commented.

David laughed, "Well tone deaf or not, I still like to sing."

Debra, again, consented to let him observe her doing Healing Touch on Edna. David asked her to join him on the porch and share a pot of tea after Edna fell asleep.

Once they were settled on the porch with their tea, he said, "So, tell me more about Healing Touch. How did you know you had a gift for healing people?"

"Actually, everybody does. It's just a matter of whether or not we use it." She told him about her friendship with Liz and how Liz had introduced her to Healing Touch. She explained that she had learned through doing a joint session on Kurt.

"Do you treat many people?"

"Not really. Hardly anybody even knows that I do it. It's not exactly well accepted. We taught it to a Bible Study Group, but other than that, I've only tried it on your mother, Liz, her husband, and my children."

"You have children, too? How old are they?"

Debra noticed he said, "too" and she glanced over at his ring finger. He didn't wear a wedding ring, but that didn't necessarily mean anything.

She told him the names and ages of her children. "How old are your children?"

"I only have one, a son. Chad's twenty-one. He's attending college in Boulder, Colorado, but he'll be coming to visit his grandmother as soon as he can get away. They're very close."

They talked a bit about their jobs. David was an architect. "I enjoy the challenge of my work, but I don't let it consume me. There are lots more important things in life."

It was refreshing to talk to someone who shared her point of view. She wished she felt able to pry enough to ask what those things were.

She found herself thinking about David and wondering whether or not he was married or involved with anybody as she walked down the sidewalk toward Liz's home Wednesday morning.

"You're looking particularly chipper this morning. What you been up to?"

"Nothing much."

"What is it. Cough it up?"

"What?" Debra asked her.

"You look like the cat that swallowed the canary. What's that all about?"

"Well, you know how I've been doing Healing Touch on Edna every evening, her son's been there a couple of evenings and I enjoy talking with him."

"Are you falling for an older man?" Liz asked.

"Actually, he's our age. I guess Edna had him late in life."

"H-m-m-m. What's he like?"

Debra started to blush and Liz burst into laughter. "Oh, that's how it is!"

"Well, not really. I hardly know him!" Debra protested.

"But, you'd sure like to! Come on. What's he like?"

"I don't know he's maybe six foot one or two. He's got dark brown hair...broad shoulders...he looks fit. He's got blue eyes. He's very clean cut looking."

Liz snickered, "So, is he single?"

"I don't know. I haven't had enough nerve to ask."

"You have to find out."

"No kidding. And exactly how do I do that?"

"Ask his mother!"

"I couldn't do that. She'd tell him. I might as well ask him myself, if I do that!"

"Might as well." Liz responded.

"Easy for you to say. How do I go about it?"

"I don't know. What's the worse that could happen?"

"Now you sound like Elizabeth. I'm always asking myself that question now...whenever I'm about to take a risk. All that does is make it so that nothing is impossible, but it doesn't make it any less scary!"

Liz laughed as she swung her arm around Debra's shoulders. "You've got to find out and that's all there is to it."

Debra groaned, "I know."

CHAPTER FOURTEEN

The opportunity to find out about David's marital status came sooner than she had expected. She was chatting with Edna in Edna's kitchen, when she was told that David would be visiting that evening, "I wasn't expecting him. David's coming to visit more often and I don't think it's to see me." Her eyes twinkled.

Debra was pleased that David might be visiting more frequently because he wanted to spend time with her and she couldn't stop a telltale blush from spreading across her face, so she turned in her chair and bent over to re-tie one of her shoes. She tried to brush it off, "He's worried about you."

Edna said, "Well, in that case he could simply use the phone. So, do you fancy him, too?"

"I don't even know whether or not he's attached."

"He's not."

Debra couldn't help but smile, "Well, in that case, then...yes, he seems very nice."

"Nice!" Edna chuckled, "Is that the term they use nowadays?"

Debra laughed, too. "I don't know, it's been a long time since I had to describe my feelings about a man."

"Well, I know I'm a little biased being as I'm his mother, but David's a lot more than 'nice'. His wife died of leukemia, when their son was only five years old, and David did a bang up job of raising him, if I don't say so myself. He's a right responsible young man—as a matter of fact, they both are."

Just then they heard the front door open and David called out, "Hello!"

"We're in the kitchen!" Edna called back.

David walked in, bent over to kiss his mother's cheek and then looked over at Debra and said, "It's nice to see you again, Debra." She could almost feel his eyes caress her face. Damn, Debra could feel all of her senses perk up. She couldn't believe the effect he had on her.

He asked them both how they were and then he looked down at the pillow his mother was sitting on in the kitchen chair and asked why she wasn't sitting somewhere more comfortable.

"I wanted a change of scenery. I can only look at those four bedroom walls for so long."

"Well, how about we take you for a drive then? How does the La Jolla oceanview from the top of Mount Soledad sound?" He looked at Debra, "Are you able to join us?"

"I don't want to intrude...I..."

"Nonsense," Edna interrupted. "We'd love for you to come along."

"Well, if you're sure," she looked at both of them for confirmation. When they both nodded, she added, "I need to run home for a minute and let the kids know I'm going."

Debra soon returned to find David lifting Edna into the back seat of his Explorer, amid her squeals of laughter. She was such a tiny little thing that it was easy for him, but Edna wasn't accustomed to such treatment. Debra and David laughed along with her. Once he got his mother settled, David opened the door so Debra could climb in the front, "Mom insisted on sitting in the back so she could stack some pillows against the door and sit with her legs up across the seat."

Humph. Sounded to Debra like she was matchmaking!

Edna asked whether Debra had ever been to the top of Mount Soledad. Debra admitted that she hadn't and Edna commented, "It's lovely." After that Edna was so quiet in the backseat that Debra almost forgot she was there. She and David talked about some of the other siteseeing places in the San Diego area. Debra had to admit that she hadn't been to many of them.

After a while, David looked toward the back seat, "Mom's asleep."

As they drove up the windy mountain road, the houses became larger and spaced further apart, until all that was left were gated estates. Debra noticed a long, sleek black limousine gliding through the darkness in the opposite direction down the mountain road. It could hardly be seen and it if hadn't been for the sidelights near the rear of the vehicle, she probably would have missed it. David commented, "Looks like they're slumming it," and Debra laughed.

David pulled into one of the parking spaces at the top of the road. There were several other vehicles there and Debra noticed the couple in the car beside them was locked in a passionate embrace. Debra felt a little uncomfortable when David nodded toward another couple hugging and kissing as they stood against a nearby fence. "I guess this spot is a bit of a lover's lane in the evening," he said.

Edna didn't so much as stir. They decided to walk around the site and agreed they shouldn't wake her. There was almost a three hundred and sixty-degree view around the mountaintop. As they looked down at the multitude of lights throughout San Diego and surrounding areas, David pointed out Mission Bay, Miramar Marine Corps Air Station, and the well-lit Mormon Temple just off of I-5 which was beautiful and pristine with its many spires.

They rounded the bend and the faint odor of skunk assailed them. "The delicate scent of skunk," David commented. They both chuckled.

Debra gasped when they walked around to the side overlooking the ocean. It was a crystal clear evening and the view extended as far as the eye could see. Lights twinkled and reflected onto the water from the buildings on the land curving around the ocean's edge. They could also see the occasional light from a boat far out in the ocean.

When Debra commented on the beauty and peacefulness, David told her that he used to sail with his son, Chad. "We both liked to fish and enjoyed the different ports we stopped at, but my favorite time was always the evening...it's so quiet at night. The only sound is the rhythmic slap of waves against the boat. It's like there's nobody else in the world."

"It sounds incredibly peaceful," Debra commented. "Do you still sail?"

"No, Chad's away and I prefer not to go out alone, so I sold the sailboat."

"Are you and Chad very close?"

"Actually we are. I pretty much raised him myself. His mother died of leukemia when he was five years old."

"Your mother mentioned that today. I'm sorry, that must have been really hard."

"It certainly had its moments, but it gave me a chance to have a closer relationship with my son than I might have had otherwise."

"Good for you. For a while there, I thought Ted, my ex-husband, was going to abandon the kids completely, but they get together about once a month, now."

"That's good. Does he live in San Diego?"

"He moved to Fair Oaks, a suburb just outside of Sacramento where we used to live."

David raised his eyebrows.

"My impression was that he wanted to get away from responsibility and the rat race of San Diego."

"And you?" he asked softly.

"So it seems."

"That must have been tough. When did he leave?"

"In January of this year."

"Not that long ago," he said.

"It feels like it has been years...A lot has happened since then and I've changed so much."

He looked at her. "For the better?"

"Definitely. I don't think I could have found myself if I was still with Ted. I certainly wouldn't have gotten into Healing Touch and I wouldn't feel as good about myself as I do now."

David looked at her with admiration, "Good for you."

They decided they should get Edna home to her own bed where she could sleep more comfortably. They drove back in companionable silence. David parked the Explorer in front of Edna's house. Debra leaned around the front seat and supported Edna and the pillows while David opened the back door. Edna stirred slightly when he lifted her out, but remained asleep. "She always was a sound sleeper."

He had given Debra the keys to Edna's house. Rueben was waiting outside for them and he brushed back and forth against Debra's legs as she opened the door and let them in. Edna woke when one of her feet lightly knocked against the doorframe as David carried her through.

She was a little startled and confused about her whereabouts. David spoke softly to her, "You're home, Mom. We just returned from Soledad Mountain." That reassured her and she instantly became wide awake.

"Isn't it time you put me down, then?"

"Just let me get you into your bedroom." He laid her on the bed and went into the kitchen to get a glass of water so she could take her medication. Debra assisted Edna in getting changed and ready for bed. "Edna, would you like Healing Touch?"

"I wouldn't mind, Dear. It was nice to get out even though I didn't stay awake for most of it," she chuckled. "But, I'm a little sore from that trip."

David joined them shortly afterwards and Debra told him what she was going to do. "Would you like to give your mother Healing Touch with me?"

He hesitated, "I would like to, but I don't know what to do."

"You've watched me a couple of times. Just stand on the opposite side and copy whatever I do." She instructed him to share a hand/heart connection. When he placed his hand over hers on his mother's chest, Debra felt a strong bond with him and Edna at that moment. He looked into her eyes and she could tell he felt it, too.

Edna was asleep within minutes, but they continued with the session, with Debra coaching him, where necessary. At one point, she briefly opened her eyes to see how David was doing. His eyes were closed and he had a look of rapture on his face. The association that Debra made with the look on his face made her feel flushed all over. She quickly forced herself to return to thinking about the task at hand. "Honestly," she thought to herself, "you're with his mother in her bedroom for crying out loud!"

David soon whispered to her, "Debra, I'm seeing the most incredible colors in my head. What is that all about?"

"Aura layers. I see them, too. Purple, right? Now, blue?"

"Yes... now, orange tinged with yellow."

"Uh-huh."

When they were finished and left Edna's bedroom, David commented, "Now I can see why you enjoy doing it. The colors were incredible and I don't know how to describe the feeling."

"I know what you mean. It's like a very special connection that I can't describe either."

He nodded. "Thanks for sharing that with me...so what are the colors from?"

Debra explained about the different chakras and layers of the aura and then added, "Thanks for including me for the drive to Soledad. It was a lovely evening."

"It was, wasn't it?" David agreed as they shared eye contact.

Just as Debra's hand was on the door to leave, David called out, "Debra."

"Yes."

"I'm going to be away in Malaysia for a few weeks on a consulting trip. I'd really appreciate it if you could look in on my mother. She's very fond of you."

"I will definitely do that. I'm fond of her, too."

They said goodbye and Debra went home with a sense of disappointment as she realized she didn't know when or if she would see him again.

She continued to stop by regularly to visit with Edna. During one of her visits, she had a chance to meet David's son. He came to spend a weekend with Edna just before the start of the next school semester. He looked like a younger version of David, except with blond hair. When Edna introduced them, Debra was disappointed that Chad seemed unfamiliar with who she was, which meant David had never mentioned her.

Chad was friendly and talkative, but seemed a little surprised that his grandmother had insisted that Debra stay and visit with them. It was well into the conversation before his grandmother made a comment about Debra having done Healing Touch on her.

"Oh, you're that neighbor!" He looked her up and down and seemed impressed by what he saw. "Dad told me about you."

Edna chuckled. "I've always said you have all the finesse of a bulldozer!"

Chad looked embarrassed, but Debra reassured him. "That's okay. It's nice to know I was worthy of mention."

Edna picked up her knitting from the basket beside her chair and they became involved talking about Healing Touch. Chad was fascinated by the topic. He explained that he hoped to practice sports medicine from a holistic perspective and he wondered about the practicality of combining massage with Healing Touch. A discussion ensued with Edna occasionally contributing her viewpoint accompanied by the clickety-clack of her knitting needles.

As they talked, Debra couldn't help but notice the close relationship that Chad shared with his grandmother. Chad was very respectful and they tended to affectionately tease each other. At one point, he asked his grandmother what number the sweater was that she was knitting.

Edna answered, "Eight, I believe…maybe, nine." Debra didn't know what they meant.

Chad explained, "Grandma loves to knit sweaters, but she never sews them together. She rips them apart and knits another one as soon as she's finished. This is the eighth or ninth go around for that wool," he chuckled.

Debra laughed. "That explains why we ripped apart a perfectly good sweater."

Edna kept smiling, "You never mind. It keeps me out of mischief."

Debra was genuine when she told him she enjoyed meeting him and headed for home.

Things were particularly busy at work during the first few weeks of September. The consultants tended to drum up new workshop ideas, which required extra preparation time for the upcoming conferences. Soccer season started up again and Debra was also preoccupied helping Leanne and Jonathan get set up for the new school term.

Edna was now getting around with the use of only a cane and was taking care of herself, with the exception of the occasional visit from a housekeeper. She had even resumed caring for her own garden, although Debra insisted on helping her with the hose. It was too much for her to hobble around with her cane and drag a hose, too, although Debra was sure Edna would have tried it, if she hadn't intervened.

Debra was pleased to return to ballroom dance classes toward the end of September. She noticed that Jean arrived with Tom. Tom had his arm around Jean and she was looking into his eyes as he said something to her. The two of them appeared smitten with each other. Debra was reluctant to intrude, but just then, Jean saw her and walked over with Tom. She gave Debra an exuberant hug.

They took turns pointing out the people they recognized, as many of the students they had met in the earlier lessons had also continued on. Debra was calling their attention to the reappearance of the cowboy she had seen at registration when she, all of a sudden, looked startled and stopped talking mid-sentence.

"What's the matter?" Jean asked her as she saw Debra's face become flushed. Debra was looking at an attractive dark-haired man who had just entered the doorway. He was talking with the disapproving blonde from the first ballroom dance class.

"That's my neighbor's son. I didn't know he was involved in ballroom dancing," she whispered. "As a matter of fact, I didn't even realize he had returned from his trip to Malaysia."

Just then David noticed her, also. He, at first, looked surprised, but then his face broke into a grin of pleasure. He excused himself and walked toward her. "Debra, I didn't know you were taking ballroom dance lessons. It's nice to see you here. How have you been?"

Debra responded and, once she had introduced Jean and Tom, she asked him how he had ended up signing up for intermediate lessons.

"I took the beginner lessons over the summer and I enjoyed it so much, I decided to continue on."

She and Jean exchanged looks and both said at the same time, "We didn't see you in the beginner lessons."

"There's more than one class. I took them Thursday evenings. Were you in the Tuesday classes?"

"Yes, I didn't know there was more than one set of classes during the week," Debra responded.

"The only reason I knew is that Valerie, the woman I was talking to a minute ago, was in my Thursday class. She told me she had switched from Tuesday evenings."

As soon as Frank used the microphone to welcome everybody and Debra and Jean were separated from the men, Debra asked, "So are you and Tom an 'item' now?"

Jean smirked and said, "I guess so. We've seen each other almost every day since the lessons ended."

"I'm happy for you. Tom seems really nice."

"Thanks. What about David? What's the story there?"

Debra didn't get a chance to answer because Frank called everybody to attention. Jean groaned, "Don't you dare leave without talking to me before the evening's over." Debra smiled. There wasn't that much to tell, but it would be fun making Jean wait.

Classes started out with a review of the steps they had learned in the beginner lessons. As soon as Frank instructed them to get a partner, Debra noticed that David headed toward her, but a short balding fellow who darted in between them and grabbed Debra's arm, intercepted him. Debra looked over at David and they exchanged rueful grins. David mouthed the words, "Next time," and Debra smiled back at him.

It was a while before they connected successfully. Debra felt both excited and anxious as she put one hand on David's shoulder and the other in his left hand. She hoped he couldn't feel her trembling, but when he placed his other hand on the small of her back and knowingly looked into her eyes, she knew he could. He provided a firm lead and it was just as well because Debra found she could hardly think straight. None of the other partners had affected her this way!

She felt so distracted, she had to focus on timing and breathing in order to keep from making an absolute fool of herself. She, however, soon became more relaxed as David, too, made errors and chuckled at himself. It was with mixed feelings that Debra returned to the other side of the room. She was relieved to have a chance to get herself together, but disappointed because she had discovered that David was fun to dance with.

Jean sidled up to her, "I saw you and David dancing and laughing together. Just how well do the two of you know each other anyway?"

Debra couldn't help but laugh when Frank's voice interrupted once more. Debra felt shy, but she finally managed to get enough nerve to approach David to dance. He winked at her when she asked him to be her partner. Debra cursed herself as she, once again, broke into a full blush. He teasingly bowed before saying, "I would be honored, mademoiselle."

David had style and presentation when it came to ballroom dancing, but nonetheless, he struggled with some of the dance sequences, too. At one point, he twirled them to the left instead of the right, they collided with another couple, and all four of them almost ended up falling to the floor. Once they stopped laughing, he apologized to the others. Debra was pleased that he had a strong enough sense of self that he wasn't put off when he made mistakes. She couldn't help but compare him to Ted who had lost the ability to laugh at himself during their last year together.

Debra's next partner was a man who had been in her beginner classes and had a crush on her. She was polite to him, but dancing with him was like dancing with an automaton. He never looked up from his feet, he counted his steps out loud, and his arms and body were rigid so he was difficult to follow. She was relieved when the time finally came for him to return to the other side of the room.

Debra noticed that Valerie was dancing with David. Valerie exhibited a touch of class that Debra knew she herself did not have. Valerie carried herself well and she was always dressed in the latest fashions, with the finest ballroom dance shoes to match each of her outfits. Debra felt at least a little threatened as she saw the two of them laughing together.

The class was much faster paced because they were reviewing previous steps. Jean did not get a chance to pin Debra down until the end of the lessons. "I got stuck with that balding guy you danced with first tonight. He was a toe stomper. If I had had to hear him apologize one more time, I was going to rip my hair out." Then she chuckled, "Maybe that's what happened to his hair.

173

Some poor women ripped it out in frustration!…Now are you going to tell me what the deal is between you and David or not?!"

Debra laughed. "There really isn't that much to report. I've run into him a few times over at my neighbor's house."

"Well, there might not be that much to report, as you put it, but there's enough chemistry between the two of you to ignite a bonfire!"

David and Tom met up with them at the door and the four of them walked out to the parking lot together. They chatted for a few minutes before Jean and Tom said goodbye and drove off together in Tom's car.

David walked Debra to her car. "Have you known them long?" David asked, nodding in their direction.

"Just since classes started. I met Jean in the registration line up. Jean and I have been each other's security blanket," she laughed.

"I can see where that would come in handy. I nearly turned around and walked right back out again when I saw the size of my class."

"Me, too. If Jean hadn't been there, I probably would have. It's been fun though, hasn't it? I really look forward to the classes."

"Yes, and I will even more now. See you next week," he said, as he helped her shut her car door. Debra felt a thrill of excitement at the thought that David might look more forward to the lessons because of her.

Ballroom dance classes became the highlight of Debra's week. She always enjoyed seeing Jean and Tom, but she particularly anticipated spending time with David. Once she was feeling more comfortable with David, she became more aggressive about reaching him on the other side of the room and, combined with David approaching her, they usually ended up dancing together several times throughout the evening. Nonetheless, Valerie seemed enamoured with David and she, often beat Debra to it. On one occasion, Valerie looked over her shoulder and gave Debra a smug look as she took David's arm. Debra wished she hadn't been caught noticing. David appeared oblivious to the tension between the two women.

They eventually discovered that several of the couples had paired off and the teaching assistants no longer objected to them dancing the evening together, provided they occasionally changed partners. The four of them solved that by exchanging partners with each other. Debra had to admit to herself that she was relieved once David was no longer dancing with Valerie.

They had a great deal of fun together when it came time to learn the two-step. It was more casual, the music was upbeat, and there was lots of hooting and hollering as people got into the steps.

David and Debra teased each other and laughed as they paraded around the dance floor. Some of the steps required that they dance side by side and at other times, David would swing Debra around so that they were facing each other. It took them a while to learn the "windmill" which involved a complicated sequence of arm placements while keeping their hands joined. Many of the others were unable to get the hang of it, but David and Debra caught on quickly. Tom eventually asked David to demonstrate for him and Jean. Debra noticed David was patient when showing them what to do and they were thrilled when they finally figured it out.

They covered lots of dance floor during the two-step lessons and all four of them were breathless by the end of the class. Jean commented, "I finally know why step classes are considered aerobic exercise."

The rest of them laughed and Debra responded, "It's pathetic. We haven't even been using step machines and we're all winded." That brought on more laughter.

When they learned the tango, Debra discovered David had a flair for the dramatic. At one point, he pretended he had a long-stem rose between his teeth as he turned his head this way and that. She was impressed with the way he held his body and seemed to know instinctively when to turn his head away. It didn't take her long to get into the role of playing "hard to get" which was distinctive of the tango. They had such fun! It was even more entertaining when they noticed Tom and Jean playing out their own rendition.

At the end of the class, Frank announced that one of the San Diego dance clubs had invited anybody interested to join their weekend mambo workshop two weeks away. The four of them didn't hesitate to sign up. They were all in agreement that the Latin American dances were their favorite.

The slow foxtrot was scheduled for the following week's lesson. The foxtrot was one of Debra's least favorite, but she was at least looking forward to spending the evening with David. Debra soon discovered that the slow foxtrot wasn't even remotely similar to the regular foxtrot. It had also been appropriately coined the "disco waltz". Once Frank called for them to partner up, he advised them that this dance was intended to be danced close. He pulled his partner toward him so that their pelvises were touching. Everybody gasped.

Once the men and women were asked to join each other, he waited for the men to pull their partners in close. When he instructed them to swivel their hips simultaneously in a figure eight motion, Debra was unbearably aware of David's body. They practiced the steps...slow, quick, quick...which were danced almost on the spot, then, with David's hand firmly placed on the small of her back, their pelvises swayed in unison in a figure eight. Debra was aware that the fabric of her silk dress and his black dress pants did not create much of a barrier between his pelvis and hers.

The more they practiced, the more rhythmic it became and, as the night progressed, she could feel the heat emanating from his body. They didn't even consider exchanging partners. David had incredible style and, with their bodies pressed against each other, it didn't matter that the lights weren't dimmed, nor that there were almost two hundred people in the room. The only things Debra was aware of were David and the sensual tempo of the music. The sensations she experienced were only heightened by each new step they shared and, by the end of the evening, her knees were just about buckling and her body was humming from head to toe.

As the four of them walked out to the parking lot together, none of them spoke a word, except for Jean's one whispered comment to all of them, "Did you ever see *Dirty Dancing*?"

Debra briefly thought David was going to lean forward and kiss her when he said goodnight to her at the side of her car, but he seemed to change his mind and instead walked away. She drove away disappointed. She started to wonder whether or not he was attracted to her.

Debra was wired all night and couldn't sleep. She drug herself out of bed the next morning to join Liz for their Wednesday walk.

"What happened to you? You look like you were in a train wreck!" Liz said.

Debra tried to explain the previous evening to Liz. "So, what you're trying to tell me is that you've never been so hot and bothered in your life!" Liz summarized for her.

Debra laughed. "That's about it in a nutshell. But, I don't know what's going on with David. I thought he was going to kiss me goodnight, but he didn't. I don't know how he feels about me."

Liz reassured her, "Debra, he's probably trying not to rush you. You and Ted only separated nine months ago. There's no way David would spend most of every class dancing with you, if he wasn't interested."

"I guess so, but it's hard not knowing for sure."

Debra struggled to get through the day at work. She was exhausted. She managed to sleep well the rest of the week and was feeling rested by the time Saturday morning arrived. As this was the day of the mambo workshop, she had cancelled her walk with Liz. It was also the day that Ted was coming by to pick up Leanne and Jonathan.

Debra was running out to her car dressed in a black petticoated full-skirted dress printed with rosy red blossoms, with her high-heeled ballroom dance shoes dangling from one hand, when Ted drove up and got out of his car. Ted stood there in disbelief when he saw her.

"The kids are just getting ready. Sorry, but I have to get going or I'll be late for my dancing lessons. See you later," she said as she rushed off.

Debra was feeling nervous and excited when David joined her at the gymnasium where the workshop was being held. Tom and Jean soon arrived and the conversation was light and fun, which helped her to relax. Once David took her in his arms to practice the mambo steps that had just been demonstrated, she remembered how seductive their dancing had been. It didn't help that he looked down at her and said, "You look particularly fantastic, today."

"Thank you." He was wearing black chino pants and a silk shirt that she figured he had purchased just for the mambo workshop. "You look pretty sharp yourself." He looked damned sexy is what he looked.

She managed to collect herself so that she could follow the dance steps. The mambo involved a tricky combination of steps which, fortunately, soon had her distracted.

"Four, three, two, one...four, three, two, one," they counted together so they could stay synchronized. Debra rolled back and forth on the ball of her right foot, making her hips swivel, as she first stepped forward with the left foot and then backwards.

Everybody in the class was paired up and, as usual, there was lots of laughter and chatter off and on throughout the lessons.

The class broke for lunch and David and Debra joined Tom and Jean at a table. Debra was surprised to see that David had packed himself an appetizing lunch. He had pita bread loaded with grated carrot, shredded lettuce, chopped tomatoes, sliced cucumber, and alfalfa sprouts. He opened a small Tupperware container and added a tantalizing smelling mustard sauce.

"Whoa, do you cook, David?" Jean asked him.

"As a matter of fact, I consider myself to be a bit of a gourmet," David responded.

Jean raised her eyebrows at Debra and nodded approvingly. "So, David, how is it that you're still single?"

David became serious, "To tell you the truth, over the years I met lots of women who would make good wives and lots of women who would make good mothers, but I never met anybody who I thought would be good at both. I wasn't willing to settle for less. And..." he paused, "I don't know what my excuse has been since my son became an adult and moved out on his own." He laughed and everybody joined in. Tom liked to cook, too, and they all spent the rest of the break talking about some of their favorite dishes.

As the day progressed, the steps became more advanced. There were lots of swivels and turns. Debra's favorite sequence was one in which David held one of her hands high and she walked around him in a circle, seductively dragging her other hand across the back of his shoulders until she came around to face him, again. At the close of the lessons, the instructing couple left to change into flashy competition outfits. When they returned they gave a mambo demonstration. They were stunning!

Jean chattered away in excitement as the four of them walked through the parking lot. When she and Tom drove off, it became very quiet. David walked Debra to her car and he seemed to have something on his mind.

"Debra, I know it's only been a little while since you and Ted separated, and I don't want to hurry you, but I'd really like to spend some time together outside of dance classes. Maybe take a drive up the coast, have dinner, spend some time talking..."

"I'd like that very much."

He breathed an audible sigh of relief. "How does next Saturday sound? I could pick you up around one o-clock."

"That sounds perfect."

He smiled. "See you at dance classes, Tuesday?"

"Uh-huh, see you then," she smiled back at him. As Debra got into her car and drove away, she felt excitement bubble up inside her, until she thought she would burst. She drove straight to Liz's house.

"Oh-ho! Don't we look sexy?" Liz looked her up and down. "What's happening?"

Debra grabbed one of Liz's arms with both hands. She was almost bouncing on the pavement. "David and I are spending next Saturday together! He wants to go for a drive...and eat...and talk. You were right. He just didn't want to rush me!"

Liz hugged her, "Okay, okay. You're going to burst a gasket!" she laughed. "That's great. What are you going to wear?"

"I need to shop for something. I'm going to get a new outfit. Could you come with me tomorrow?"

Liz couldn't help but laugh. "How could I say 'no'?"

When Debra arrived home, the Bergers were pulling up at the same time, "Hello George and Nancy," she called out. This time, it didn't even faze her when they didn't respond.

Debra was relaxing in her swing when Leanne and Jonathan returned home with their father. They greeted her and, with coaching from their father, said goodbye to him and went inside.

Ted looked tentative when he approached her. "Okay if I sit down?"

"Sure," she replied.

"I might as well get to the point," he started.

"Oh-oh, this is not going to be good," Debra thought to herself.

"Look, I know I behaved like a jack ass. I'm sorry."

This wasn't at all what she had expected. "Yes, you did...but, I accept your apology." She hesitated, "I could have been easier to get along with, too. I'm sorry."

He nodded. "I think I may have made too many changes in my life. I thought it would be better back in Sacramento, but it's not."

"Unfortunately, there's no such thing as a geographical cure," Debra responded.

"I miss you and the kids. I miss the life we had. I miss...Is it too late to try again?"

This was definitely not what she had expected. "I don't think it would work."

He still looked hopeful.

"No, what I really mean to say is, I know it wouldn't work. I've changed too much. So have you. We're not a good fit for each other anymore. I'm sorry."

He was hunched over likc an old man when he got out of the wicker seat. Debra gulped as she watched him walk toward his car. There really was no way to let him down gently. They had had a lot of good years together, but Ted was no longer the man she had loved all those years and she had come too far to go back.

CHAPTER FIFTEEN

They went to Nordstroms the following afternoon. Debra tried on several outfits, but they were both in agreement about which one to buy. She was dressed in soft turquoise capri pants and a sleeveless blouse, with a matching jacket. She removed the jacket, laid it over her arm, and turned around slowly for Liz's perusal.

"You look fabulous. It's casual and dressy at the same time."

"I really like it, too."

Debra paid for her purchase and as soon as they were away from the checkout, Liz asked her, "Do you have sexy lingerie?"

"Liz, we're only going for a drive and dinner!"

"Yes, but you never know. Even if you don't need it this time. I, personally, would want to be prepared. By the sound of the fire smoldering between you two, you won't have it on long, anyway, but first impressions and all..."

Debra laughed, "Fine, let's go take a look."

When they were finished shopping, they stopped at Starbucks for iced tea. The afternoon passed pleasantly and Debra was feeling satisfied when she returned home and started to prepare dinner.

She looked out of her kitchen window as she was rinsing the vegetables and noticed a red and black hummingbird dart toward her hummingbird feeder. It must have been startled by something because it flew away before it had a chance to light on one of the perches. Debra had seen several green hummingbirds, but she had never seen a red one before. It was such a pretty little bird, she hoped it would return.

Debra called her parents after dinner that evening. She had talked to them several times since receiving her mother's written reply to her letter. The conversations usually went fairly well, although Debra's mother slipped in the occasional barb. She found the comments didn't get to her as much now and were a welcome relief in comparison to the lectures her mother used to give her. She wondered what her mother would say about her seeing David, but decided there was no need to bring it up yet.

She talked about the ballroom dance lessons, but she didn't mention dancing with David. Her mother's one response when she had first mentioned ballroom dance lessons in a previous phone conversation had been, "I wouldn't want a bunch of strange men pawing me."

Her father, who had been on the extension line had interjected, "Oh, is that what they're doing? I thought they were ballroom dancing." Debra couldn't help but smile when she recalled how he had jumped to her defense. It seemed to bother Debra's mother that Debra was having so much fun at this stage of her life, but Debra was accustomed to her mother's jealous nature and she wasn't going to let it get to her.

Leanne and Jonathan each took a turn chatting with their grandparents although they were old enough that they were no longer eager to participate. Jonathan did want them to visit, though. When the call was over, he asked why his grandparents never came to San Diego.

"Mom, doesn't like to travel. She feels more comfortable at home in her own bed," Debra told him. She also realized that her children were past the age where they were willing to leave their friends to spend a weekend visiting their grandparents in Sacramento, if they could avoid it. The phone contact would have to do for now.

She had a great time learning how to dance the West Coast Swing Tuesday evening. Even though it was the first Swing lesson, there was carryover from some of the other dance steps and they all caught on quickly. She enjoyed the many tuck-in turns whereby David would wind her up and then spin her in the opposite direction. The music was upbeat with a quick tempo, but David didn't have any trouble keeping time. It was hard for her to understand how someone who had such good timing dancing was unable to sing well.

When he dropped her off at her car that evening, he winked and said, "See you Saturday."

Debra, all of a sudden, felt shy and only nodded a response.

She was a bundle of nerves by the time Saturday arrived. Liz had to slow her down on their walk. "You're going to wear out the pavement and me, too. Save some energy for the rest of the day."

"What if he decides he doesn't like me?"

"What's there not to like? Now you're being ridiculous. It's not as if this is a blind date. He's already spent time with you and now he wants to spend more time with you." She slipped an arm around Debra as she walked beside her. "You'll be fine."

Debra did a few chores and had a quick lunch before showering and dressing in her new outfit. Not that she could eat much. Her stomach felt like it was in her throat.

Leanne thought she looked great in her new clothes. Jonathan wasn't willing to comment. He just groaned, "Chick stuff."

Debra tried not to pace as one o'clock approached. When the doorbell finally rang, she just about jumped out of her skin. Leanne rushed to answer the door. She was dying to meet her mother's "date".

"Hello, you must be Leanne." David introduced himself.

"Hi, come on in, I'll get my Mom." She looked him up and down. He must have passed inspection because Debra noticed Leanne smiled when she turned around and saw her mother behind her in the doorway.

He looked over Leanne's shoulder, "Hi, Debra." Damn, he had a warm voice. She just about melted.

Debra took him around the corner and introduced him to Jonathan who was sitting in an armchair watching sports on the television. "So I hear you're the soccer player in the family."

Jonathan shrugged, "I play a bit."

"What did you think of that first World Cup game when the U.S. upset Portugal?"

Jonathan looked surprised that David was familiar with the World Cup. "It was pretty cool…you like soccer?"

"I played it all the way through into my early adult years."

Jonathan just nodded and went back to watching the television, although Debra could tell he was impressed. Debra was aware that his nose was a little out of joint because she was going out with a man other than his father.

Debra picked up her jacket. "You ready to go?"

David nodded and they said goodbye to Leanne and Jonathan. Debra had given them money to order pizza, so they didn't mind that she wouldn't be home to cook dinner, although Jonathan would have preferred that she dine with a female friend.

David opened the door to his Explorer and closed it behind her after she got in. It had been years since a man had done that for Debra.

"I thought we'd drive along the coast to Encinitas, stop off in Del Mar and walk along the cliffs, and then stroll along the beach in Encinitas before we go to dinner at one of my favorite restaurants. Does that sound okay?"

"Sounds wonderful."

They chatted about inconsequential things while David maneuvered through the Pacific Beach traffic and onto Interstate 5. Once they were on the highway, David asked Debra what she liked to do in her spare time.

She laughed. "I never used to have spare time. I always thought there was something that needed to be done…and, I don't know…maybe there was, but I'm learning to enjoy life and it sure makes getting up in the morning a lot easier."

David smiled which encouraged her to continue.

"I enjoy spending time with my female friends, your mother, Liz, Jean. I like to garden and kayak. I even enjoyed decorating my home and making it my own. I'm a voracious reader. I love to sit on my porch swing with a good novel and I really like to read in bed." He looked interested, so she continued. "Although I didn't use to, now that I feel like I have more time, I enjoy cooking. And, as you already know, I like to ballroom dance and do energy work. It seems that the things that matter most in my life are different now…Life is good."

"Ah-h-h, doesn't it feel good to say and feel that?"

"It's wonderful."

"I used to be a workaholic."

Debra was surprised. "What made you change?"

"My wife's cancer. There she was, only twenty-seven years old having the very life squeezed out of her. It really made me take stock of things. I don't think that once we're old and gray sitting in our rocking chairs we're going to wish we had worked more."

Debra grinned, "Isn't that the truth? So what's important to you in life?"

"People, the outdoors, nature. I've discovered that no matter where a person lives, there are places of beauty and peacefulness nearby. It's a matter of seeking them out and taking the time to enjoy them. Most of us don't do that enough. And, we need to do it with the people we care about."

"That's what you and Chad got out of sailing."

He nodded.

"One of the other things I do in my spare time is meditate. I think the peace I get from meditating has helped me to feel more centered," Debra told him.

"You like to meditate? There's a place I'd like to show you. It's in Encinitas and we could stop there if you'd like."

David turned off onto Carmel Mountain Road and they drove along Highway 101. As they came into Del Mar, they drove along a street lined with quaint little shops and restaurants. David turned left and parked on the side of the road just before it came to a dead end. They had to walk across railroad tracks and a ditch to get to the path, but the view was worth the effort.

As they walked along the bluffs, the sun glistened off of the ocean. On one side of the path there were several homes, ranging from small beachfront properties to elaborate multi-windowed mansions, their yards decorated with palm trees and colorful bougainvillea. On the other side they looked down upon an expanse of beach and a never-ending view of the ocean. The occasional sea gull swooped down to the beachfront and a multitude of sandpipers walked along the water's edge.

David took Debra's hand and pulled her closer to him as they were walking along the path. She liked the feel of her hand in his. She smiled.

"Penny for your thoughts," he said.

"I was just thinking about how little touching most of us share even though it feels so good."

He smiled back at her. "Most people crave it, but there's not much permission in our society to touch each other. Lots of other cultures exchange hugs or kisses on each cheek when greeting each other, but Americans usually only shake each other's hand, if that."

"Energy work can be done without touching, but Liz and I agree that most people don't get enough touching in their lives, so we prefer to do hands on energy work. Touching is so nurturing."

"I'd like you to give me Healing Touch some day. I could even do it for you, if you're willing to bear with me while I learn how."

Debra was touched that David would be willing to reciprocate. "I would really enjoy that."

After a while they turned around and walked back. As they drove along Highway 101, they could see stretches of beach and ocean. It was very scenic.

Debra was intrigued when they entered Encinitas, as she knew David lived somewhere in the area. David made a couple of turns before driving down San Rafael Avenue and finding a parking space on the side of the road.

"This is the Self-Realization Fellowship Retreat," he said, gesturing toward a large wrought-iron fenced enclosure with multiple buildings. "The grounds are open for the public to visit and meditate."

He pointed out a huge white stucco building with a red tile roof and told her it was one of the retreat buildings. They then walked through an intricate labyrinth of tiny paths winding up and down through the grounds. The pathways were lined with flowers, shrubs, and trees, with a variety of ponds enroute that were stocked with colorful Koi fish. They came across the occasional individual seated on the various benches provided for the purpose of meditation. They kept their voices low so as not to disturb them.

"It's so beautiful and serene," Debra whispered to David. She gasped when they reached the top of one of the paths, walked up three broad terrazo steps, and saw the ocean expanse before them. "This is absolutely incredible."

David told her that a small open-air temple similar to the Taj Mahal was once situated at the top of the steps with a reflecting pond, however, the shoreline eroded to the point that the temple slid from its foundation. As they toured the grounds, they also came across a small pool, drained of water, that David informed her the founder Paramahansa Yognanda had previously used.

They eventually returned to David's Explorer. "Thank you for bringing me. I didn't know such places existed."

"There are actually several in California."

Debra was surprised.

David drove up and down the streets of Encinitas until he found a parking space close to the cliffs. He lifted a small soft-sided cooler out of the back of his Explorer. "There's a park here on the bluffs overlooking the ocean. How about we share a small picnic before we go down to the beach and watch the surfers?" he asked.

"Sounds good to me—you thought of everything didn't you?"

He chuckled, "I aim to please."

They found an empty bench in the park and sat down. David opened the cooler and poured them each a glass of tangy raspberry herbal iced tea. He then placed a selection of fresh grapes, strawberries, and sliced mango on a plate and spread out cheese and crackers on another plate before offering Debra a napkin.

Debra teased him. "You forgot the checkered tablecloth."

"Next time," he promised and winked at her.

Debra grinned back at him. It was a wonderful place to enjoy a picnic. There was green grass, lots of fresh air, and a scenic view of the beach and ocean. Debra let out a heavy sigh, "What a great way to spend a day!" she exclaimed. Her face was lit up and the sun shone off of her hair.

David looked over at Debra and said, "You're beautiful."

Debra had been described as "cute", and "good-looking", but never as "beautiful". It took her by surprise and a few seconds passed before she said, "Thank you." She looked back at him and truly felt he saw her as beautiful. She let out a sigh.

"What's the sigh for."

"I feel beautiful when I'm with you."

He moved over and put his arm around Debra, pulling her closer. She rested her head on his shoulder. They sat quietly enjoying the view and making the occasional comment about the people that they observed. After a while, Debra helped him pack the leftovers into the cooler and they returned to the Explorer. David left the cooler in the back and picked up a blanket so they could sit on the beach. They climbed down a series of wooden stairs that wound to the beach below. It was difficult trudging through the sand so they decided to remove their shoes and leave them nearby.

David took Debra's hand and as they walked along the water's edge, the occasional wave broke and ran along the sand, almost reaching their feet. David tried to drag her close enough for the waves to splash over her feet. They made a game out of Debra jumping and trying to evade getting her feet wet, but it was almost impossible to time it right. They both ended up laughing at her efforts. Debra eventually gave up and they walked through the wash together.

David maneuvered them both around the many clumps of kelp lying along the water's edge. After a while, they chose a spot at the end of the beach where it was less crowded, spread out the blanket, and sat down on the sand to watch the surfers.

Debra called David's attention to a tiny female, probably only ten years old. She looked like she could surf circles around the older guys. It was amazing.

"Children who start early tend to be fearless and catch on quickly. Do your children like to surf?" David asked.

"They've never tried it."

"What!? They can't live in San Diego and not know how to surf!"

"I guess they haven't had the opportunity yet," Debra responded.

"We've got to do something about that. Chad has several boards at home that aren't being used while he's in Colorado. We could rent some wetsuits and have some fun."

"I bet they'd love it. Jonathan might be a little difficult as he's not too happy about me spending time with you, but I could ask them."

"How about you? Would you be open to trying it?"

"I think I'd prefer to watch."

"You sure?"

"M-m-h-m-m."

"Okay, fair enough."

It was getting to be early evening. David folded up the blanket and they strolled back along the beach together. A small group of people had gathered and was listening to a woman who was singing softly as she strummed a guitar. With the exception of the group and a few stragglers, most of the people had left.

David drove to a small restaurant. It looked like a European house and was decorated with window boxes overflowing with colorful flowers. The hostess greeted David by name and smiled warmly when he introduced Debra. She seated them in a quiet corner of the tiny restaurant.

Small trellis dividers decorated with silk flowers and vines separated the room into sections. A dark cherry wood floor provided a rich contrast to the white tablecloths. Burgundy valances trimmed with lace and matching Chantilly lamps gave it a homey atmosphere.

"You come here often?"

"Yes, I like the way it's a small Mom and Pop establishment. They're an Austrian couple and their specialty is home-cooked meals flavored with just the right herbs and spices."

The waitress came by to offer drinks and review the specials with them. With Debra's agreement, David chose a bottle of Merlot.

Debra asked for suggestions from him when it came time to choose from the menu. They both ended up ordering Oscar Schnitzel, which David described as tender breaded pork smothered with seafood and cream sauce, accompanied by baby asparagus and the cook's specialty, cooked red cabbage.

Once they had ordered, David reached over and covered Debra's hand with his. "I'm really enjoying spending the day with you. You're a very special woman."

Debra, who wasn't accustomed to compliments, blushed, but managed to remember her manners to thank him. "I'm really enjoying the day, too."

They talked a bit about their siblings and the fact that, in both of their families, they were separated by geographical distance. In David's case, though, he and his sisters shared regular contact through email and long distance phone calls, whereas Debra's siblings rarely bothered with each other.

The food was delicious, but Debra had difficulty eating. Although she found him easy to talk to and felt relatively relaxed in his presence, there was an edge of excitement. The butterflies in her stomach seemed to have replaced her appetite.

They both declined dessert. David, again, held her hand as they walked to his Explorer. When they stopped beside his vehicle, David took her in his arms and kissed her, a long, slow kiss. Debra's knees got weak and she had to hang on to him to remain standing.

"I'd love to take you back to my house, but I don't think I could trust myself to behave," he said, as he pulled away and opened the door for her.

Debra wasn't sure she wanted him to behave. David held her hand as he drove down the highway. They didn't say much. The scenery was beautiful and peaceful with the occasional light reflecting off of glimpses of ocean. As they drove up to Debra's house, she was disappointed that the evening was coming to a close.

David walked her to the door and, as he kissed her goodnight, she wanted to invite him to hang out on the porch swing with her and neck up a storm. God, she was sick of being so contained. To heck with it, she wanted to rip her clothes off and attack him! With a husky voice, she told him so.

He chuckled and wrapped his arms around her, again. "Later. Much as I'd love to, there's lots of time for that."

It was late, both kids were home, and that would be no way for them to get to know David. Debra thanked him for the wonderful day.

As he walked down the sidewalk toward his Explorer, he looked over his shoulder and said, "Don't forget to ask the kids about surfing."

"I won't." Debra sighed from a combination of bliss and wistfulness as he drove off. Damn, he could kiss! She didn't go back in the house immediately, she wanted time to herself to savor the moment.

Leanne eventually came to the door. "What are you doing?"

"Relaxing."

"Did you have a good time?"

"Definitely."

Leanne looked like she was going to ask another question, but instead she said, "Good," and walked back into the house. Debra followed her inside.

Debra didn't think she would sleep, but she never heard another thing until morning. She had just finished her shower when the phone rang at nine o'clock. It was Liz.

"Well, how was it? It was all I could do to wait to call you!"

"What if David had been here?"

"I knew he wasn't. His Explorer wasn't out front. Not that I thought it would be anyway, with the kids home and all, but I checked. Now, how was it?"

Debra laughed, "You got time for tea?"

"Yeah, I'll be right down." Debra heard the phone disconnect.

"I bet you will," she said, chuckling, as she placed the receiver back in its cradle and plugged in the kettle.

Liz came through the front door in next to no time. "Look at you! I bet I couldn't wipe that smile off your face if I tried."

"Probably not."

"Okay, okay, tell me all about it."

Debra told her about walking along the bluffs, touring the Fellowship Center, and spending time at the beach. She also told her about the picnic lunch and dinner.

"Yeah, yeah, so what happened? There had to be more to it than that, to get that look on your face!"

Debra couldn't help but laugh. "Well, he kissed me. Not once, but twice."

"Can he kiss? No, never mind, I can already tell. So are you going to go out with him, again."

"He wants to teach the kids how to surf."

"No kidding! That's great!"

Liz got up off of her chair and hugged Debra. "I'm so happy for you. When do we get to meet him?"

"I was thinking that, if the kids agreed to go surfing, I could barbecue afterwards and you and Kurt could join us. Even if

Leanne and Jonathan don't agree to the surfing, we could get together for a barbecue. Of course, I'd have to check with David."

"Sounds good to me."

They chatted for a while before Liz decided to return home and Debra went into the yard to garden. Everything was filling out and her yard was beautiful. Her feeders were frequently visited by a variety of small birds. She noticed that Twitchy had returned. He was feeding himself, but he never allowed himself to get more than four inches away from his mother. Each time she hopped down to a different branch, he was right behind her with his wings twitching. They ended up perched side by side on the feeder. It looked like it was all they could do to hang on, due to the fluttering of his wings. With all of the birds singing and chirping among the beauty, Debra's yard sounded and looked like a small paradise.

After a while, she went inside to make a batch of waffles. Jonathan and Leanne were both up.

"What's the occasion?" Jonathan asked.

"I just felt like having breakfast together as a family."

Leanne looked sideways at her. "Was that the David that I've heard you talk about ballroom dancing with?"

"Uh-huh."

"Where'd you go yesterday?"

Debra told them. Jonathan looked away and pretended he wasn't listening. When Debra got to the part where she talked about watching the surfers at Encinitas, she told them about the young girl they had observed.

"David would like to teach us how to surf." She noticed Jonathan perk up a little. "His son has some boards you could use. Would you like to learn how to surf?"

Leanne was quick to answer. "I'd love to! That would be so cool. Lisa is going to take lessons next summer. She'll die if she finds out I'm going to learn before her!"

"What do you think, Jonathan?"

"What do you mean 'you'?"

Debra raised her eyebrows. Jonathan explained, "Well, you said he wants to teach 'us', but then you said his son had some boards 'you' could use—aren't you going to come, too?"

"I think I'd rather watch. But, I could try it, if you really want me to."

"Nah, I guess that's okay. As long as you're there, too.—How are we going to explain to Dad that your boyfriend is teaching us to surf?" There was heavy emphasis on the word 'boyfriend'.

"Jonathan, your father is probably dating, too. We're just not there to know about it."

Jonathan looked doubtful. "Look, Jonathan, I really like David and I don't know if anything is going to come of this. But, I sure think it's nice that he wants to teach you two how to surf. Can I tell him you're interested or not?"

"Please Jonathan," Leanne pleaded. "I want to, but I don't want to be the only one learning. If Dad questions it, you can tell him I made you." She smiled and he smiled too because Jonathan had grown and they both knew there was no way she could "make" him do anything.

"Okay. But remember, it wasn't my idea."

They talked about their weekend schedules. It turned out that Leanne had the following Saturday off. Debra didn't know whether that was too short notice for David, but if it was, they would have to wait a couple of weeks for Leanne to get her next work schedule.

The following week's dance session was another cha-cha lesson. Debra enjoyed this dance step because it was so much fun. Frank taught them how to do a "chase" whereby they danced a sequence of steps and then the man followed closely behind the woman as if he were chasing her. At one point when they reunited immediately following the chase step, David whispered to her, "That's it, wiggle that cute little behind in front of me." Debra laughed. There was nothing "cute and little" about her "behind", but she enjoyed the flattery anyway.

Jean was wearing a saucy little number, a wrap around skirt that tied just above the hip and left one thigh bare. She actually did have a cute, little figure and it seemed as if she was having a great time flaunting it. Tom looked like he was going to take her right there on the dance floor!

The four of them were all laughing when they got together at the end of the night. They had had a great time. After Tom and Jean had driven off and they were standing by Debra's car, David wrapped his arms around Debra, "How about I leave work early next week so I have enough time to pick you up for the lesson? It's silly taking two vehicles every week."

Debra was hardly paying attention as she agreed to the plan. She was waiting for him to kiss her.

Then he said, "Did you ask the kids about surfing?"

"Yes, they're both free on Saturday, but otherwise we would have to wait for Leanne to get her next work schedule."

"This Saturday is fine. How does ten o'clock sound?"

"Great. I'll bring the picnic this time. How about I barbecue afterwards and ask my friends, Liz and Kurt, over so you can meet them?"

"That sounds like a good plan. What would you like me to bring?"

"Just yourself...Now, are you going to kiss me, or not?" she smiled, teasingly.

"Just prolonging the agony," he said, cocking one eyebrow at her.

She leaned into him, "What if I told you that I'm not finding you very funny?"

He groaned. "You don't play fair."

"Neither do you." He stopped her from saying anything further by pressing his lips against hers. Debra just knew she was going to have another restless night.

CHAPTER SIXTEEN

Debra had no problem getting the kids up Saturday morning. They were excited about going surfing. She put a picnic lunch together after she returned from her walk with Liz. The lawns were already trimmed and the house was tidy. Debra had prepared a frozen chocolate mousse laced with coffee liqueur the previous evening. There were chicken breasts and vegetables marinating in the fridge to be barbecued for dinner and Liz had offered to bring potato salad. Debra was planning to prepare the vegetables when she returned home from the beach.

Debra was dressed in an attractive new swimsuit with a matching wraparound skirt. David's eyes lit up and he gave a low whistle when she met him at the door. Debra, as usual, blushed. David was wearing board shorts and a T-shirt. He looked good enough to eat.

David greeted each of the children. Leanne's face shone with eagerness when she said hello to him. Jonathan was more reserved and tossed a casual "Hey," his way.

The surfboards were strapped to the roof racks of David's Explorer. They stopped off at a surf rental shop to get wetsuits before heading to Tourmaline Beach. It was still early so they were able to find parking relatively close to the beach. The three of them put on their wetsuits over their swimsuits and lathered themselves with sunscreen wherever their skin was exposed.

David brought the surfboards down off of the roof racks and handed one to each of Debra's children. Debra carried the towels and cooler. Once they found a spot on the beach, David showed them how to wax their boards.

David turned to leave, "I'll be back in a minute, I have to get something out of the Explorer." He returned with a large folded down canopy and set it up to keep Debra shaded. Debra was overwhelmed by his thoughtfulness. When she thanked him, he was modest. "I wouldn't want you to burn your lovely skin."

He turned to Leanne and Jonathan, "Are you ready to show the surf's who's boss?"

They both nodded. David bent over and gave Debra a quick kiss on the cheek, and said, "See you soon." Jonathan looked disgruntled when he saw David kiss his mother and Debra thought for a minute that he was going to refuse to join in, but he trudged off behind David and Leanne.

It was a beautiful sunny day. Debra was wearing sunglasses that helped shade her eyes so she could see them in the water. They carried their boards out to thigh-high depth where the water was frothy after the waves had broken. David showed them how to push the board out in front, flop on it, and try to ride the board in on their bellies. Jonathan's board tipped almost immediately and he fell into the water. He looked over toward Leanne. He seemed relieved to see that she had also fallen off and they grinned at each other. They carried their boards back and tried again. This time they stayed on a little longer. They were both laughing when they walked back to try it again. David rode his in with them this time. He got off of his board once they had both dumped into the water and he walked back with them. Debra could see they were all laughing and chatting. They kept trying until they were able to stay on their boards almost all the way up to the beach.

David next showed them how to get up on their knees. Debra heard him give the command, "Okay, get ready!" They all flopped on their boards together and tried to rise onto their knees. It looked like it was difficult to stay balanced and Leanne and Jonathan took several spills before they were successful. David even fell off a couple of times.

They eventually headed back to Debra, carrying their boards, laughing, and panting. Jonathan grabbed his towel, laid it out, and flopped onto it. "That was so cool!" he said gasping for breath.

Leanne said, "Mom, it's so much fun. I can hardly wait to tell Lisa!"

David came, dragging himself behind them, "They've got too much energy for me." He gave Debra a quick kiss. "How about lunch?"

Debra opened the cooler. She offered everyone a drink before pulling out several plastic containers with tomatoes, shredded lettuce, spicy breaded chicken strips, and ranch dressing. She constructed them each a wrapped sandwich, using soft whole-wheat burrito shells.

"M-m-m. Looks good." David said, as he bit into his.

"I am so-o-o hungry," Leanne said, "This is delicious!"

Jonathan nodded with his mouth full, "Me, too. Do you have enough for us to have two of these?"

Debra laughed, "Yes, I figured you'd be hungry." David smiled and gave her an affectionate look. Debra felt her heart flutter. She could love this guy.

After they finished eating, the four of them rested, meanwhile talking and laughing with each other. Debra was pleased that they all appeared to be enjoying themselves.

David asked, "So, are you ready to go out further?"

Both Leanne and Jonathan hopped up. "Let's go," Jonathan responded.

"Okay, but let me show you what to do here on the beach first." David had them lay on their boards on the sand. Then he demonstrated how to push up with both hands and quickly get into a surfer stance. They both tried it before carrying their boards and wading out almost up to their waists. There were lots of flops and screams, followed by laughter as they tried to get up on their boards. Debra kept watching and couldn't help but root out loud even though they couldn't hear her. After several tries, Jonathan managed to briefly stand up on his board. It took Leanne longer, but she finally did it.

The three of them went out deeper. They turned around and paddled like crazy trying to catch waves as they broke. On the last go around, David stood on his board, weaving back and forth, until he rode it in as far as he could. He almost made it to the beach. Debra was impressed.

Once he stopped, he picked up his board and came to sit beside Debra. The kids eventually paddled in behind him. When they finally returned to the beach, they looked exhausted, but content.

"Mom, he's trying to kill us," Jonathan said as he fell onto the sand.

"I'm trying to kill you?!—You're trying to kill me!" Then he turned to Debra. "They did well, didn't they?"

"I'll say. I got tired just watching all of you!"

They rested for a while before using the outdoor showers to clean themselves up. Debra was worried about them getting into David's vehicle in their wet swimsuits, but he didn't seem concerned and simply suggested that they sit on their towels.

When they pulled up in front of Debra's house after returning the wetsuits, the Bergers were sitting on their front porch. "Good afternoon, George and Nancy!" Debra called out. They didn't so much as bat an eyelid. Leanne and Jonathan tumbled into the house, laughing.

"What was that all about?" David asked.

"Oh, they have yet to speak to me since we moved in so Leanne bet me ten dollars I couldn't get a response from them before the end of year. I can't quit trying," she said, chuckling.

David smiled. "I bet you can't. That sounds like a challenge that would be hard to resist."

David used Debra's bathroom to change into dry clothing. As soon as Leanne had changed, she grabbed the telephone so she could tell Lisa about their day. Jonathan rushed down the block toward Tim's house, calling out that he would be home in a few minutes.

David joined Debra in the kitchen and she offered him a drink. They both decided to have a glass of wine.

Debra turned to David, "Your lessons were sure a big hit! Thanks for teaching them how to surf."

"No problem. They're great kids! They didn't give up easily and they were good sports about all the spills they took."

Debra smiled at him. "You were wonderful with them."

This time David was the one to blush. "Aw shucks, it was nothin'," he said, joking to cover his embarrassment. "Now, what can I do to help?"

"I was thinking of cutting up some vegetables and wrapping them in tinfoil to barbecue. Do you want to take care of the mushrooms?"

David cleaned the mushrooms while Debra sliced the zucchini. David picked up a large onion off of the counter. "Would you like me to slice this?"

"Thanks, that would be great." She laid the prepared vegetables on tinfoil and David added the onions as he sliced them. She then sprinkled them with salt, pepper, and fresh basil before adding dots of butter. They meanwhile chatted and teased each other. It was pleasant sharing the kitchen with David. Ted had never been comfortable with domestic duties.

The doorbell rang and Liz and Kurt came through the front door. Debra yelled, "We're in the kitchen!"

Liz and Kurt joined them. Liz put her potato salad on the counter and hugged Debra in greeting. Kurt was carrying a bottle of wine and swung it against Debra's back when he gave her a hug. She jumped, "Oh, it's cold!"

"Sorry," he sang out, but his laugh said he wasn't.

Debra gave him a shove and introduced both of them to David. "These are my rotten neighbors, Liz and Kurt."

Kurt greeted him with a handshake, but Liz gave him a brief hug, "I feel like I already know you, I've heard so much about you."

"Liz!" Debra exclaimed from embarrassment.

David chuckled. "I can see why you call them rotten."

"Hey!" Liz and Kurt said together in protest.

Debra took a sectioned Tupperware out of the fridge and opened it to reveal a selection of chopped veggies and dip.

"M-m-m-m," Kurt said, helping himself. He turned to David. "Liz never feeds me. I have to come over here to eat. See how skinny I am?" Everybody laughed as he stuck out his stomach and pretended to be malnutritioned.

Debra put Liz's potato salad inside the fridge. David meanwhile poured drinks for Liz and Kurt and topped up his and Debra's wine glasses before they headed outside to the backyard patio. Debra carried the veggie platter and David brought her glass of wine. Debra had recently purchased a huge umbrella, with a table and chairs for them to sit at. It added an elegant touch to her backyard.

David looked impressed as he surveyed her yard. "Looks like you've got a green thumb."

Liz piped up, "She sure does. She even helped us to make our yard more beautiful."

"Oh, come off if. All I did was make some suggestions for plants."

"Well, they were good suggestions."

Leanne and Jonathan soon joined them. David offered to light the gas barbecue. He and Kurt decided they would do the barbecuing. Liz and Debra looked at each other. They weren't going to protest.

After a while, Jonathan and Leanne helped Liz and Debra carry everything they needed outside. There was lots of chatter and joking around. Even Jonathan and Leanne appeared to be having a good time. Dinner was a success. The vegetables and meat had a pleasant smoked flavor and were cooked to perfection. Liz's potato salad was exactly what they needed to complete the meal. Jonathan was a huge fan of potato salad and he didn't hesitate to let her know he thought it was delicious. The frozen chocolate mousse added a finishing touch.

Once they were finished eating, Debra told Jonathan and Leanne that they didn't have to stick around and could spend the evening with their friends, provided they helped carry some of the dishes back inside the house. They didn't need a second invitation. It was Saturday night, after all!

The adults finished cleaning up and then retired to the livingroom. They asked David to turn on some music, but Debra was quick to point out that she didn't have much of a selection of CD's and he instead turned on San Diego's new 80's radio station. Before you know it, they were all singing. David didn't look at all abashed and every once in a while he would even accompany them with whistling, which made his inability to carry a tune even more obvious.

Actually, none of them were particularly melodious, but they didn't care. Liz's attempts at harmonizing were hilarious. There was a lot of teasing. They almost rolled on the floor laughing when one or more of them sang the wrong words or continued to sing during instrumental sections.

At one point, Kurt said, "I don't think we'd better give up our day jobs." They even competed over who could guess the names of the songs and singers or bands.

David finally said, "Kurt you've obviously had way too much time on your hands listening to the radio. You've guessed almost all of these!"

"Maybe I was listening while I was working!" he responded, which brought on lots of laughter.

Liz and Kurt eventually left for home. Liz had insisted that Debra keep the remainder of the potato salad being as Jonathan had liked it so much. David helped Debra carry the glasses into the kitchen where he soon had her pinned up against the kitchen counter while he kissed her. Not that Debra was putting up any kind of a struggle as she kissed him back, "I wish you didn't have to go home."

"Me, too. How about I come by in the morning? We could go to Lake Poway and rent a tandem kayak early while it's still nice and peaceful."

"I would really like that."

He kissed her again, but just at the point when Debra whimpered and was about to throw all of her morals out the window, they heard the door open. It was Jonathan. They pulled apart.

"Is seven o'clock tomorrow too early?" David asked.

"No, I'll be waiting on the front porch."

He called goodbye to Jonathan and ran his hand down Debra's back as he gave her a light kiss on the cheek before departing.

"Tease," she whispered.

He smirked, "Tomorrow."

Debra slept like a baby. Even though she hadn't had lots of exercise like the rest of them, she had had lots of fresh air. Fortunately, she had set the alarm. She showered and donned shorts and a T-shirt and was sitting on the porch before seven o'clock arrived. David was on time.

There were hardly any signs of life on the streets until they reached Interstate 15, but it was early enough that the traffic was light. They soon arrived at Lake Poway. David took a bag and a cooler out of the back of the Explorer, "Blanket and refreshments," he explained.

David was disappointed when they went to the rental shop and discovered that the shop did not rent kayaks. "We have canoes and rowboats," the clerk told them.

David looked over at Debra, "What do you think? Rowboat or canoe?"

They both said together, "Canoe."

"It's cozier," David said as he put his arm around Debra.

David paid for the rental and the clerk handed him a couple of wooden paddles. They then followed him down the hill to where the back of the boathouse rested on stilts. The clerk walked under the raised wooden floor, carried a canoe out, and placed it in the water. They removed their sandals and David put the shoes, bag, cooler, and paddles in the canoe. Before she knew what was happening, he put his arm around her back, swung his other arm under her legs and picked her up. Debra let out a squeal of surprise. They both ended up laughing as he placed her in the canoe.

"You all settled?" He grinned at her.

Debra nodded. The canoe rocked back and forth as David got in and she thought for a minute that they were going to tip, but he sat down, grinning. They each picked up a paddle and headed the boat into deeper water.

Debra finally took the time to look around. The lake was a beautiful shade of emerald green, outlined by a small beach of reddish coarse sand that was almost surrounded by hills scattered with scrub brush. There was a lovely hillside park covered in green grass along the bank beside the boathouse. The small lake with its many leafy Eucalyptus trees and hillside park looked like a small oasis among the desert hills. A few ducks floating here and there and the occasional fisherman in a rowboat on the outside edge of the lake were the only signs of life. It was very peaceful.

They paddled around the outer shores, making sure they left enough room so as not to disturb the fishermen.

After a while, David said, "Come over here." He helped her sit with her back to him on the floor between his knees. Then he tipped her head back and kissed her forehead. When he bent over her, nuzzled her neck, and slid his hands down her bare arms, she ached to turn around and face him.

"I think we'd better head for shore," David said huskily.

Debra went back to her seat. There was an inlet lagoon on the far side of the lake. They soon stopped by the edge, hopped out, and pulled the boat up onto the beach. Once they found a secluded place under a huge Eucalyptus tree and spread out the blanket, David tossed the breakfast cooler onto the ground and took Debra in his arms. As he kissed her, he caressed her back and Debra ran her hands through his hair. It was luxurious and thick just like she had thought it would be. When he bent to kiss her neck, she folded into him. The two of them ended up lying in a tangled heap on the blanket. "You didn't think I'd be able to support you did you?"

Debra choked out a giggle, "No."

It was excruciating not being free to undress. The spot was secluded, but there was no guarantee that they wouldn't be interrupted. Debra could hardly breathe she wanted him so much and it only became more difficult when she pressed herself against him and discovered how aroused he was.

His breathing was jagged when he finally said, "Okay, okay, I give up." He pulled away from her. "Uncle."

Debra couldn't help but laugh. She hadn't heard anyone use that term to indicate surrender since she had been in her early teens. He ended up laughing, too.

"Maybe we should check out the cooler," David said as he pulled it toward him. He took the lid off and lifted out a lightly wrapped plate of croissants. Then he spread a checkered tablecloth on the blanket, which made Debra chuckle remembering her comment the last time he had brought a picnic. He flashed a proud grin her way. He then placed a variety of jarred homemade preserves on the cloth and took out a knife. Finally, he pulled out a bottle of champagne, orange juice, two champagne glasses, and a corkscrew.

"Oh my! You're incredible!"

David beamed. "Thank you, thank you." He opened the champagne with a pop and poured them each a glass combined with orange juice.

"M-m-m-m," Debra said as she took a sip of hers. "I've always heard this is great in the morning for breakfast, but I've never tried it before."

David took a drink from his glass, too, before kissing her. "M-m-m, m-m-m, m-m-m, it is delicious." They grinned at each other.

He sliced a croissant and spread it with apricot jam at Debra's request before preparing one for himself. Debra thought it was the best croissant she had ever tasted.

"Hey! It just occurred to me! How did you manage to get fresh croissants this early in the morning?" Debra asked.

"Remember the Austrian couple? Gustaf starts baking at 5:00 in the morning on Sundays. This is their Sunday morning special. I sort of dropped by before the restaurant opened."

"You're amazing!" Debra said, shaking her head.

They chatted while they finished their breakfast and then packed everything back into the canoe before paddling back across the lake.

While they were traveling back to San Diego, David told Debra he would be spending the remainder of the day with his mother and that he planned to take her out shopping. He asked Debra about her parents. She told him they lived in Sacramento. She gave him a brief description of her relationship with each of her parents, being careful not to be too expressive so as to avoid swaying his opinion of her mother before he even had a chance to meet her.

When they pulled up to the front of Debra's house, she thanked him for the lovely morning and kissed him.

"Don't forget, I'll pick you up Tuesday for ballroom dance classes," he said as he walked toward his mother's house.

The week's lesson featured the waltz. Debra was almost relieved it wasn't one of the seductive Latin American dances. Her body felt like it had been tuned to a fever pitch for long enough. She didn't need to provoke things further. She and David enjoyed a pleasant evening of elegant dancing, with gliding steps and lovely slow turns.

There was one point in the evening, though, when Jean managed to get all four of them going. One of the new dance sequences involved the man holding the woman's hand high above her head. She was expected to bend her knee and lift her right toe while pointed, and slowly kick her foot out with her toe still pointed, before gradually stepping down on the floor and rising up on her tiptoes. Jean, of course, had to ham it up with exaggerated steps and arm gestures. She had everybody in stitches as she made fun of what she called a "prissy" step.

David kissed Debra goodnight at the end of the evening and asked whether he could cook dinner for her at his home Saturday evening. She agreed and, although he offered to pick her up, she insisted that she would drive to his place so he wouldn't be interrupted while cooking dinner. He wrote directions, drew a map for her, and gave her his phone number so she could call if she had trouble finding his house. It sounded simple. He lived on the cliffs above the beach they had visited two weeks ago. Just as she was leaving, he told her, "Bring your swimsuit. I have a Jacuzzi."

When Debra arrived home, she told Leanne and Jonathan that she wouldn't be home for dinner on Saturday. Leanne reminded her that it didn't matter. This was the weekend their father was taking them camping at Lake Morena. He would be in town for a weeklong conference and had given Leanne enough notice that she had the weekend off. She and her boyfriend had terminated their relationship after only a few weeks and Leanne had decided it wouldn't kill her to have a weekend break from her friends. Jonathan was looking forward to boating with his father.

They had everything ready when their father stopped by to pick them up Friday evening. It was a little awkward seeing Ted after their previous discussion, but he acted as if nothing had happened as he helped the children carry their camping gear out to the car. After Debra said goodbye to the children, she yelled, "Have fun!"

Jonathan called back to her, ""Yeah, you, too!"

Debra thought it was generous of him. He was truly ambivalent about her dating.

After they left, Debra went next door to Edna's for tea. Edna had finished knitting her sweater and Debra was helping her rewind the wool, although Rueben was complicating things a bit. He wanted to play!

"My son's got a soft spot for you Debra. I've never seen him look happier. Thank you, my dear."

Debra said, "He's making me happy, too. He's very kind and considerate and he makes everything fun."

Edna chuckled, "That's my David."

"Wouldn't it be easier to knit a sweater with new wool?" Debra asked, changing the subject, as she rolled a tiny furry toy across the floor past Rueben.

"It might, but what a waste of wool that would be." Debra couldn't argue with that.

Debra was excited as she got dressed before going to David's Saturday evening. She wore a soft cotton floral print sundress that hung down to her ankles and had open pleats all the way up to her lower thighs. The jade green fabric showed off her golden tanned limbs. The neckline was round and revealed just enough to be provocative. She had painted her fingernails and toenails in a delicate shade of pink to match the flowers on her dress.

Shortly after Debra drove into Encinitas, she pulled up to a two-storey house with stained wood siding. It had a striking architectural design, with skylight windows in the roof, an octagonal shaped window on the side, and beautiful double wooden doors. She supposed David had designed it himself.

David greeted her with a warm kiss at the door, looked her up and down, and said, "M-m-m, I like what I see."

He led her through the foyer into a room. It was compact, but spacious enough for convenience. The far wall was in the shape of a ship's front that was completely paned in glass and overlooked the ocean. The ceiling was open-beam and the kitchen, dinette, and great room were open to each other. Wood stained in a rich golden honey hue had been used for the floors and ceiling. It was so warm looking!

His furniture consisted of an overstuffed couch, loveseat, and chair in a forest green/gold weave and were placed around a beautiful stone fireplace. A large imitation polar bear rug lay on the floor in front of the fireplace. L-shaped cabinets and an island that faced into the rest of the room made the kitchen appealing. There was a half bath down the hallway.

David poured her a glass of white wine. "Would you like a tour?"

He walked her up a set of wooden stairs to a loft bedroom. It was masculine looking, but very tasteful, with a huge four poster bed and matching dressers. They could look down over the wooden railing and view almost the entire main floor or look out the windows to the ocean and beach below.

"The view is incredible!" Debra gasped.

He showed her a small nicely decorated ensuite bath off to the side. He then took her down the stairs, through the great room, and down a set of stairs to the basement. There were two bedrooms, a bathroom, and a storage room. Each of the bedrooms had a large window facing the ocean as the basement was semi-walkout. Debra was impressed and she told him so.

When asked, he admitted that he had designed the house himself, although he told her, "At work, I design large multi-storey buildings made of cement, steel, and glass, so this was kind of fun for me. I bought the property before the prices skyrocketed and it's a small lot, but the location makes up for that."

They returned to the main floor and he took her out double glass garden doors and onto a deck that wrapped around the building. The deck was enclosed with waist high glass so as not to block the view. There was a jut out on the corner with a built in Jacuzzi.

Debra sighed as she breathed in the salted ocean air.

"They should bottle this, shouldn't they?" David said as he came up behind her and wrapped his arms around her. "I love the smell of fresh air. That's one of my favorite parts about paragliding, that and the peacefulness."

"You paraglide?" She turned slightly, with a questioning look on her face.

"Yes, it's one of the things that helps me to feel one with nature."

"What exactly is paragliding? Is that the thing I've seen where people are up in the air behind a boat?"

"No actually that's parasailing. A paraglider is much higher performance and we run off of hills or mountains. We can fly for miles and stay up for hours, if the air conditions are right."

"You have got to be kidding me!" This man never ceased to amaze her.

"The views are indescribable. It's peaceful. The sound of the air passing our ears is the only thing we hear."

"Sounds wonderful. I'd like to experience that."

"I could take you for a tandem flight some day, if you'd like. We could go to Torrey Pines."

She turned to face him. "Oh, I know what you're talking about! I've seen them floating around above Black's Beach at Torrey. It would probably scare the heck out of me, but I think I'd like to try it anyway."

"Really? That's wonderful!" he gave her a tight squeeze. "I thought that being as you didn't want to surf that there was no chance you would ever try paragliding."

"I'm not crazy about water sports because I'm not a strong swimmer, but floating around in the air…that sounds appealing."

"I'd love to share paragliding with you. We have to go when the winds are right so it's hard to plan in advance, but it's pleasant hanging out at Torrey Pines even when it's not flyable." He took her hand, "Now how about dinner?"

They went back inside and David slipped a covered casserole dish into the oven. Debra was curious about what he was cooking, but decided to wait to find out. There were already a couple of dishes in the oven and they smelled delicious!

He wouldn't let her lift a finger as he spread a white linen tablecloth over the dinette table, set out the dishes and silverware, and added a small vase with a red rose in it. He lit a few candles and dimmed the lights before turning on some soft instrumental music.

They started with a salad garnished with mandarin oranges and hazelnuts. He next served baked soft-shell crab in tomatoes, dilled carrots, and roasted red potatoes. Everything was wonderful. After dinner, David pulled out a stool at the island so Debra could be nearby as he prepared dessert. He tossed a few ingredients in a saucepan on the stove. Debra watched as he spooned a boiling mixture over fresh raspberries he had placed in custard cups. He sprinkled each of the cups with brown sugar and broiled them in the oven until the sugar melted.

"Raspberry brulee," he said in explanation. It was absolutely scrumptious!

After dinner, they changed into their swimsuits and David brought her a towel. He refilled their wineglasses, turned the music up enough to hear it outdoors, and carried a couple of candles out to the Jacuzzi.

Debra leaned against David as they sat in the bubbling water and looked out over the ocean. They spent the time sharing their dreams and teasing each other between occasional kisses and quiet laughter.

After a while Debra sighed. "If someone had told me even a year ago, that I would be feeling this relaxed and content in my life, I would have laughed myself silly."

David wrapped his arms even tighter around her. "H-m-m-m. Life is good, isn't it?"

After a while they dried off and went back inside. David fetched silk robes for each of them. "My sister has the habit of sending me silk robes from Japan for Christmas every few years." He handed her one. "We might as well get some use out of them."

Debra went into the bathroom to take off her swimsuit. She felt a combination of anxiety and excitement as she slipped into the robe, rolled up the sleeves, and tied the silk sash around her waist. When she reunited with David in the living room he was also dressed in a robe and was building a fire in the fireplace. A marine layer was rolling in from the ocean and it was becoming chilly.

He lit the kindling and walked over to put his arms around her. He looked down at her. "Nervous?"

She nodded.

"Me, too."

He turned the music low and added several logs to the fire, "Care to dance?"

It was a melodious slow waltz. It felt so good to be in his arms swaying back and forth to the music that Debra soon lost her nervousness. A rhumba selection started to play and David led her through the multitude of steps they had learned together. It was such a seductive dance style. The next music piece was immediately recognizable. Slow foxtrot.

"M-m-m, our favorite music," he whispered in her ear and pulled her closer. As David led her into the figure eight pattern and their pelvises swayed together in unison, Debra became achingly aware that neither of them wore anything under their robes. She trembled as he kissed her neck and almost crumbled when he looked into her eyes and took his time unwrapping her robe before slipping it off her shoulders. The silk slid to the floor.

Debra was quivering and fumbled slightly as she untied the sash on his robe. She could see the passion in his eyes as he looked down at her. She slid her hands up through the dark curly hair on his chest and slipped his robe off. He groaned.

He took her hand and led her to the bear rug where they laid down together. Debra's entire body was vibrating as he caressed her face and kissed her breasts. She wanted to feel him inside her and she wanted it from the very core of her being. She was even prepared to beg, if she had to.

Afterwards, they lay satiated in each other's arms. Debra felt overwhelmed with warmth in her heart. She looked into David's eyes and smiled softly. "You're very special, you know.

David hugged her tight. They lay there for a while before Debra suggested that they go up to his bed where it was more comfortable.

"What time do you have to leave for home?" he asked.

Debra smiled wickedly at him. "Sometime before noon tomorrow…the kids are camping overnight with their father."

"Here I've been dreading you leaving and you knew all along!"

"I didn't want to be presumptuous."

"You can assume that I want to spend as much time as possible with you."

"M-m-m, that sounds delightful." She said as she traced the outline of his lips with her finger before kissing him.

Debra followed David up to his bedroom. They made love again, but this time, the pace was slower. Debra later fell asleep curled up in front of David with one of his arms wrapped around her.

CHAPTER SEVENTEEN

Debra woke to the sound of birds chirping. She slowly became aware of her surroundings. She rolled over to watch David sleep. His dark lashes fluttered and he soon opened his eyes, "Good morning, beautiful."

Debra smiled. She slid over closer to him and he slipped his arms around her.

"How about we cuddle for a while and then I'll get up and make you an omelet?" he asked.

"Do you think that's possible for the two of us?"

"Oh, yeah I could make an omelet for the two of us," he smirked.

Debra ran a hand up the outside of his thigh to his buttock. "You're not half as humorous as you think you are."

He groaned, "I guess not." All of a sudden he rolled her onto her back. "Neither are you."

Debra tried to come back with a witty remark, but the words died in her throat as he kissed her lips. He kissed her neck, between her breasts, and down past her navel until she was on fire. As he bent over her, he whispered, "So which will it be, an omelet or me?"

Debra gasped, "David, please..."

When they were both spent, they lay facing each other. David stroked her arm and shoulder as she played with his hair.

David looked into Debra's eyes, "Thank you."

"For what?"

"For being you."

They held each other close. Debra knew what he meant. She felt blessed, too.

After a while they got up and showered. David asked Debra to show him how to do a grounding ritual and they did the routine together. Their conversation was light and teasing as they cooked breakfast and went out on the deck to eat.

Debra found it difficult to leave, but she knew she had to. David was also reluctant. "I'll pick you up for dancing Tuesday. We'll plan to get together on the weekend then, okay?"

Debra nodded. He kissed her goodbye and waved as she backed out of the driveway.

She spent part of the afternoon doing chores and picked up some groceries so she could make Leanne and Jonathan a special Sunday meal. Liz was out in her yard when Debra drove by on her return from the grocery store so she stopped to chat.

Liz looked up from gardening. "I was wondering when I would hear from you. How was dinner?"

"Fantastic." Liz gave her a questioning look. "Yes, I stayed the night. After dinner we soaked in the Jacuzzi and then he lit a fire in the fireplace, and we danced for a while."

"It looks like the fireplace wasn't the only thing he lit."

"Liz!"

"Well, you've got that look of contentment that only a great night in the sack can give you."

"Let's put it this way. Once we started dancing the slow foxtrot, it was all over but the crying. Now are you happy?!"

Liz smirked. "I'm just looking out for you. Besides if good friends can't vicariously live through each other's experiences, what can they do?"

Debra smiled. "How about we get together and exchange some energy work one evening this week?" she asked as she got back into her car.

"Sounds good. Call me." She held her thumb and baby finger out in a "V" shape to imitate a phone receiver.

Jonathan was grouchy when they returned home just before dinner. Apparently their father had spent a good part of the weekend on his cell phone talking to a "new lady friend".

That didn't take him long. It was only four weeks ago that he had said he wanted to get back together with her. But, she remembered that she was supposed to encourage the children to accept a new partner in their father's life.

"I'm sorry, Jonathan. I know it was a big disappointment for you, but your father needs to get on with his life, too. Someday when you have a girlfriend, you'll understand how hard it is to spend time apart in the beginning of a relationship." Jonathan went off sulking to his bedroom.

Leanne had met a guy her age at the campground so she wasn't affected at all by her father's lack of involvement. She thought it had been a great weekend.

Jonathan could be moody, but he always made a quick recovery. By the time they had unpacked and showered, he arrived excited at the dinner table because Debra had made meat lasagna.

He took a huge portion and wolfed it down before helping himself to seconds. After dinner, Leanne and Jonathan were busy getting their homework done and catching up with friends on the phone, so Debra went out to do some gardening and dream about the night she had spent with David.

Monday was a particularly stressful day for Debra. Her employer had hired a new presenter—a woman.

Emily marched into Debra's office in her tailored suit and high heels, her red lacquered finger wagging back and forth, "I just don't think round tables are going to work. I'd much rather have rectangular. Put fewer people at each table and spread them out."

Debra had to arrange for a larger room in order to have enough space. She had just managed to do that and had faxed in a new room set up diagram when Emily returned, "You know, I've thought about it, and I think I'd prefer round tables after all. I'd also like two TV/VCR stands for greater visibility for the workshop participants." Debra sent a new set up diagram to the hotel and requested the smaller room, again.

Then Emily reappeared in her office doorway. "I'd like my session videotaped. It would give me a good opportunity to review the tape and see where I need to make changes in my presentation."

So Debra made the necessary arrangements. Emily soon called her, "Maybe it would be better, if I waited until a later date to videotape a session." Debra cancelled the equipment and crew. And so the rest of the morning went.

Debra's clerical staff was all up in arms over the number of revisions Emily demanded. She repeatedly asked them to make additions or deletions to the information in her handouts. Debra did everything she could to appease them, but, frankly, she was fed up herself.

Then, to top it all off, the phone rang in the middle of the afternoon. It was her mother. She was crying and Debra couldn't make head nor tail of what she was blubbering into the phone.

"I don't know what I'm going to do," she sobbed. "It's all so horrible." Debra tried to interrupt, but her mother went on, "Everything was fine one minute and then it wasn't." Debra heard her blow her nose loudly into the phone receiver. Between the sobs and yammering, she heard two words that got her attention. "Father" and "hospital". Something had happened to her father!

"Mom get a hold of yourself! What has happened to Dad?" Her mother just sobbed more loudly. "Mom, is there someone else there I can talk to? You're not making any sense at all!"

The phone was completely silent for a while, and then a voice she didn't recognize came on the line. "Hi, Debra. It's Mrs. Cross, your mother's neighbor." Debra remembered her.

"I'm afraid your father's ill. He's got an infection and he's in Intensive Care. Your mother's distraught."

"It must be serious if he's in Intensive Care."

"Oh, it's not good, at all. He's right out of it. You might want to come to Sacramento right away."

"Mrs. Cross, is there someone there I could talk to. A nurse or a doctor?"

"Let me see…" She handed the phone back to Debra's mother, who kept sobbing uncontrollably.

Then there was quiet and another voice soon said, "Hello. Angela Walker here. I'm one of Mr. Logan's nurses."

Debra told her who she was and asked about her father's condition.

"It's critical right now. We're giving him antibiotics and oxygen, but he's got a serious case of septicemia."

"Okay, I'll come as soon as I can, but I need to know, what exactly is septicemia?"

"It's like poison in the blood from an untreated infection. Your father injured his hand. It became infected and spread into his blood."

Debra gasped, "Could he die from it?"

"He could, but we're doing our best to get things under control."

"I'll get there as soon as I can. Thank you. Would you please put my mother back on the line?"

Her mother was quiet as Debra told her that she and the kids would fly to Sacramento as soon as possible. Debra called a travel agent that she used regularly for the organization and arranged flights for herself and her children.

She called both of the children at school, waited while they were called out of their classrooms, and then told them their grandfather was ill. They agreed to hurry home to pack their travel bags. Fortunately, her boss was in and she was able to explain the situation. She also spoke to one of her assistants and passed on any important information that she would need in Debra's absence.

Debra felt sick. There was really no telling how critical her father was and whether or not they would get there in time to see him alive. It would be another couple of hours before the plane would leave for Sacramento.

Both Leanne and Jonathan didn't say much when they returned home. She explained the situation and reassured them that at least he was being taken care of. She packed her bag. Neither she nor the children felt like eating anything, so she threw a few snacks into her on-flight bag in case they wanted something later.

She wished David were there. All of a sudden she realized that he would be coming to pick her up for dance classes the following evening. She called his phone number and left a message on his answering machine explaining that she was rushing to Mercy Hospital in Sacramento because her father was seriously ill. At the end of the message, she added, "I miss you." Debra also left a message on Liz's answering machine asking her to keep an eye on the house and then called to arrange for a taxi.

Just as the taxicab arrived, she hurried into her "sanctuary", grabbed her pendulum, and shoved it into her purse.

"Hurry, Mom. It's time to go," Jonathan yelled.

"I'm coming." She picked up her travel bag and, after locking the house door, followed them out to the car. All three of them were quiet and subdued throughout the entire trip to Sacramento.

Debra's stomach was churning by the time their taxi pulled up to the hospital doors. It seemed to take forever for the elevator to reach her father's floor once she received directions to her father's room from the information desk.

As she was asking about him at the nursing station, her mother came around the corner. She burst into tears as soon as she saw Debra and waylaid her from going into her father's room. If it had been anyone other than her mother, she would have panicked and thought she had arrived too late to see her father alive, but she knew only too well how histrionic her mother could be. Debra felt sympathetic, but she needed to see her father for herself.

"Mom, just a minute. I need to go in and see Dad." She directed Leanne and Jonathan to some chairs outside her father's room where Mrs. Cross was already sitting. "I'll come out soon and let you know how he's doing."

The sight of her father laying pale and helpless in a hospital bed with oxygen nasal prongs coming out of his nose, an I.V. drip attached to the back of one hand, and the other heavily bandaged, was more than she could bear. Whereas her father had always been robust and healthy, he looked lifeless. The only sounds she heard were the beep of the monitor and the whoosh of the I.V. pump.

She knelt beside his bed, laid her head on his leg, and began to cry softly. "Dad, please don't die. I never had a chance to get to know you. God, please don't take him away from me now." She said another silent prayer and sat for a while before going out to talk to medical staff.

His prognosis remained uncertain. Because of his age, they were concerned about the impact on his heart. He had apparently sliced his hand with a carpet knife and had received stitches. The incision had become infected and, left untreated, had spread into his blood. Debra's mother had noticed that he had become increasingly lethargic and then feverish with intermittent chills during the previous couple of days. She had panicked that morning when he had become disoriented and had not known where he was, so she had called an ambulance. Debra could not for the life of her figure out why her mother hadn't gotten medical attention for her father sooner.

Debra hugged her children and asked if they would mind if she left them long enough to give their grandfather Healing Touch. Both felt that would be a comfort to them and they agreed to wait for her outside his room.

Debra talked with her father's nurse, "I do energy work and I'd like to help my father. Would it be okay with you, if I do it right after you check his blood pressure and vital signs so that we won't be disturbed."

She gave Debra a comforting smile. "I'll call you in just as soon as I'm finished. We won't interrupt you unless his monitor alarm goes off."

Debra soon went back into her father's room and took out her pendulum. Energy flow was problematic almost everywhere. Debra felt sick with grief. When she did a body scan, she, for the first time, felt a difference. She knew with certainty that she should perform a pain drain on his injured hand and his heart. She unruffled her father, being even more careful than usual to be smooth in her movements.

She later sealed and brought in energy to both his heart and his injured hand and then gave her father a mind clearing. Debra had never in her life felt as loving toward her father as she did when she kissed his forehead at the end of the mind clearing. The pendulum indicated good energy flow at all points and Debra was relieved.

She went out and hugged Leanne and Jonathan. The hallway lights had been dimmed and the ICU area was the only area left that was well lit. The nurse suggested that they might want to go home and get some sleep. She would call if there were any changes. Debra was adamant that she would take everybody home, but then she would return to spend the night with her father. Mrs. Cross had long since returned home.

Debra made sure everybody was settled in bed. She gave Jonathan and Leanne mind clearings to help them sleep. Her mother was still fretting and was pacing the hallway. Debra was tired, but decided she would help her mother anyway.

"Mom, come get into bed. I'm going to help you fall asleep."

"What are you going to do?" She was so childlike.

"I'm just going to place my hands on your head and shoulders. It will help you sleep. Trust me."

Her mother climbed into bed and Debra covered her up before proceeding. "Close your eyes and try to relax. Think pleasant thoughts." She took her mother to a fantasy meadow near a brook. Within minutes her mother was snoring softly.

Debra was weary when she locked the door and used her parents' car to return to the hospital. The parking lot was almost deserted. Her tennis shoes squeaked on the polished floors as she walked down the darkened hallways. It was disquieting, but Debra was too tired to care.

The nurse gave her permission to stay in her father's room. Debra parked herself in the rocker glider chair that had apparently been donated to the hospital. It had no padding because of health regulations, but it didn't matter. Debra soon fell asleep with her head resting on her arm on the side of her father's bed.

She was disturbed many times as nursing staff came in to check his vital signs and she was up and about early as the hospital came to life. It was time to do their morning routine and Debra was asked to leave her father's room. She used the toothbrush she had brought with her and ran water over her hands so she could tousle her hair. She next visited the cafeteria to get a cup of tea. Her throat was dry and the warmth of the tea felt good, but she still didn't feel like eating. She walked back to sit outside her father's room in case there was any news.

A familiar figure sat outside his door. It was David!

She rushed to him. "Am I ever glad to see you." Debra buried her face in his chest and he squeezed her tight.

"If your phone message hadn't said, 'I miss you', I might have wondered whether or not I should come, but I thought you might like some support."

Debra nodded with tears in her eyes. She filled him in on what had happened. It was great to have him there.

They checked at the nursing station to get her father's status. "It will be a while before I can give you an update. The doctor will be doing rounds later this morning and we may know more then," the nurse told her.

"We might as well go to my parents' place and pick up my mother and children. It'll also give me a chance to get cleaned up." She ran her hands through her hair, "I guess I must look a sight."

"You look just fine." He kissed her on the end of her nose. "A little tired maybe, but you're still a sight for sore eyes."

Debra smiled, weakly. "Okay, I guess you're about to meet my mother."

Her mother looked about to dissolve into tears when Debra arrived, until she noticed they had company. Debra introduced David. He gently took her mother's hand and held it for a while before commenting that he wished they could have met under better circumstances. Debra could tell her mother was touched by this gesture when she didn't try to remove her hand.

"Jonathan and Leanne are still in bed. I don't know how they can sleep in at a time like this," her mother complained.

"Mom, people have different ways of handling worry and sadness." Her mother looked about to argue, but Debra asked, "How about I make you a cup of tea before I have a shower and change my clothes."

"Mrs. Logan, why don't you show me where the kitchen is and I'll make you a cup of tea. Debra looks about ready to drop on her feet and it would give us a chance to get to know each other."

Her mother looked a little surprised and even a little wary, but she accepted. Debra gave David a grateful look as he followed her mother into the kitchen. The children got up while Debra was in the shower and, after she dressed, she found everybody sitting around the kitchen table.

They took turns showering and hurried off to the hospital. There was still no change in her father's condition. Debra and her mother went in to see him while David sat outside with Leanne and Jonathan. Debra asked her mother to sit quietly while she did some energy work and, to Debra's surprise, she did.

When they left her father's room, Debra found her children and David standing together outside the door with David's arms wrapped around them. Both children were crying. It moved her to tears as she remembered the second gift in her waterfall/pond fantasy.

Apparently Leanne and Jonathan had been sharing stories with David about special times with their grandfather and Jonathan had become choked up which had led to both children crying. They all sat down and Leanne and Jonathan managed to pull themselves together. David told them some stories about times with his grandfather, which actually made them laugh.

About an hour later, her father's day shift nurse came out of his room with a smile on her face. "His temperature has dropped two degrees and his vital signs are stable. He may be coming out of the woods." Everybody smiled and Jonathan started to chatter. Debra and her mother went back into his room.

Debra unruffled her father again. "What's the purpose in doing it again?" her mother asked.

"I need to do something. I can't stand feeling so helpless. Energy work helps to reduce body temperature and also clears toxins and infection. I don't know whether it will help to do it again, but it can't do any harm." This time her mother watched intently as Debra moved around the bed. She even complied when Debra asked her to share a hand/heart connection with her.

They were standing on each side of the bed with one of his hands in each of theirs and Debra's mother's hand covering hers on her father's chest when he coughed and opened his eyes. They both started to cry and Debra squeezed his hand tight.

He looked a little startled when he saw where he was and he asked for a drink of water. Debra went out to tell the others and asked the nurse whether he could have a drink. She came in to check his vital signs. His temperature had dropped another two degrees. Everybody was relieved to hear the good news. David took Leanne and Jonathan to the cafeteria to have lunch while Debra and her mother returned to her father's bedside.

He was only semi-awake and you could tell the infection had worn him out, but he asked how long he had been in the hospital and how Debra happened to be there. They gave him an update and, at the end, her mother commented, "Debra performed her witchcraft on you…" Debra was about to protest, but her mother looked over at her, winked and finished with, "and here we all are." They squeezed each other's hand across the bed.

Once he showed signs of needing to fall back to sleep, they joined the others in the cafeteria. It was agreed they would go back to the house to rest and the nurse would call if there were any changes or he woke. Debra didn't want to be separated from David so when the rest went to their bedrooms, she curled up on the couch with her head on David's lap. He stroked her hair until she fell asleep and then nodded off while sitting up.

David later helped Debra and her mother make a simple meal of soup and sandwiches. Everybody was so relieved by the improvement in Debra's father's health. There was lots of chatting and teasing. Debra's mother even joined in. Debra noticed her mother watching David and she seemed impressed by what she saw. He offered to stay behind and play board games with the kids while Debra and her mother made another quick visit to the hospital.

Debra's father was a little more alert this time. Debra gave her mother some time alone with him before they left to go home for the night.

Jonathan insisted that David use his bed and he slept on the couch that night. David was complimented by the gesture and, although he tried to get Jonathan to keep the bed, Jonathan would not take "no" for an answer. It was unanimous that everybody wanted to go to sleep early.

Debra was pleasantly surprised when her mother asked if she would give her Healing Touch to help her fall asleep. Even though Debra was tired, she didn't refuse. "You get into bed and I'll be there shortly. I just want to say goodnight to David."

She and David kissed each other goodnight in the hallway. He went into the bedroom, but Debra called him out, again. She hugged him. "Thanks for being here."

He hugged her back, "You're welcome."

Her father was moved to the general ward the next morning so visits were no longer restricted to immediate family. He had a semi-private room and there wasn't anyone in the other bed so they broke the rules and all went in at once. Debra was pleased that her father had more color in his cheeks and the oxygen was no longer necessary.

They took turns hugging him and then Debra introduced David. The two men shook hands, "Eileen said you've been a good support to the family. I'm glad to hear somebody was holding down the fort while I was away," he chortled.

Jonathan was the first to give his grandfather a hard time. "You know, if you wanted us to visit that bad, all you had to do was call."

"I'll keep that in mind next time. Sometimes I forget about Alexander Graham Bell's invention."

"You'd better not ever give us another scare like this," Leanne said, hugging him, again. He patted her hair.

"I'd better not ever give myself another scare like this," he chuckled. "It's not fun waking up in ICU with your family looking over you as if you've died." He glanced back and forth between his wife and daughter with fondness.

They kept the visit brief to avoid wearing him out. Her mother spent some time alone with him and then Debra went in to do energy work. When she left, her father was sleeping.

"Mom, why didn't any of the rest of the family come?"

"Steve is coming out tomorrow, he couldn't get away sooner. I didn't call the ones out east. They wouldn't have come and there would have been no point in getting them worried for nothing."

"For nothing! What if Dad had died?"

"Oh, he wasn't going to die. He just wasn't himself, that's all."

"It was a lot more serious than that. Just make sure you call me any time he's ill. I don't want to find out that I didn't get to say goodbye because you didn't think it was serious enough."

Her mother looked disturbed, but she didn't respond. "Talk about denial!" Debra thought. David squeezed her hand to help calm her.

The following day, David told Debra that it was time for him to return home and get back to work. "This house is going to get mighty crowded with your Dad returning home and your brother coming. It's time I went home and got back to work."

"Are you sure?"

"Well, you know what they say? Guests are like fish—after three days they start to stink."

Debra laughed. "I've really appreciated you being here. It made a big difference for the kids, too…and you even managed to calm my Mom down."

David kissed her. "You're exaggerating, but I was glad to have a chance to spend some time with your family."

"I'm just going to stay one more day so I can help Dad get settled in at home and make sure Mom's not overwhelmed." It was agreed he would make flight arrangements and she would drop him off at the airport.

They held hands all the way out to the airport. "Debra, how about I take you for that tandem paragliding flight this weekend. It's a great time for you to have an escape from reality."

"Really, David, that sounds wonderful! I am a little scared, though."

"You'll be fine. I won't do anything outrageous. We'll just float and enjoy the view."

She quickly agreed. He said he would check wind conditions for Saturday and would call to arrange a time. They gave each other a kiss and a hug and he waved goodbye as she drove away.

Her father's intravenous was discontinued and he was sent home with oral antibiotics later that morning. Once he was settled in bed, he fell asleep. Debra and the children helped her mother to tidy the house. They spent the rest of the day quietly playing board games and visiting off and on with her father.

He looked like his normal self by the time they left for the airport, although he was still confined to bed rest. Debra's mother had offered to drive them, but Debra felt her mother had had enough stress for the week without battling traffic. She told her parents she loved them. "I promise we'll visit more often now that our lives are more settled."

Her father gave her a warm hug goodbye and also told her he loved her. That brought a tear to her eye. Her mother was the most surprising, though.

"Debra thanks for coming. Thanks so much for helping your father with the Healing Touch. It was lovely to see all of you. And, that David, he seems like a wonderful fellow. You hang on to him!" she said as she gave her a hug and a kiss goodbye.

"I will, Mom. I will."

She breathed a heavy sigh as they left in the taxi. What a week!

CHAPTER EIGHTEEN

Jonathan played with his Game Boy for most of the trip home and Leanne read her book. Debra eventually realized her mind was going a mile a minute. She hadn't grounded herself since she had left San Diego! She could remedy that situation right away and she did. Then she settled in to read the book she had brought.

Both kids decided to go to school to collect their homework assignments and books. They were also pleased to be reunited with their classmates. Debra unpacked her things and went kayaking.

When she called to let Liz know she was home, she gave her a quick update and they agreed they would chat the following morning during their walk.

David called that evening. They asked each other how they were and David also inquired about her family.

"The forecast looks good at Torrey tomorrow. I'd like to pick you up at ten o'clock. Would that be okay?"

"I can hardly wait."

"Wear pants and make sure you have a jacket. It will be fairly breezy. I'll bring lunch."

Debra appreciated the chance to talk with Liz the next day. She told her about David's supportiveness, the effect it had on her mother and children, and her mother's response to Healing Touch.

"Wow, that must have been a shock! I wish my parents would be more open-minded about it. They think I'm brain-washed."

Just before they parted, Debra told her she was going paragliding with David. Liz was astonished. "Kurt is going to be so envious! He's always wanted to go paragliding."

Debra was surprised by that news. She figured most people didn't even know what it was.

She was humming when she walked up the sidewalk to her home. The Bergers were out in their yard.

"Good morning, Nancy and George."

Nancy looked up from her roses, "Good morning." Debra just about fell over from shock. She was doubly shocked when George echoed his wife, "Good morning."

Debra was beaming as she went into the house and told Leanne what had happened.

Leanne looked up from watching Much Music, "I guess you finally wore them down. You win."

"I guess so. Don't worry about paying off the bet, though. Having them respond was reward enough."

Debra went to have her shower and get dressed. She was anxious and excited at the same time. It seemed spending time with David always had that impact on her. She was looking forward to things becoming more even keel some day, but for now they were having too much fun discovering new things together, so that would have to wait.

Jonathan was up by the time David arrived. Both he and Leanne greeted David enthusiastically.

"David, would you mind taking me paragliding some day?" Jonathan asked.

"I'd love to, if it's okay with your mother," he looked over at Debra and she nodded in agreement.

"Awesome!"

"What about you, Leanne? Would you be open to trying it?" David asked.

Leanne's eyes glistened, "That would be the best. Lisa would burst a gasket!"

David laughed. "Your friends aren't going to like me much if we keep making them envious."

"Sure they will. They'll just wish they were us."

He and Debra drove off in his Explorer. The closer they got to Torrey Pines, the more anxious she became. David reached over and took her hand. He lifted it to his lips and kissed the back of her hand. "I know you're nervous, but you'll be fine."

Once they had parked in the dirt lot, he hauled his paraglider bag out. It looked like a huge backpack. Debra followed him up an embankment and onto the grass, where David dropped his bag. They went into the shop to sign in.

Debra sat on the grass and looked around while David pulled his gear out of the bag. There were five or six patio chairs and umbrellas beside an outdoor snack bar. Several bags and gliders lay in a heap on the side of the lawn. Colorful flags and windsocks were placed along the front of the hill and two paragliders were in the air floating back and forth in front of the cliffs. Just then, she noticed someone pulling his paraglider up. He took only a couple of steps forward and was lifted into the air. Debra was astounded. "It's that easy.

"Yes, it's that easy. All you have to do is remember to run whenever your feet are close to the ground. We run when we launch and we run when we land."

He spread his glider out on the grass. It was turquoise blue with a black design. There were lots of different colored lines attached to the glider, which were connected to webbing that David referred to as "risers". Half of the lines were attached to one riser and the rest were attached to another one. He showed her how to make sure that the lines were clear and then laid them on the grass.

"There are so many lines! Don't they get tangled?"

"Once you spend enough time around a paraglider, you learn how to avoid that as much as possible or it can be a real hassle."

He strapped a helmet on her and put one on himself. Then, he slipped a harness over her shoulders like a vest and fastened the straps around her legs and waist. He put one on himself and used two foam-covered bars to attach their harnesses together. The two of them practiced running while connected, with David running right on Debra's heels. Debra almost felt like she was in a three-legged race, they were so close together! David was coaching her, "Run, run." What a hoot!

He then attached one of the two glider risers to each side of his harness with carabiners and they stood there waiting with David holding the top of the risers in his hands.

"Is that all that's going to be holding us up?"

"Believe me, you'll feel like you're being held up by a crane once we're in the air…We're waiting for the wind to come straight in. As soon as it does, I'm going to blow my whistle so people know we're launching and we're going to run toward the edge."

Debra's heart jumped up into her throat when he said that.

"Just remember, all you have to do is run. If we lift up and touch down again, just run, okay?" Debra nodded.

Seconds later he said, "Okay, run."

It was hard to go forward, but David pulled the risers, the glider came up over their heads and all of a sudden it was easy. David tooted his whistle a few times and within a few steps Debra's feet were lifted off of the ground. They were flying! Once they were out in front of the cliffs David turned right and told her to lift herself into her harness. It was just like sitting in a comfortable baby swing! Debra felt David pull himself into his harness behind her. She was perched in her harness between his knees.

They flew above the ridge, gradually getting higher until they were a couple of hundred feet above it. "Now you can resume breathing and look around," David told her.

She didn't even realize she was holding her breath. How had he noticed? She tried to look back at him, but he just laughed. "Everybody holds their breath the first time."

Debra looked around as they floated along. She could see and hear the waves crashing into shore. The people below looked like little ants, especially the ones down on the beach and in the water. They had a bird's eye view of a beautiful golf course. Some of the golfers looked up and waved. Debra waved back and chuckled. This was great!

David turned the glider around and they flew back. They passed a couple of paraglider pilots going in the opposite direction and smiled at each other. Debra figured she must look silly. She had a huge goofy grin on her face.

David blew his whistle as they passed a flag and entered the area for the Remote Control Aircraft pad. After they passed launch, Debra noticed groups of people standing along the cliffs looking up at them. Debra felt lucky to be one of the people in the air.

As they floated along, she looked down upon several extravagant mansions with swimming pools. They gradually lost altitude as they passed the cliff area and flew toward Scripps Pier. There was no beach along this section and they were flying so low that Debra could hear the surf pounding on the rocks. Debra was a little worried they would end up landing in the water, but David turned the glider back and they regained their height as they resumed flying near the cliffs, again.

"What makes us fly at different heights?"

"We're ridgesoaring. The air lifts when the wind hits the hill or cliff because it can't go through it. That's why we can only fly back and forth here. We have to stay in the ridge band just in front of the cliff because that is where the air is lifting." He added, "Some day I'd like to take you thermal soaring in the mountains. We can fly distances with thermals because we get our lift from warm pockets of air that are rising."

They flew from one end of the ridge to the other a couple of times before David blew his whistle and turned the glider in towards the grassy knoll launch area. He reminded Debra that she would need to run once they touched down. He turned the glider, again, so they were flying toward the front. They touched down and Debra only had to run two steps before they ended up standing still. David then turned his body and pulled the glider down. He drew the glider in, looping the lines into one hand, and then bunched up the fabric.

Debra was ecstatic. "That was sensational! Can we do it again some time?"

David laughed. "Sure."

He unhooked Debra's harness so she could walk freely. He then slung the glider over his shoulder and they walked toward the area where there were a bunch of gliders on the ground. David took off his helmet and so did Debra.

Debra couldn't stop chattering about how wonderful it was. As a matter of fact, she didn't stop until he kissed her. He walked her over to where there were several patio tables and umbrellas. "Would you like some lunch, now?"

"I'm too excited to eat!"

"That's okay. I guess it's too early for lunch anyway. Nobody else is sitting here eating."

Debra leaned toward him and kissed him. "Thank you. Thank you so much. I can't believe you took me flying!"

"I once took a psychology course and the professor told us about some research where they had men take their dates across a swinging bridge to see if they would confuse the racing of their heart and pulse with being in love. I was hoping the excitement and fear of paragliding would make you think you're in love with me," he teased.

"I don't need other stimulus to make me think I'm in love with you." She looked into his eyes, "I already know I am."

He took her in his arms and gave her a deep, passionate kiss. "Then why don't we get married? I love you and I want to spend the rest of my life with you."

Debra couldn't speak. She gulped and nodded as a tear rolled down her cheek.

David squeezed her tight. "Let's go home."

They packed up his gear and decided to go back to his house so they could be alone. It was only a matter of minutes before they were in the bedroom. They made slow, passionate love.

Afterwards they lay in each other's arms and talked about how their children might feel when they announced their intentions to get married. Debra thought Jonathan might be a little worried about how his father would feel, but that he would be pleased on his own account. She was sure Leanne would be happy.

"Chad liked you in the little amount of time you spent together and he always wanted brothers and sisters. I can't see him ever living at home, again, but he might enjoy having siblings anyway."

"David, would it be okay if we lived in my house? I promised the kids I wouldn't uproot them."

"It wouldn't make sense to move the three of you when there's only one of me. I can commute to my job. We could keep this house as a weekend retreat. Your kids could bring their friends on weekends and go surfing and whatever. They'd like that wouldn't they?" Debra nodded.

"I bet I know one person who's going to be tickled pink," Debra said.

"Who?"

"Your mother." He laughed and couldn't help but agree. It also occurred to them that living next door to his mother would be convenient as she got older. Being as she tended to be non-interfering, neither of them thought living nearby would be a hardship.

They talked about what kind of wedding they would like. Both were in agreement that a small garden wedding attended only by close family and friends would be ideal.

"We could even get married in your back yard. You've done a lovely job of it."

"And I could pretty up the yard here some day. I'd really enjoy a new gardening project."

He smiled. "That would be nice. I'm not much of a gardener, but I could help you set up the dirt beds and things."

"H-m-m-m, I'm looking forward to spending my life with you."

"I hope so," he said. "You did just agree to marry me."

They both laughed.

"So how about you get me home so I can share the news with Leanne and Jonathan?"

Debra was excited and nervous as she waited for her children to come home for dinner. "Here I go again," she thought. "I'm going to be a basket case if this doesn't stop." It was agreed she would meet alone with them so they would feel free to share their honest reactions. David was having dinner next door with his mother.

Leanne came home first, but Debra decided not to say anything until she had them both together. It nearly killed her to wait until they were settled around the dinner table. Of course, they wanted to hear all about her paragliding experience so she answered those questions first.

"You must have had a great time, you've got a smile like a Cheshire cat," Leanne exclaimed.

"Well actually, I've got some news to tell you."

They both looked up.

"David asked me to marry him."

Leanne jumped up and hugged her, "Congratulations, Mom. That's wonderful!"

Jonathan's first reaction was, "Cool!" But then he became sober, "How are you going to tell Dad?"

"He'll be okay, Jonathan. He can take care of himself."

"I guess so."

Leanne suddenly looked apprehensive. "Where are we going to live after you get married?"

"We thought we'd live here being as you two are all settled in school." Their faces lit up. "We could use his house as a weekend getaway. David said you could even bring your friends for weekends to go surfing."

"That would be awesome!" Jonathan exclaimed.

Debra looked at Jonathan. "Well despite the fact that you gain a surfing getaway, what do you think about having David around full-time?"

"I think David's cool. I'm just worried about Dad."

"David's not going to try to replace him, he'll still be your father. This shouldn't change anything in your relationship with your Dad."

"When's the wedding?" Leanne asked.

"We thought we would wait to see whether or not the two of you are ready, so we haven't set a date yet. It's important in life for people to do whatever makes them happy. But making you unhappy, would not make me happy."

"Well you don't need to hold back on account of me," Leanne said.

Debra looked at Jonathan, "You don't have to hold back on account of me, either. Dad's a big boy and, like you said, he can take care of himself, right?"

Leanne and Debra both nodded.

"Okay, it's cool," he said.

Debra later overheard Leanne on the phone telling one of her friends that she was getting a "big brother." She would have to find out from David when they would get a chance to meet him.

Leanne and Jonathan soon left to get on with their usual weekend activities. Debra went next door. Edna greeted her with a hearty "Congratulations!" and a warm hug.

David was quick to ask how the conversation went with the children and was pleased with her response. "I actually managed to reach Chad on the phone before he went out for the evening. He asked me to welcome you to the family on his behalf."

Debra was touched. "That's sweet of him."

Edna chuckled, "Don't ever let Chad hear you refer to him in those terms. You'd spoil his macho image of himself!"

Debra and David both laughed.

Debra asked whether he would mind if she spent the evening alone. She could hardly wait to phone her friends and family to tell them the news.

He looked at his mother, "How do you like that? I only just asked her to marry me and she's already trying to get rid of me!"

Edna chuckled, "Don't look at me! I'm just going to mind my own business."

"I guess it won't hurt anything. We still have the rest of our lives to spend together."

"Oh, I like the ring of that," Debra gave him a quick kiss and departed.

Liz was ecstatic about the news and just about deafened Debra when she yelled to Kurt, "Hey, guess what? David and Debra are getting married!"

Debra heard him yell, "Great, tell her congratulations!"

When she called her parents, her mother was pleased, although she wasn't impressed that they would have to travel to San Diego for the wedding. Her father was feeling better and got on the line to congratulate her.

She realized, with disappointment, that she and Jean had never exchanged phone numbers so she couldn't talk to Jean and Tom. Oh well, she and David could tell them together Tuesday evening. They would definitely be invited to the wedding.

It occurred to her that Terri would probably be pleased to hear her news, too, but she decided that could wait for now. She wasn't going to spoil a perfectly good evening by turning on the computer. She was looking forward to spending a quiet evening alone with her thoughts and feelings.

She changed into her robe, poured herself a glass of wine, and curled up on the sofa with the fleece blanket from her sanctuary. She was so content, she felt like purring.

As she began to reflect about the events of the past year, she found it hard to believe that everything had been set off by a one-word response from Ted.

So many changes. She had a multitude of strengths she hadn't known about before. She had discovered she was capable of raising and supporting a family by herself. She could attract and keep good people in her life, David, Liz, Jean, and Edna. She was a risk-taker who could try new things and, if they didn't work out, still try something new. She had become in touch with spirituality through energy work and she had even improved her relationships with her mother and Ted. Most importantly, she had learned the value of enjoying life and taking care of herself.

Debra knew herself better and she liked what she saw. There was no doubt about it. Life was good.